"What's your name?" came the dreaded question.

For a split second, Yusuf thought about using an American version of his name. Joseph? Joe? How hard could it be? After all, Kamran had managed the transformation into Cameron in fifth grade without any trouble. It was the first day of middle school. He could do this, if he wanted.

No. Abba always said, "Be proud of who you are. Be proud of the name and everything that comes with it." He took a deep breath and said, enunciating each syllable clearly, "Yusuf Azeem, sir."

To my father, who always pushed me to do better.

1

You suck.

The paper lay faceup on the locker floor. White lined notebook paper. Black ink.

Yusuf blinked and read it again. *You suck.*

He wasn't sure if the paper was meant for him or was left over by the last person to use locker 130A. He looked at the other kids walking around, smiling and high-fiving. The student lockers in the south hallway of Frey Middle School were painted blue. Not a light sky blue, which everyone knew was for babies, but a deep grayish blue. A color that announced "Welcome to middle school!" without being cheesy.

Just a few seconds ago, Yusuf had been thrilled at opening his locker for the first time. Lockers were for big kids. They meant something more than storage: they meant you were old enough. He'd been grinning as he'd spun the dial carefully to make sure he got the numbers right. Seven zero two zero. Easy. He'd already memorized the combination written on the class schedule he'd been emailed the night before. That was also a middle school thing, apparently. An email account from the school, where he'd now get school announcements directly. His username was YUSUF_AZEEM, it said on the schedule, right next to the locker code.

Yusuf Azeem. Son of the famous Mohammad Azeem from A to Z Dollar Store on Marbury Street.

And now this. He pushed his glasses higher up his nose. Then he looked down and studied the inside of the locker. *You suck.* The paper made everything go quiet, like a movie suddenly on mute. He bent his head and studied the paper the way he studied a new LEGO instruction manual. The K had a flourish that turned into a long, straight line. The Y had a curl, as if the writer had tried to learn cursive but had given up.

His breathing slowed. The hair on the back of his neck bristled. What should he do?

Only for a minute, though. Someone jostled his side lightly as they passed. The world began to move again.

Yusuf let out his breath in a whoosh. He decided the paper was a mistake. Students were streaming into the gym from the hallways, their faces bent to their schedules to figure out where to go. Nobody could have decided he sucked in the ten minutes since the school bell rang. It had to be a mistake. Middle school was going to be awesome. He knew that 2021 was going to be his year. Cafeteria food. Chromebooks. Robotics club. This blue-gray locker.

And most important, the annual Texas Robotics Competition. Yusuf couldn't wait for things to get started. He'd been preparing for the TRC his entire life.

It was time for life to get interesting.

Principal Williamson was short and energetic, with bouncy brown hair tied in a ponytail and her face thick with makeup that shone under the gym lights. She wore a silky blue jumpsuit with sequins on the collar and held a microphone in her hands like a deejay.

At least, that was what Yusuf thought deejays dressed like. You needed to go to Houston or Austin for an actual concert, and Amma and Abba would faint if he ever suggested it. Good Muslim kids didn't go to concerts, they'd say, frowning with disappointment.

Danial had found a space on the floor all the way in the far corner of the gym. "Over here!" He waved to Yusuf.

Yusuf sank down into the empty spot next to his best

friend. "Why didn't you walk to school with me?" he grumbled, fiddling with his glasses.

Danial shrugged, his floppy black hair spilling onto his forehead and around his ears. "My mom wanted to drop me off, since it was the first day and all. I think she just wanted to show off her new Jeep."

Yusuf squished the tiny spark of envy inside his chest. Danial's parents were computer engineers, and they worked in the new Exxon regional headquarters about twenty miles out of town. This was his mom's third new car since Danial was born.

"Come home with me after school?" Danial asked. "I got a new LEGO set we can build together."

Yusuf stared straight ahead at Principal Williamson. She stood on a little wooden stage, checking her microphone, whispering, "Hello? Hello?"

"Can't," he replied reluctantly. "My mamoo is visiting at dinner."

"The uncle from Houston? He's cool."

Yusuf didn't say that a LEGO set sounded cooler. That was a given. But Uncle Rahman came a close second.

"Did you set up your email yet?" Danial continued. "I'm thinking of changing my username to legomaniac2021."

Yusuf didn't know you could change your username.

Why would anyone want to do that? "I'm okay with mine. Besides, what will you do next year? Change it to 2022?"

Danial obviously hadn't thought of that. He shrugged like he didn't care, but his face was scrunched up as if he'd swallowed a pickle.

"This is so childish," he complained, nodding to the front of the gym.

"What? It's middle school. It's what they do on the first day." Yusuf was sure this welcome assembly was a time-honored tradition. At least, that was what the email last night had said.

The sound system crackled, making them jump. "Helloooo, boys and girls, welcome to Frey Middle! I'm your principal, Mrs. Williamson, and I'll be your pilot for the duration of your flight."

There was silence. A few groans.

Principal Williamson looked around with a pained face. "Wow, tough crowd! Okay, no worries. I realize it's the first day of middle school for some of you, and you're probably still in summer vacation mode. Not a problem! Now, let me go over some rules before y'all head on to your classrooms. . . ."

Yusuf tried to listen to the rules. He really did. There were easy ones, like no running in the hallways, and no fighting ever. Wandering the school without a hall pass was the biggest crime a kid could commit, apparently. There was something about bathroom breaks, and a great deal about the sports teams you could join.

But the note in his locker kept swimming into his vision, until Mrs. Williamson's face resembled a lined notebook paper with black letters on it. "Did you open your locker yet?" he whispered to Danial.

Danial was jotting down the names of all the sports clubs on the palm of his hand. Soccer on Monday. Basketball on Tuesday and Friday. Wrestling on Wednesday. Yoga on Thursday. "Why would anybody choose yoga?" he whispered back. "Yoga is for old ladies."

"Yoga is meditation from ancient India."

"I really don't care. It's for old ladies."

Yusuf decided there was no use arguing. He chewed on the inside of his cheek, then asked again. "Locker?"

"Dude, I didn't even *get* to my locker yet," Danial replied. "I think the last class can still access them in the first week of school."

Yusuf didn't ask how Danial knew this. His father, Mr. Khan, was on the school board, so all sorts of school secrets were probably discussed at their dinner table. A wave of relief washed over Yusuf. The note in his locker could have been left over from the year before. It was meant for somebody else. Maybe someone who actually sucked.

Definitely not Yusuf.

"Okay, who can tell me the three values of Frey Middle School?" shouted Mrs. Williamson, the sequins on her jumpsuit glinting brightly. "The first one starts with a P."

The gym erupted into laughter.

"It's perseverance," whispered Yusuf, but nobody could hear him over the noise.

2

After the assembly was over, Yusuf and Danial stood in the hallway outside the gym comparing class schedules. They weren't in any classes together, which was the worst news. They'd been together ever since kindergarten, except in third grade, which Danial had labeled the Year of Sorrows.

"This is a bad sign," Danial pronounced, pushing his hair out of his eyes. "How will you function without me?"

Yusuf ducked his head to hide his smile. "I'll manage somehow, don't worry."

They were standing right under a big white banner that said WELCOME, NEW STUDENTS! and a smaller black one that said NEVER FORGET—TWENTY

YEARS. Yusuf examined the black one. Twenty years was a very long time to keep remembering something.

Danial hefted his new Star Wars backpack higher on his shoulder. It was so shiny new, it still had the plastic wire of the tag attached to one strap. "I think this will be the middle school of sorrows."

Yusuf looked back at Danial. "Don't be silly. We'll get to see each other in lunch and PE and library."

"Those are all baby classes."

"No, they're not," Yusuf replied cheerfully. Firmly. "They're the most essential classes. Nourishing the body and the brain and the spirit."

"Ugh, you're so positive, it's disgusting."

Yusuf said, "Remember over the summer, how we built LEGO robots and watched Texas News Network with Abba at the store?"

"Man, those were some messed-up news reports on TNN. People hating on anybody who's different," Danial replied. "Why does your dad watch that all the time?"

"He says we should know what's going on around us. Learn about the worst and hope for the best."

Danial chortled. "Yeah, he's always saying that. He should make a poster and hang it over his checkout counter next to that plaque of his. Or maybe even replace that old plaque. It's getting rusty."

"He'll never replace the plaque, not in a million years."

Yusuf started walking. "Anyway, what I'm saying is, that's how we should begin middle school. Learn the worst and hope for the best."

Danial followed, his backbone bent. "I repeat: ugh."

They separated in the hallway outside the gym and went in opposite directions. Yusuf watched for a minute as Danial grew smaller in the distance. "Good luck!" he called out, but Danial was too far away to hear him. He hefted his backpack and walked slowly. *YUSUF_AZEEM reporting for duty!*

Despite his positivity, his stomach was grumbling. Classes without his best friend. A locker with a mean note inside. And it wasn't even nine o'clock in the morning yet. He wished he hadn't eaten the fried eggs Amma had cooked. They always left his mouth feeling greasy.

Pretty soon, though, the morning improved, because first period was science.

Yusuf's science teacher was Mr. Parker, which was the best news on the class schedule. Mr. Parker had been voted Teacher of the Year seven years in a row, his name proudly displayed on a billboard on El Paso Street where the twin buildings of Frey Elementary and Frey Middle stood. The evening news had sent a reporter to interview him this past summer. That was how Yusuf knew the teacher held a degree in chemistry from the University of Houston, had two teenage sons, and liked strawberry shortcake ice cream.

"Science is going to be very interesting this year, kids," Mr. Parker announced, his clipped brown mustache stretching with his smile. "We'll do some cool science experiments right here in the classroom. How much do you know about slime?"

A few of the kids groaned, as if Mr. Parker was being cheesy. Yusuf wanted to smile back at him, but he hesitated. Maybe smiling at teachers in middle school was frowned upon by the others? He sneaked a peek at the rest of the class. There were a few kids he already knew, like Madison Ensley, who was always picked line leader in every elementary grade class, and Cameron Abdullah, who wore one shiny earring and made the weirdest jokes. Of course, in a town the size of Frey, there were hardly ever any new kids. They all knew one another.

Mr. Parker was writing safety instructions on the whiteboard with a blue dry-erase marker. Number one, follow rules. Number two, notify the teacher IMMEDIATELY if there's a fire or a spill. Number three, wear safety goggles for lab activities.

Yusuf thought the rules looked like code. Everybody knew programming code came in steps, or sequences. His hands itched to write some code, but he forced himself to copy down Mr. Parker's safety rules instead.

When he looked up, his eyes met Cameron's, aka Kamran. Cameron wiggled his eyebrows and rolled his eyes at Mr. Parker. "Boring!" he mouthed.

Yusuf shook his head. Mr. Parker's safety instructions might not be exciting, but they were essential. On his last visit to Frey, Uncle Rahman had told Yusuf about a lab technician in his hospital who mixed some chemicals wrong. Not only was there a mini lab explosion, but the tech's eyebrows had gotten singed because he forgot to wear goggles. The image made Yusuf grin. He could just imagine the poor lab assistant without eyebrows.

"Glad my safety rules are making you laugh, young man."

Yusuf gulped and looked carefully at Mr. Parker. "Uh, I was thinking of something I'd heard," he confessed. He tapped the frame of his glasses with a finger.

"About . . . ?"

Yusuf had no intention of starting sixth grade on the wrong foot. He ducked his head. "Nothing, sir. I'm sorry."

"What's your name?" came the dreaded question.

For a split second, Yusuf thought about using an American version of his name. Joseph? Joe? How hard could it be? After all, Kamran had managed the transformation into Cameron in fifth grade without any trouble. It was the first day of middle school. He could do this, if he wanted.

No. Abba always said, "Be proud of who you are. Be proud of the name and everything that comes with it." He took a deep breath and said, enunciating each syllable clearly, "Yusuf Azeem, sir."

Then Mr. Parker said, "Well, Yusuf Azeem sir, please listen carefully, because your first assignment will be on these safety rules."

Yusuf stared at Mr. Parker, and Mr. Parker stared back solemnly for six whole seconds before turning to the whiteboard. Cameron made a shocked face with both hands over his cheeks and mouthed, "Busted!"

Yusuf stared straight ahead for the rest of the class, focusing all his energy like a laser beam at Mr. Parker's shiny forehead.

3

Amma was cleaning out the garage when Yusuf got home from school. "Salaam alaikum! Just the boy I wanted to see," she said, giving him a quick hug. Her knee-length white tunic had smudges of dirt on it.

"I'm starving," he announced, before she could give him a box to lug out. She'd been cleaning and reorganizing the garage all summer, bit by bit, to make room for her desk and file cabinets. She had even put in new shelves and painted the walls a cream color. Her little garage office, she called it, where she'd write her newspaper articles and essays and do all her other freelance work. The year before, she'd edited a book for a famous writer in New York. That was when she'd decided she needed a real office, not just the kitchen table.

The garage project had taken *all* summer. Every day of the seventy-five-day vacation. Yusuf had been on cleaning duty with her most of those days. Not today, though. Garage-cleaning duties had officially ended. "Can I eat something?" he asked.

"Of course." Amma wiped dust from her cheek. "There's chicken pulao on the counter. Wash your hands before you eat."

"And raita?" he asked as he headed inside. Every plate of pulao needed a side of spicy-sweet yogurt poured over it.

"And raita," she replied. Then, as an afterthought: "Don't fill your stomach, though. Rahman mamoo is already on his way here, and he promised to bring Chinese food."

Yusuf's heart jumped. He'd almost forgotten. He hurried inside and put his backpack in the hallway closet, then lined up all the shoes correctly before heading to the kitchen. Aleena sat at the kitchen counter, playing with her toys. She squealed when she saw him. "Salaam, bhai!"

"Hey, goosey, how's my favorite baby sister?" he cooed at her, ruffling her curly hair.

"My dolly say hi," she told him solemnly. There were at least five dolls in front of her, so he said hello to all of them just to be safe. Aleena beamed at him.

Yusuf washed his hands at the kitchen sink, then sat at the counter eating a steaming pile of rice with chicken. His laptop—a present from Amma and Abba on his birthday last year—was nearby, and he pulled it toward him. "Make me a game," Aleena commanded. He opened a window to his favorite website, Scratch, and began dragging boxes of code to please her. An animated unicorn? Aleena loved unicorns.

"Make him glow," Aleena said.

Yusuf ate with one hand and worked with the other. Coding with blocks was one giant shortcut, but it got the job done and made Aleena happy. She laughed at the glowing yellow unicorn dancing on its front legs, shooting rainbow farts every ten seconds.

"Unicorns are a myth, you know, Aleena?"

She looked up. "What's a myth?"

"Something a lot of people think is true, but it's really not."

Aleena wagged her finger at him. "I know it true. Unicorns real."

He grinned at her. "You're right, of course."

She grinned back. "Me hungry," she said. He speared a piece of chicken with his fork and popped it into her open mouth.

Abba came home an hour later, grumbling about his new assistant at the dollar store. "He said he had a year's experience when I hired him, but the way he stocks the shelves, it seems like he's never done it before."

Yusuf had moved into the living room, watching a documentary about a new type of robot that assembled cars in half the time it took human engineers. Aleena snuggled next to him, singing under her breath. It was either the Barney song or something from the Muppets. They all sounded the same to Yusuf. "Maybe the guy knows a better way to stock shelves," he told Abba. "Like, by colors or size or something."

Abba took off his socks and leaned against the couch back next to Yusuf. "No, his system makes no sense," he said, shaking his head. "Not that I can see, anyway."

The robots were just a long arm and a slim metal body, but they had pushed sixty-five engineers out of an auto plant in Michigan. "New systems often don't make sense to the old generation," Yusuf murmured.

"What's that?" Abba asked, frowning.

Yusuf shook his head. Thankfully, at that moment Aleena noticed Abba. She scrambled off the couch and launched herself at him. "Abba! Abba!" she shouted. "You came home!"

Abba picked her up and whirled her around. "How's my favorite little gurya?"

"I'm not a dolly!" she replied, laughing.

"Sorry, you look just like one!"

Yusuf went back to his documentary, lost in a dream world where he could build robots that functioned like brilliant metallic geniuses. Abba and Aleena sat next to him, but he hardly noticed.

At a quarter to six, Amma came in from the garage holding a big brown box with torn edges. "I need to get cleaned up," she announced. "Yusuf, be a darling and put this box in the front hallway for your uncle Rahman. They're his old books, and he keeps forgetting to take them with him whenever he visits."

"Only if you promise never to call me darling again," Yusuf replied without looking away from the television screen.

Amma dumped the box on his lap. It gave off a faint cloud of dust. "I gave birth to you, so I can call you whatever I like."

"Yes, ma'am." Yusuf sighed.

Abba stood up as well, holding a dangling Aleena from his arm. "And take your sister in to get her changed, please. She stinks."

Aleena thought that was hilarious, and she went into a peal of giggles and sniffed her armpits in an exaggerated way. Yusuf switched off the television. He took the box with one hand and his sister with another, and marched out of the living room. The robots were lucky. They didn't have any family to take care of. No wonder they could get so much done so quickly.

Uncle Rahman arrived at six o'clock, holding warm plastic bags full of food. He was Amma's younger brother by six years, and a research scientist in a university hospital in Houston. Every six months, he traveled along I-45 to Dallas to teach a week-long course in something called genetic mutation. On his way back, he always stopped in Frey. Like clockwork.

This was the second visit of the year. Yusuf couldn't wait to hear about his class. There was always something interesting going on at Uncle Rahman's work.

But first Amma showed off her new garage office. "It's got a working fan and everything now!" she boasted, while Abba muttered under his breath. Yusuf had to admit the place was quite comfy. There was a bright patterned carpet on the floor, and a little area for Aleena's toys. "Very nice, Farrah baji," Uncle Rahman said, smiling.

"Nice, yeah, but where am I going to park my car now?" Abba grumbled.

"That piece of junk can stay in the driveway," Amma told him. "Nobody will steal it even if you ask them to!"

Aleena pulled at Uncle Rahman's hand. "Now see my

room," she said, and they all moved back to the house.

Yusuf set the table while Amma poured the Chinese food into porcelain dishes. "In movies they just eat straight out of the takeout boxes with chopsticks," he complained.

"Television isn't real life, my boy." Amma licked a spot of soy sauce on her finger. "I prefer to have my meal look nice, even if it's takeout."

Uncle Rahman coming over was always fun, but the Chinese food in Frey was terrible. China Star on the corner of Rochester and First was run by a Mexican family, and their signature dish of kung pao was laced with cilantro. Somehow this made the food even more endearing to Yusuf's family. "Who doesn't like a good sprinkling of cilantro?" Abba would always say.

Not Yusuf. Cilantro belonged in Pakistani food, mixed with chickpeas or curry, or sprinkled over a hearty daal. It had no business being mixed into Chinese food. Still, everything tasted better when Uncle Rahman was around, and Yusuf was glad he hadn't eaten too much pulao.

He counted the dishes. Vegetable fried rice. Beef with broccoli. Ginger chicken. Uncle Rahman always brought enough to last the next day too. "Where's the kung pao?" Yusuf asked, disappointed.

"Don't be ungrateful; there's plenty of food," Amma

told him. "Go call everyone for dinner."

Uncle Rahman smiled at Amma when he saw the porcelain dishes. "We could have eaten from the takeout boxes, you know. Less dishes to wash."

She smiled back and ruffled his hair. "I don't mind doing dishes for my little brother."

They ate in silence for a while, the only sounds the slurping of milk from Aleena's sippy cup. Yusuf tried to block his ears, but she was sitting right next to him, grinning.

"The twentieth anniversary of the attacks is coming up soon," Uncle Rahman announced.

Abba drank some water. "Does it matter? It's been twenty years."

Uncle Rahman looked stern. "You don't mean that. You know it still affects us every single day. At work. On the street. At the airport."

Abba shoveled pieces of ginger chicken into his mouth. Yusuf could tell by the speed of his fork-to-mouth action that he was annoyed. "Work never stops because of an anniversary. Just keep working and ignore all the noise, that's my philosophy."

"Philosophy . . . ?" Uncle Rahman's voice rose to an alarming level.

Amma put her hand on his arm. "Let's not talk politics, please. Not in front of the kids."

Immediately her brother took a deep breath and tried to smile. "Of course, Farrah baji, you're right. Tell me, Aleena jaan, how old are you now?"

Aleena laughed with her mouth open, specks of rice on her tongue like snowflakes. "Guess," she said, holding up three fingers.

"Three?" Uncle Rahman's black beard quivered in surprise. "I can't believe it! You're such a big girl now."

"And Yusuf is twelve now," Amma interjected proudly.

Uncle Rahman turned to him, startled. "Really? When did that happen?"

Yusuf rolled his eyes. "Almost twelve," he corrected. "Today was the first day of middle school." He pushed his glasses up his nose. "What did you mean, the attacks?"

Abba made a noise in his throat, like he was irritated. But Uncle Rahman shook his head at him, took a minute to swallow his food, and then replied seriously. "Twenty years ago our country was attacked by terrorists. The date was September 11, 2001. Next month will be the twentieth anniversary of that event."

Yusuf wrinkled his nose. He wasn't a baby. He knew about 9/11. He thought about the blue banner in his school hallway. Never forget. "Twenty years? That's ancient history."

Uncle Rahman lost his smile. "Don't tell me you

don't learn about 9/11 in school?"

Amma waved a fork in the air. "They do, just a little bit. A small lesson here and there. Not the way they teach it in other states. Sarah was saying they have units in social studies every year."

Yusuf hadn't known this. His cousins in California learned about 9/11 in school every year? Here in Frey, they hardly discussed it. He looked up. Uncle Rahman was staring at him like it was his fault. "History informs the present, my dear nephew, and so it affects the future," Uncle Rahman told him.

Yusuf spent the rest of dinner thinking about this statement, while the adults talked. Aleena fell asleep with her face on the table, snoring lightly. Yusuf finished his food and went to his bedroom to work on Scratch. Aleena's unicorn had been glitching, but he knew how to fix it.

Uncle Rahman came to say goodbye just before bedtime. The box of old books from the garage was tucked under his arm. "I found something of a relic in this box of books, and I thought you should have it," he told Yusuf, holding out a battered leather journal.

Yusuf switched off his laptop. "What is it?"

Uncle Rahman tapped his finger on the cover of the journal. "I was your age when 9/11 happened. It was an emotional time for everyone, and it was hard for me to process. My English class project that year included journaling, and I ended up writing about some of my experiences in here, trying to figure things out."

Yusuf squinted through his glasses. "Figure what out?"

"Everything. Life. My place in the world. How it all changed in an instant, how I became a stranger in my own country."

Yusuf had so many questions. He opened his mouth to speak, but Uncle Rahman had already turned away, leaving the journal on his bed. "Please . . . don't tell anyone about this. It'll be our secret."

And then he was gone.

Journal entry 1

August 28, 2001

It's exactly one week since sixth grade began. It's the first time I have a locker, and I'm going to decorate it with mini posters of Harry Potter and Hermione. Jonathan thinks that's too silly. He says characters in books can't be our idols. I am 100 percent sure he's going to put up pictures of football players or something. The best thing is that our lockers are next to each other, and we're together in every single one of our classes too, including English with Mrs. Clifton, who's making us keep this journal as writing practice. Jonathan thinks it doesn't really matter, because she said we don't need to turn it in. I think I should definitely make my weekly entries, just in case she wants to take a look at some point. Plus, she said it's ten extra credit points. "Who cares?" was Jonathan's predictable response.

Jonathan O'Reilly is weird, but in a good way. He makes me laugh when I'm sad, by telling jokes about the chicken crossing the road or something. Corny, is what I tell him. He shrugs and replies, "Who says corny is bad?"

He's right, of course. Corny is good.

Getting ten extra credit points is even better. I want to keep my track record of all As, because Abba gives me money for each A I get on my final report card. This year I've got my eye on a brand-new Discman from Sony, and I need all As to make it happen.

Mrs. Clifton gave us some examples of what to write about in the journal. For instance, you could write about your summer vacation, she said in class when she announced the journaling project.

So here goes.

My family went to Pakistan for summer vacation, just like we do every single year since I can remember. Abba never goes, because he can't leave work at the university for so long, but our cat, Silky, keeps him company. Amma takes the three of us—Farrah baji,

Sarah, and me—on our annual vacations.

It's always super-hot in the summer, but that also means mango season. Mangoes are the supreme fruit, but not the ones we get here from Mexico. The real mangoes are the ones in Pakistan . . . soft and delicious, so that the juice runs down your chin when you bite into them. Oh, and we also get to see all the people Amma and Abba left behind when they came to the U.S. a thousand years ago.

Okay, it wasn't a thousand years. More like twenty years ago. Abba came as a student, and then got married after graduation to Amma and brought her here to Houston. I've seen their wedding pictures: lots of dancing and smiling, and tons of food. Seems like fun!

Another thing that's definitely going to be fun: middle school. In fact, I predict that 2001 is going to be the best year of my entire life.

4

The next morning, there was another paper in Yusuf's locker.

Go home.

It was the exact same paper as last time. White. Lined. The same cursive writing in black pen. He swallowed. Then he closed the locker door and studied the front of it. There was one long vent on the top, to let in air. Anyone could have slipped the paper inside without even having to slow down as they passed. He gripped the locker door and swallowed again. It was clear that the messages were meant for him.

Or were they? He'd just had this locker for two days. How did anyone find out it was his? Was someone stalking him? Was the locker list on a bulletin board somewhere in the school? Yusuf's stomach lurched.

He opened the locker door and stared at the paper some more. *Go home?* What did that even mean? He'd just gotten to school; it was almost time for science class. He took the paper—and the one from yesterday—and hid them on the top shelf of the locker. Abba always said, "Out of sight, out of mind." Maybe that would do the trick.

In science class, Mr. Parker gave a quiz on yesterday's safety rules. Then they watched a short video about how to conduct science experiments. "Who knows the first step of the scientific method?" Mr. Parker asked with arched eyebrows when the video finished.

Yusuf raised his hand. "Making an observation," he said.

"Nerd," someone coughed from the back of the class.

Mr. Parker ignored everyone and started to write the steps of the scientific method on the whiteboard. Yusuf could recite them backward in his sleep, but he took notes anyway.

Just before class ended, Mr. Parker passed out flyers about the robotics club. "Tuesdays and Thursdays from three to four, right here in this room!" he called out. "It's really fun, I promise!" Most of the students were already talking and packing their books. Nobody took a flyer except Yusuf.

He waited until the bell rang and everybody had left. Then he went up to the teacher's desk, flyer in hand. "It doesn't say anything about the club fees," he asked quietly. "How much are the fees?"

Mr. Parker looked at him without speaking. Up close, the wrinkles around his eyes were mini craters. Then he answered, "The club is free for now. I usually don't get enough kids interested in robotics here. They'd rather play football."

Yusuf nodded. Football was the lifeblood of Frey. "Will we be prepping for the TRC in this club? That's what we did in elementary school. As practice, anyway."

Mr. Parker narrowed his eyes. "The Texas Robotics Competition is a serious event, son. It requires at least six kids on the team, and not just any kids. They'd have to be really good at robotics and building things. I haven't been able to get that many to sign up since 2012. Do you think this year will be any different?"

Yusuf nodded so vigorously his backpack slid down his arm and onto the floor. "Yes, sir. My friend Danial and I have been working toward TRC since third grade. You can ask our science teacher, Mrs. Oldham, from Frey Elementary School."

Mr. Parker nibbled on his mustache. "We'll see. All I can tell you is, join the after-school club and hope for the best. That's where you'll practice programming basics using LEGO Mindstorms. If we get enough kids for the TRC, we'll begin meeting on Saturdays to work on our robot."

Yusuf didn't tell him he'd already programmed LEGO Mindstorms at least thirty times. He nodded his thanks and turned to leave, then paused. "Who's the mentor for TRC?"

"Me." Mr. Parker gave a little smile. "Guess you'll be seeing a whole lot of me this year."

As Yusuf was leaving, Mr. Parker called out, "You're Azeem's son, aren't you? From A to Z Dollar Store?"

Yusuf turned around and nodded. There was only one dollar store in Frey, and there was only one Azeem. "Yes, sir."

Mr. Parker nodded thoughtfully and went back to the papers on his desk. "Welcome to sixth grade."

In the cafeteria at lunchtime, Yusuf and Danial pored over the robotics club flyer. "The worst part of this entire thing is the TRC club on Saturdays," Danial complained. "My dad will never let me skip the mosque for that." He was eating paratha and omelet he'd brought from home, because his parents didn't allow non-halal food.

Yusuf, on the other hand, was chomping on a chicken barbecue sandwich straight from the cafeteria. No longer bringing lunch from home was the ultimate sign that he was cool. He looked dreamily at the chalkboard menu above the lunch counters. Pizza day was Friday. Tomorrow.

"Are you listening to me?" Danial hissed. "The TRC club is on Saturdays, which is when we all go to the masjid for Sunday school. Did you forget?"

Yusuf hadn't forgotten. Sunday school at their masjid had temporarily shifted to Saturdays because of construction, but they still called it Sunday school out of habit. "Don't worry, I'll figure something out. Maybe my amma can convince yours. That way we can bypass the fathers altogether."

Danial grunted. "Your mom's no fool. Remember how last year she made you go to Sunday school in the middle of a tropical storm? You were the only kid there that day."

Yusuf hadn't forgotten. "It wasn't raining so badly when we left the house," he protested. "Anyway, it's been an entire year since that happened. I'm going to try talking to her over the weekend."

Danial pushed his egg pieces around in disgust. "Whatever."

Yusuf polished off the last of his sandwich and jabbed a barbecue-smudged finger on the robotics flyer. "The bigger problem is that we need more players to form a team. Mr. Parker said he can never get enough kids to join the competition."

"Really?" Danial pushed his lunch box away with a groan. "Where will we find other kids as much into LEGO and robots as we are?"

"You mean obsessed like us?"

"Have you noticed how most kids would rather play football or even watch a football game than write code?" Danial asked. "And they're so rude here. Nobody says hello, and one kid pushed me as we were leaving the class. Forget about saying sorry. Middle school is hard, dude."

"It's about to get harder," Yusuf replied, looking over his shoulder. A group of boys stood near the entrance in a tight circle, laughing loudly. Someone was in the center of that circle, but all Yusuf could see was a head of black hair. "Who is that?"

A minute later, the circle began to move, and then morphed into a line. The black head in the center came into view. Cameron. He was laughing with his mouth open, his T-shirt untucked over too-loose pants. His hair was spiked with what seemed to Yusuf like a ton of gel. He wasn't the only one, though. All the boys in the group looked the same. They moved like a school of sharks through the cafeteria, Cameron in the middle. One boy purposefully bumped into a table, spilling milks and juices. Another boy snatched a cap off someone's head and put it on his own. Cameron laughed some more.

"What is his problem?" Danial whispered furiously.

"What do you mean?" Yusuf was still staring at the group.

"He acts so . . . white." Danial said the last word as if it was an insult. "Like, changing his name, talking in an accent, hanging out with those guys . . ."

Yusuf looked at his friend in surprise. "What do you care who he hangs out with?"

"I don't care. I'm just pointing out that it's not very smart. Does he think they like him? They all probably make fun of him behind his back."

The bell rang. Lunchtime was over. Danial stood up, a hard look on his face. "Like they probably make fun of all of us."

Yusuf paused. "Not all of us."

Danial gave him a pitying look. "Keep fooling yourself, my friend. Just because you're your father's son doesn't mean you're golden."

Yusuf wanted to protest, but then he thought of the paper in his locker and closed his mouth.

5

Frey, Texas, was a small town of eight point five square miles, approximately two hundred miles from Dallas and fifty miles from Houston. It lay closest to the city of Conroe, off Interstate 45, but you needed to take a two-lane farm road for another ten miles before you got to Frey. The local population, including Yusuf and his family, was 12,845.

Yusuf knew the story of the town as well as any resident: how two brothers, George and Henry Frey, had traveled there from England in 1832 with their families. Their portraits hung in the entryway of the city hall building, two mustachioed and bearded men with identical frowns and faraway looks in their eyes. The original village didn't have a name, but it had an orchard, a winery, and a cotton gin. And cattle, of course.

Yusuf always wondered if the Frey brothers were ranchers in England, but Abba told him ranching was a Texan thing. They must have learned, though, and quickly. The village grew, and with it the Frey family. And sometime in the early 1900s, they gave their home an official name: Frey, Texas.

Frey boasted a lot of typical small-town things. A nineteenth-century courthouse that now also included the Frey Family Museum. A corn maze that was open all night in the fall, if you dared to enter it. A still-functioning stone fountain and three quaint little bed-and-breakfasts. Groves of peaches that supplied many of the grocery stores in southeast Texas. And sixteen churches in a variety of denominations.

The Freys were Quakers. The church they'd built in 1835 was still standing in the middle of the town square. Over time, the town had grown, and many people with different traditions had settled here. Abba often talked about the Hindu family that lived next door to them when Yusuf was a toddler. Gita and Krishna Bannerjee, their three sons, and Krishna's eighty-year-old father. They'd moved away when Gita got a medical residency in Conroe. The last thing they told Abba before they left was, "This town is only big enough for one kind of people."

"What did they mean?" Yusuf had once asked Abba, and Abba only shrugged with sad eyes. There were a total of eleven Muslim families now, up from five in 2001. They prayed together on Fridays and took every opportunity to mingle. The children went to Sunday school on the weekends, every single one of them, even if they didn't want to. That was how things were done.

On Friday night after dinner, Yusuf showed Amma the flyer about the robotics club. She shook her head firmly. "Nahi beta. I'm sorry, but I won't let you miss Saturday classes just so you can go to a LEGO club."

Yusuf felt his heart thud in his chest, but he went on anyway. "Amma, please. You know how hard we've been working to prepare for the championship. It's a great opportunity."

"Any other day would be fine," she replied, turning away as if the matter was decided. "Saturday mornings are busy for all of us."

He could feel his eyebrows gather together into a scowl. "Why can't we have Sunday school like before? It's not fair."

She gave him a sideways look. "You know why. Everybody's busy at the construction site on Sundays. We all have to sacrifice something to build our new mosque."

He opened his mouth, but she beat him to it, saying, "Bus, end of discussion."

He closed his mouth with a snap. What could he say? Amma's face softened, and she turned back to hug him. "It's not forever, jaan. Soon the construction will finish and we can go back to the way things were before."

He stood tense in the circle of her arms. He didn't tell her it would be too late by then. He just swallowed his feelings.

Saturday school had an odd sound to it, but that was how they'd been meeting for the last two years. Their "mosque" was a dingy mobile trailer at the back of Abba's dollar store. It was small and hot and dark, and smelled like old newspapers even when you opened every single window at the back. It was no longer a viable option, as Abba was fond of saying. Yusuf was sure the option had been unviable for at least a decade. The number of Muslims living in Frey had grown and grown until they spilled out of the trailer and into the parking lot at Friday prayers.

Mayor Taylor Frey Chesterton, great-great-great-great-grand-nephew of the original Freys, had come around to Abba's dollar store three times last year to tell him something must be done. He liked to remind people he'd worked hard to establish the town as a modern, state-of-the-art place. "It's unseemly to be praying like heathens in the parking lot of a decent business," he'd said gently one time. "It may scare away the customers."

Abba didn't tell him that they were Muslims, not heathens. In Frey, anyone not worshipping at a church with a pointy steeple was a heathen. "No offense," Mayor Chesterton assured Abba. Everybody always assured Abba that they loved him, that he was their favorite store owner ever. "Our hero," the *Frey Weekly* had proclaimed him in last year's report on the local economy.

Abba had nodded and smiled and told the mayor that they were building their very own mosque more than a mile away from town, near the railway tracks. "That's far," the mayor had replied, pleased. "How long you reckon it will take to build?"

The mayor should have known all this. He'd approved the plans and signed all the permits just months before. Still, he always spoke with everyone with the utmost respect, leaning down until you could see the white hairs growing out of his nose. So Abba told him, "Not long now."

Yusuf knew the truth. Nobody was sure how long the mosque would take to build, because they were all building it together. Cameron's father was a construction foreman, and he was the only one who had any clue about what they were doing. He'd brought a small crew with him in the early days of building. They'd done the major work like laying the foundation and putting in the plumbing. After that, Mr. Khan's fundraising efforts had stalled, and the crew had stopped coming every day. On the weekends, the crew worked twelve hours. That's when the entire Muslim community— men, women, and children—showed up to help.

In the meantime, Sunday school continued. That week, Amma was the only teacher. The other teacher, Sameena Aunty, had a terrible cold. "No Busybody Aunty today," Danial whispered gleefully to Yusuf. "I hope she never recovers."

"That's awful!" Yusuf whispered back, but secretly he agreed. Sameena Aunty was a dragon, handing out punishments with righteous glee. She knew everything about everyone: who was sick and who'd gotten all As and which family was going on vacation six months from now. It was freaky how much she knew.

"Your mom is the best teacher, dude."

It was true. Amma gave out candy to anyone who sat quietly or answered correctly. She made all the kids seem smart. "MashAllah!" She beamed when a child recited the Arabic alphabet. "Good job!" she told the class when they did even a little bit of their homework.

Yusuf always did his homework. Danial always copied off him in the parking lot before they took deep breaths and entered the trailer. Today was no different. Check homework, breathe deeply, enter, take your shoes off, say salaam.

Today Amma was wearing a long checkered blouse and black pants, with a black hijab covering her head casually. She only wore it in the mosque and when praying, unlike Sameena Aunty, who wore it 24/7, even in 110-degree weather. Danial speculated that she even wore it to sleep. Yusuf told him that was ridiculous, that he was no better than those people on TNN whose information about Muslims was 100 percent incorrect.

"So what do we learn from the story of Prophet Moses?" Amma asked the class.

"Pharaoh's a baddie?" Aleena guessed.

"Correct!" Amma smiled a huge smile and handed her a snack-sized Twix. "What else?"

Danial raised his hand. "Prophet Moses was so brave. He couldn't even speak properly, but he gathered the courage to go before the king."

Amma beamed and handed him a tiny Mars bar. "Faith makes us strong, doesn't it? It helps us do scary things because we believe in our mission."

Yusuf couldn't really imagine a young Moses going before the Pharaoh to demand anything. It seemed impossibly terrifying. He watched Danial unwrap his Mars bar and gobble it up.

"Anything else?" Amma prodded, looking at Yusuf.

He shook his head, and Amma went back to her book. Danial rolled his eyes and whispered, "Forgot the lesson, did you?"

Yusuf glared at him. "You have chocolate on your teeth."

6

Abba was cleaning the plaque on the wall when Yusuf came into the store. Rusty the cat sat in the window, ignoring the humans around her. A football game played on the little television in the corner. "It's not dirty, Abba," Yusuf told his father severely.

Abba stood back from the plaque and read the words as if they weren't etched into his heart already.

> TO MOHAMMAD AZEEM,
> FOR YOUR COURAGEOUS BRAVERY
> IN THE FACE OF DANGER.
> APRIL 18, 2011

"It's not dirty because I clean it every day, my son."

"More like twice a day."

Abba sniffed at him. "Do you want to watch the security camera footage from that day? It will help you understand."

Yusuf groaned so loudly he startled Rusty. She stood up and stretched. "I've watched that thing a thousand times, Abba!"

It was true. He had, because Abba wanted him to. How could he ever forget the image of the masked man, his hand in his jacket pocket, shouting at Abba to give him money. The customers crouching down in the aisles, fear in their eyes. Abba hitting the man in the stomach with a cricket bat he kept under his cash register, then standing over him with legs wide apart while dialing 911 on the store phone.

"A thousand times is not enough to understand what a great day that was! What a blessing in disguise that robber was."

"Amma says he was a horrible man with a gun. How can he be a blessing?"

Abba put away the dusting cloth behind the counter. "See the way the people of this town treat me—us—because of that man?" His voice rose with excitement. "A robber came to terrorize us with a gun, but I was stronger and braver. And I defeated him!"

"Yes, I know."

Abba smiled and patted Yusuf on the head. "Inshallah,

one day you can also be a hero like your father. I have faith in you!"

Yusuf doubted that could ever happen. "Abba, do you have any work for me? Amma will be back from Conroe soon, and then I have to go do my science homework."

Abba threw an annoyed look his way. "Yes, yes. My useless assistant is off today." He started walking toward the aisles. "Aisle three is a mess. We need to clean it and make room for new stock."

Aisle three was the paper aisle. Yusuf knew all the aisles backward and forward. Aisle three had notebooks, envelopes, greeting cards, and printer paper. It was a section that depended heavily on tidiness and structure, things Abba loved.

"I'll be right there," Yusuf called.

Rusty came over to Yusuf. He knelt and scratched her back with gentle hands. She was orange and scrawny, living off the trash in the back parking lot, which wasn't a bad thing because the visitors to the mosque trailer always left behind delicious treats like chicken bones with the flesh still hanging off, and beef tendrils, and lamb hoofs. Plus, Amma always brought back the fat trimmings from her weekly treks to the halal meat market in Conroe. "Amma will be back before you know it, Rusty," he murmured to her.

She meowed loudly.

Yusuf scratched harder. "A couple of hours, max," he assured her, thinking about the cat in Uncle Rahman's journal. What was her name? Silky. What a weird name.

Rusty wasn't any better, though. She'd gotten her name because she'd wandered into the back room of Abba's store one day last year from God knows where. She was just a kitten, and on her third day in the back of the store, she'd swallowed a pallet nail from the floor. They'd thought she wouldn't survive. But she'd recovered, and Yusuf had begged to keep her. Aleena had asthma, and being around cats was bad for her lungs, so Abba allowed Rusty to stay in the shop. Yusuf thought she probably didn't mind. Rusty seemed allergic to people most of the time, unless she was hungry.

Abba sat hunched in aisle three, sorting the notebooks. A small pile of price tags lay on the floor next to him. Yusuf sat down next to him, legs crossed, and began fixing the tags on the shelves the way he'd been doing for years.

"How was school this week?" Abba asked without looking at him.

He shrugged. "Okay. Robotics club is starting next week."

"Good. Maybe you can make a robot to clean up my store."

Yusuf didn't like how Abba made that into a joke.

"I could probably do that if I put some time into it."

"Really?" Abba looked half amazed and half disbelieving.

"Not right now, but maybe if I studied robotics for a few more years."

"That's good. I like that plan. Stay in school, study hard, all that good stuff."

Yusuf debated if he should ask about Saturday school. Abba didn't really have control over his after-school activities. Those were Amma's realm, and she was the tyrant queen. Yusuf decided to keep quiet.

The bell on the door rang, and Abba stood up quickly. "Ah, a customer."

There were several. A blond woman with a toddler wanted to see if there were any diapers on sale. A man with a tired face wanted a greeting card. Abba knew all the customers by name, and he smiled and asked about their families and offered the toddler a lollipop from the big jar he kept on the shelf above his counter.

Yusuf cleaned up aisle three by himself. He affixed all the new price tags and then picked up the old products and took them to the storeroom. The supply truck came from Houston every two weeks, and as far as Yusuf remembered, the next one was due in just a few days. The storeroom was a mess, so he sighed and cleaned that up too. Rusty slid between his legs as he worked.

When he came out, the blond woman and the man with the tired face were gone, but someone else was talking with Abba—an old woman with white hair tied in a bun and gnarled hands she waved around as she talked. "I need that potting soil, Azeem; my flowers won't grow without it."

Abba nodded in time with her words. "Yes, yes, Mrs. Raymond. A few more days, I promise. The truck will be here next week. I will call you as soon as it gets here."

"See that, Jared? That's what I call good service."

Yusuf hadn't seen a boy standing next to the woman, still as a statue. Jared Tobias. He'd seen this boy in Mr. Parker's science class. He was tall, and thinner than a rake with long brown hair that fell almost to his shoulders. Yusuf couldn't help but be impressed. There was no way his parents would ever let him grow his hair long.

Abba waved Yusuf over. "This is my son, Yusuf. Say hello, beta."

Yusuf wished he could be anywhere else at that moment. "Hello."

The old woman beamed. "Well, hello, handsome fellow. You look like my Jared's age. This here is my grandson. He's staying with me now."

Yusuf nodded to Jared, then offered a little smile. "Hi."

Abba was ringing up Mrs. Raymond's purchases as he spoke. "How is your garden doing this year, Mrs. Raymond?"

"Oh, this heat is not doing us any favors! I'm keeping my precious roses in a special greenhouse this year. They'll be needed for the parade, I'm sure."

"Good idea." Abba paused, as if not knowing what to say, then continued. "Twenty years, eh?"

The woman shook her head. "I know, I can't believe it's been that long. Seems like yesterday. I still remember what I was doing when the planes hit those towers."

Abba didn't say anything. He jabbed a finger on the keys of his cash register as if they had something rude written on them.

Yusuf tried not to stare at Jared. He hadn't seen this boy in elementary school. Where had he lived before coming to Frey Middle? Yusuf had a dozen questions in his mind, but he kept quiet.

Mrs. Raymond chatted some more, then took her purchases and left. "Don't forget to call me when the soil gets here!"

When they'd gone, Abba whispered almost to himself, "Twenty years. So much time, but things haven't really changed at all."

Yusuf's ears perked up. They'd been talking about

the same thing at dinner with Uncle Rahman. "What do you mean?"

Abba shook his head as if to get rid of ugly thoughts. "Never mind, forget I said anything." He pointed a finger at Yusuf's chest. "That Jared moved here from Houston recently. You saw how he looked—like a lonely, miserable cat. You should make friends with him."

Rusty meowed as if insulted.

"I'm going to do my homework," Yusuf told Abba, before any other customers appeared. He went back to the storeroom and opened his backpack. There was only one math worksheet, which he finished in ten minutes. Then he took out Uncle Rahman's journal and settled down on the floor to read.

Journal entry 2
September 4, 2001
This week we had our first elective class of sixth grade. I'd chosen art, only because being in band for an entire year didn't sound like too much fun. I didn't think I'd like art, but it's actually okay. Mr. Levine lets us sit anywhere we want, and we use oil paints and canvas. Plus, nobody minds if I make a mess. Our first assignment is a landscape, and I'm painting Galveston Beach because that's where we're planning

to go for next weekend. I can already imagine it: the sun, the waves, the smell of meat on our portable grill.

It's going to be AWESOME!

Plus, I'm going to sit on the sand and read. Art may be fun, but I'd rather be reading, any time! Too bad library isn't an elective.

Farrah baji always tells me to be serious in my studies, like she is. She's a senior in high school this year, and she's thinking about college. She can't decide which subject to choose as her elective this year, world literature or journalism. It's strange to me . . . how can someone in high school decide what they want to be for the rest of their lives? I have zero clues about myself, although Amma and Abba keep telling everyone I'll be a doctor when I grow up. I don't want to burst their bubble, but the sight of blood makes me feel like throwing up, so I don't think that's going to happen.

Jonathan says he's seen a lot of blood on the football field. I don't doubt it. Those guys are brutal. I'm so glad he's my friend, though. I've known him since second grade, when he kicked a ball in the playground that landed on my head. "You cried like a baby for hours!" he always teases me. But it's not really true. I cried for a minute, and then we became best friends forever. End of story.

Some people think it's weird that we're friends.

He's a popular white kid with muscles and thick blond hair. I'm a first-generation Pakistani kid who wears glasses and reads a lot. And I don't have muscles. But Jonathan says to forget those haters. We have a lot in common, because secretly he reads a lot too. He just doesn't do it in public like me. He says he has a reputation to maintain.

I don't care. As long as we can hang out in school and do our homework together on the phone on weekends, I'm happy. Sometimes I can hear his mom grumbling about us in the background, but it doesn't bother me too much. We're going to be best friends forever and ever, even when we're fifty years old. I guarantee it.

7

"Look out, beta!"

"Stay out of the way, will you? Ya Allah, you kids!"

The next day, Sunday, was construction day, as always. Yusuf and Danial ducked just as a group of men—uncles they knew—huffed past with wooden beams. "Can we help?" Yusuf asked eagerly.

Danial pulled him away from the half-built structure that would one day be the Islamic Center of Frey. At the moment it was just wood planks and nails and Sheetrock. It was men and women and children of all ages milling about, carrying heavy things. It was noise and laughter. And some worried glances, like Abba's as he asked nobody in particular for the tenth time: "Are we on schedule with the construction? Because it doesn't look like we are."

Yusuf agreed with his father. It didn't look like the mosque would be finished in another few months. He opened his mouth to repeat his offer of help.

Danial gave Yusuf a hard look. "No, we can't help right now. We need to strategize."

Yusuf looked around. "But we're supposed to help. All hands on deck, remember?"

Cameron walked over to them, his lip curled in disgust. "You're such a Goody Two-shoes, Yusuf. Always doing exactly what the adults tell you to do."

Danial scowled. "Nobody asked you to be in this conversation, Kamran!" he said, stressing the correct Urdu pronunciation of Cameron's name.

Cameron shrugged. "Yet here I am." He had a backpack on his shoulder, gray and dirty, and definitely old. Yusuf couldn't help wondering what was in it. Something terrible, knowing Cameron.

Danial strode away with purposeful steps. The others followed, going through a wooden fence that marked off the construction area. "My dad told me we have to help with lunch prep. That's at least two hours away. So you can rest easy."

"Wait," Yusuf replied. "Amma said if we have nothing else to do, we need to help with the medical table."

They stopped at a clearing that would one day be

a parking lot, but was only grass and mud and trees for now. One of the Muslim doctors had set up a little table with a few supplies and a row of folding chairs. A pregnant woman was getting her blood pressure checked. Razia Begum, Frey's oldest Muslim, sat snoring in her wheelchair. She wore a yellow cotton sari, and her brilliant white hair was tied into a straggly bun at the nape of her neck. A fly buzzed around her, but she didn't seem bothered by it.

Danial waved. "See, everything is under control. We're not needed."

Yusuf looked around for Amma, but she was busy talking with a few other women in a far corner of the lot. Everything *did* seem under control. He could help out a little later, he decided.

The boys wandered to the shade of a giant oak tree and sat cross-legged under it, making sure they stayed away from the muddy bits. Cameron collapsed on the tree's exposed roots as if he was made of foam. Yusuf passed around some cinnamon gum, and they relaxed in the sunlight, looking at the workers in the distance. The uncle-workers they all knew as their neighbors and friends' fathers, and most had zero knowledge about building things. The aunty-workers assembled sandwiches and babysat the little ones and cleaned the worksite in the evenings.

The railway tracks gleamed in the distance as the sun shone over them. Yusuf checked his watch. The ten o'clock train would pass in exactly thirteen minutes.

"So, did you talk to your mom about the Saturday club?" Danial asked.

Yusuf nodded glumly. "Yes. You were right. She refused."

"Told you." Danial stared into the distance with a pleased look on his face. He loved being right.

There was a rustle from the other side of the tree. Cameron was poking a centipede with a stick, not forcefully, but just hard enough to make the centipede curl up in protest. They both watched for a minute, fascinated. "He better not hurt that thing," Danial whispered in Yusuf's ear.

"What will you do?"

"Something. I don't know."

They watched some more. Cameron left the centipede alone and began writing in the mud with his stick. Yusuf couldn't make out the letters. Were they English or Urdu? Or Arabic perhaps? He whispered again to Danial, "We need more people for TRC," and jerked his head in Cameron's direction repeatedly. "Mr. Parker said so."

Danial lost his pleased look. "No way."

"We don't have a choice," Yusuf said. "We have to

sign up a team soon or we can kiss the LEGO competition goodbye."

Cameron turned his head, pointing the stick in his hand at them. "LEGO? What are you guys, ten?"

"TRC is not for kids," Yusuf informed him. "It's a competition for middle schoolers, with regionals in Conroe every year."

Cameron went back to his sand letters. "I know what it is. It's stupid."

Yusuf sighed. Cameron had been their friend until fourth grade. They'd played catch in Danial's backyard on the weekends, or LEGOs when it was too hot to go outside. Cameron could build the most complicated thing in minutes, his hands moving so quickly over the LEGO pieces they seemed blurry.

Danial stood up and went around to stand in front of Cameron. "Forget the LEGO part. It's actually a robotics competition using Mindstorms. You've heard of that, haven't you?" It was a challenge that came out in a sneer.

"Mindstorms, huh?" Cameron pursed his lips as if he was thinking. "No thanks."

Danial made a frustrated sound in his throat. "You are so . . ."

Cameron looked up, an amused smile on his lips.

"I'm so . . . what? Not interested in being bossed around by you anymore? Not into your childish games anymore? What?"

This wasn't the first time the two had bickered. Yusuf quickly stood up between them, taking care not to step on the poor centipede curled up in the middle. "You may be interested in the prize."

There was a screech in the distance, and they all jumped slightly. The train. It came like clockwork three times a day, pulling graffiti-painted cars filled with oil. Ten o'clock, two thirty, and five thirty-five. Yusuf knew the schedule because he'd checked the city website when the mosque construction had first begun. The little kids shouted and ran to hang on to the fence, watching with wide, excited eyes. The train chugged closer with a deafening roar. It took twenty-six seconds for it to pass, and then it was gone.

"What prize?" Cameron finally asked.

Danial's face resembled a thundercloud, but Yusuf ignored him. "It's a pretty sweet prize," he told Cameron with a coaxing smile. "Cash. Video games. A laptop."

Cameron's expression eased. "A laptop, huh?"

Yusuf nudged Danial with his elbow. "We'll give you the laptop if we win. All you have to do is sign up for Mr. Parker's robotics club after school."

Danial opened his mouth to protest, but Yusuf gave him a warning look. "Yeah, sure," Danial finally choked out.

Cameron grinned, and his earring glinted in the sunlight. "Well, that sounds like fun. How do I sign up?"

Lunch was chicken salad and jalapeño sandwiches assembled by Amma's team of volunteer aunties. The food was arranged on a long white folding table, along with big bags of potato chips and gallon-sized recycled water bottles. Everyone sat around the table, either on folding chairs brought from home, or on the ground.

Yusuf gazed into the distance. A few houses were being built on the far end of the road. Close by was a church with a white steeple and a playground in the backyard. People stood in the yard in clumps, and a loud laugh rang out here and there. Yusuf imagined them talking and eating sandwiches. "I wonder if they also built their church themselves," he said.

Danial laughed. "Of course not. You only do that if you don't have enough money to hire a crew. My dad said that's the proper way."

Yusuf looked around. "Where is your dad anyway?"

"He had to work. His company has an important deadline coming up."

Yusuf chewed his lip. "I thought everyone had to be here on Sundays to help."

Danial frowned. "Look, they're coming this way."

It was a weekly ritual. The church people ended their Sunday services at exactly twelve noon, and by twelve thirty they made their way slowly in twos and threes down the street, past the construction site. Only a few came in cars that they parked on the side of the road.

"Hello."

"Good morning."

"Howdy."

Yusuf always smiled and waved. So did Abba and Amma and several others. But the church people mostly looked at their feet, as if they were worried they'd stumble if they didn't watch where they were going.

Something made Yusuf look back at the church. Only the pastor was left, standing at the door. And a tall boy with long hair. The boy saw Yusuf looking, and offered a small, reassuring smile. It wasn't even really a smile, because it vanished before Yusuf was sure it was real. He realized he'd seen the boy before.

"That's Jared," Yusuf breathed.

Danial frowned. "Who?"

"Nobody."

8

Yusuf had almost forgotten the entire note-in-his-locker situation over the weekend. He opened his locker on Monday morning with a smile, telling Danial about the cinnamon French toast Amma had cooked for breakfast. French toast was his favorite, because Amma had a secret recipe: fry the toast in a spoonful of ghee. "Ah-may-zing!" he sang.

Anything cooked in ghee was a hundred times better. It also added hundreds of unnecessary calories to the food, but who cared?

"My mom says ghee is a delicious killer," Danial said from behind him.

"Your mom needs to eat some of my amma's food," Yusuf replied. It was true. If there was ever a cooking competition among all the women of Frey, Farrah Azeem would be crowned queen.

"Whatever."

The locker door swung open, and the paper floated out to the ground gently. Yusuf tried to grab it, but Danial was quicker. "'We hate you,'" he read slowly. Then he looked up and stared accusingly at Yusuf. "Why did you write this? Who is it for?"

Yusuf swallowed the bile rising up in his throat. It didn't help that he could taste cinnamon. "I . . . it . . . I didn't write . . . Give it back."

"Then who did?"

"I said give it back!" Yusuf knew he was too loud. A few kids passing by looked at him curiously. "Someone wrote it about me," he finally admitted, hanging his head.

Danial looked aghast. He handed over the paper hastily, as if it was contaminated with a horrible disease. "Sorry."

Yusuf crumpled up the paper without looking at it. He wanted to sink into the ground, or slam the locker door and run away. But where would he go? "It's just a joke," he finally said.

"A joke? This doesn't look like a joke."

Yusuf threw the crumpled ball into the back of the locker, stuffed his backpack inside, and slammed the door shut. "Never mind. Forget it."

But he couldn't forget it. *We hate you,* the paper had said. Who was *we?* Why would they hate him? What had Yusuf ever done to anyone?

In science, Mr. Parker had to call his name three times before he looked up. "I'm sorry, sir. Can you repeat that?"

"I'm asking for an example of an insulator."

"Um, I'm not sure. . . ."

Mr. Parker waved toward the whiteboard and frowned. "It's right there, if you care to pay attention."

Yusuf focused on the whiteboard. He knew insulators inside out. He'd used rubber sheets to pad the wall he shared with Aleena's room so he couldn't hear her coughing at night. "Metal?" he read from the whiteboard.

Wait, that didn't seem right.

"Wrong column, Mr. Azeem!" Mr. Parker practically yelled.

Yusuf hung his head. "Sorry," he mumbled. He felt like puking.

Thankfully, he didn't. He kept his eyes fixed on the whiteboard the rest of science class, nodding like a broken robot every few minutes and making zero eye contact with anyone. Jared sat three desks away, and he gave Yusuf a little nod, as if to say, "It's okay, these things happen." Yusuf relaxed. It was true. Giving the wrong answer wasn't the end of the world.

Jared was also in Miss Terrance's social studies class, sitting right next to Yusuf. Miss Terrance handed out class copies of *Ancient Civilizations* and worksheets full of comprehension questions. "Read the first chapter, and then we'll discuss the questions," she told them before going back to her desk, her heels clacking on the classroom floor. She had shoulder-length hair that was dyed purple, and long nails that matched.

Yusuf turned the pages of the book, but all he could see was the paper from his locker. *We hate you. We hate you.* He pressed a finger under his glasses, touching his right eyelid. "Focus!" he hissed to himself.

"You want to say something?" Miss Terrance looked up, annoyed. She'd been writing something on her computer, her eyebrows scrunched together like an angry line of soldiers.

"No. Sorry, ma'am."

Jared leaned over as soon as Miss Terrance went back to her work. "You okay?" He had a raspy voice, so low it was almost a whisper.

Yusuf nodded. "Sure. Thanks for asking."

Jared looked at him for a second. Two seconds. Then he whispered again, shyly, "Many people think the ancient pyramids were actually built by aliens."

"That's a conspiracy theory," Yusuf told him. TNN was always full of people with conspiracy theories.

"Is it?" Jared shot back. "Or is it a truth that everyone just covers up?"

"I'm warning you, boys," Miss Terrance called out.

Yusuf didn't look up from his book until it was discussion time. But he hadn't read a word. And Jared didn't talk to him again all day.

At dinner, Amma wanted to know how school was going. "Mrs. Khan said they need volunteers in the library. I was thinking I should sign up."

Yusuf shrugged. "I haven't had library yet." He'd memorized the times for all his core classes, but not library and PE. Of course he could check his schedule to see when those were, but the schedule was in his locker, and he was pretty sure he wasn't going to open that door ever again.

Amma gave him a long look. "Is everything okay? Are you upset about the robotics club on Saturday?"

"I'm not upset."

Aleena spilled water on the table just then, so Amma stopped asking him so many questions. "WAAAHHH!" Aleena wailed. "Water gone!"

Yusuf gobbled up his leftover roti and vegetables and went off to his room, saying "Homework" over his shoulder. He wasn't lying. He had another sheet of math problems, plus a science video to watch for Mr. Parker. It was after eight o'clock when he logged into Scratch. Aleena's game was almost complete, and a bunch of users had sent comments. He clicked through the site. He loved browsing other people's projects to see what creative things they came up with.

Hey wats up? You ok?

It was Danial, sending him a message through Scratch's interface.

Yusuf: Im fine

Danial: Told you middle school was the worst

Yusuf: Stop

Danial: You looked like you saw a ghost in your locker.

Yusuf: I gotta go

Danial: Wait. Tomorrow's the robotics club. Are u ready???

Yusuf had forgotten all about the robotics club. He scrambled through his backpack for the flyer, which had a permission form on the back. He filled it out neatly, then went in search of a parent.

Abba was sitting in front of the television, dozing. The news was on, showing a hospital in some African country with wailing children and flies everywhere. Yusuf had never seen anything good on TNN. Even the animal stories were horrible.

Abba opened his eyes and looked at him. "Isn't it bedtime yet, son?"

Yusuf nodded, then said, "Can you sign this, please, Abba?"

Abba sighed. "What is this?"

"Robotics club after school." Yusuf gulped and tapped the frame of his glasses. "It's free, don't worry."

Abba read the flyer slowly, lips moving as he took it in. "Is this the year you compete in TRC?"

Yusuf was surprised his father knew what TRC was. Had Danial and he ever talked about their obsession in front of their parents? He couldn't be sure. "It's a statewide robotics competition," he said, just to be sure they were both on the same page.

Abba gave a tired smile, as if he already knew. "So, you're going to take part in that?"

"If we get enough kids to join."

Abba narrowed his eyes. "And will this help you in high school? Or college? I don't want you wasting your time on something that's not going to make you succeed."

Yusuf tried to push the form closer to Abba's face, but it was too late. Abba was on to his favorite subject.

"You know, I struggled very hard when I came to this country. I was already in my twenties. I didn't have any of the opportunities that young people who are born here do. Like your mother. Like you."

"I know, Abba."

"If I had gone to college here, taken all these science subjects, I'd be sitting in an air-conditioned office somewhere like the Khans, instead of in my shop where the AC doesn't even work most days."

"You like your shop," Yusuf protested. "Where would everyone in Frey get their . . . stuff . . . if you didn't have your shop?"

Abba was silent, staring down at the form. "There are other shops. So many of my customers have left me. Gone to the shopping center across town."

Yusuf wasn't sure he believed this. "Really? Why? You have the best things, and they're always on sale!"

Abba shrugged. "This town is changing, beta. Slowly, slowly, like a wind that's blowing through."

Yusuf frowned. "What are you talking about? Changing how?"

Abba shook his head. "Never mind. I just want a better life for you and Aleena, you know that."

Yusuf nodded. "Then can you sign the form, please? Kids who win regional science competitions get into good colleges." He didn't even need to base this claim on actual research. He was using all the buzzwords. Science. Good college.

Abba signed his name and went back to watching television, still muttering about his youth.

Yusuf returned to his room and typed on his computer.

Yusuf: Robotics club here I come!!!!!

Danial: Good, at least one thing is going right

9

Tuesday was supposed to be an excellent day. A restart. The first day of robotics club. Yusuf had decided he would be happy about the club no matter what happened with TRC.

He stood for a second outside his locker, hand on the cold metal. Then he turned away. Better not to open it and find another mean note. What could even top the last one? He didn't want to know, and he definitely didn't want his mood to be shattered so early in the morning. He could get a copy of his schedule from the front office.

His mind was wrestling with a question, though. What if the notes weren't meant for him? Nobody knew which locker belonged to which student, after all. And if they were indeed meant for Yusuf Azeem, how did the person sending them know which locker to push them into?

Danial had a doctor's appointment in the morning, so Yusuf walked the hallways alone, frowning. It was like wandering the desert, trying not to bump into a cactus. Danial was always talking about something, and Yusuf never really paid attention to his surroundings this early in the morning.

Today was different. There were still six and a half minutes until the first bell rang, so he could drag his feet and look around at the bulletin boards that lined the hallway. There was a big poster for football tryouts in the summer—the date had already passed—above the water fountain. The Frey Coyotes, only the most important team in town.

Right next to the football flyer was a long white paper with two columns. Names and locker numbers. Yusuf stared and then gulped. The mystery was solved. Everyone knew which locker belonged to which student. It was right there in black and white. Anybody could be sending him the notes. And they were definitely meant for him.

The air around him felt hot. He turned quickly and started to walk away from the bulletin board.

"Watch it, nerd!"

A big blue backpack that seemed to be stuffed with bricks hit Yusuf in the head. His breath whooshed out of him. He looked up. A chest covered in plaid. Big shoulders. A bushel of curly blond hair on a very white face. Or rather, angry pink.

"Ow, sorry!" Yusuf stammered. His head felt tender.

"You wear glasses, but still can't see?" The boy's tone was low, taunting.

Yusuf took shallow breaths and fiddled with his glasses. "Sorry," he said again, not entirely sure he needed to be apologizing so many times, since the boy didn't seem hurt. But he dipped his head and tried to move past.

"You better be, nerd," the boy growled. "I don't want the likes of you touching me. Or my backpack."

The likes of him? Did they know each other? Yusuf squinted at him, trying not to stare. Ethan Grant. He'd moved to Frey in third grade, but hadn't been in Yusuf's classroom. He'd seen him after school a few times, but that seemed like ages ago. He'd grown at least a foot over the summer, while Yusuf had grown only a quarter of an inch.

Something about this injustice made Yusuf stand taller. "You're the one who smacked me with your backpack."

Ethan's pink skin grew a darker shade of red. "Are

you kidding me?" He leaned forward and growled, as if he couldn't believe somebody would talk back to him.

Yusuf's knees quivered, but they were covered with thick gray corduroys from the Walmart in Conroe, so he was sure Ethan couldn't tell. "No."

Ethan turned around and looked at the row of lockers on either side of them. "How come you're carrying all your stuff? Which one's your locker?" He gave Yusuf a mocking look. "Let me guess. It's all the way near the gym."

Yusuf couldn't get the white paper on the bulletin board out of his mind. "How . . . ?"

The bell rang, and a group of students hurried past, talking loudly. Yusuf dipped his head and followed them, trying to blend in. Ethan howled a sudden burst of laughter at his back, but Yusuf didn't turn around.

Classes passed in a blur. In social studies, they watched a video about Alexander the Great, then answered questions about his leadership style. Yusuf couldn't stop hearing Ethan's mocking laughter in his ears. *He must be the person who's been writing the notes*, Yusuf thought. There was no other explanation.

"Yusuf Azeem, did you have breakfast this morning?" Miss Terrance asked loudly.

"Ma'am?"

Miss Terrance waved a hand with bright red nails at him. Her hair was green today, with silver barrettes holding up the right side. "You're eating your pencil as if you're starving, boy."

A few kids giggled. Jared, sitting next to him as usual, threw him a sympathetic look. Yusuf didn't really care. Ethan was the only thing he could think about.

He told Danial about the encounter at lunch. Danial shook his head sadly. "Ethan's a bully. He used to sit behind me in third grade. He'd kick my chair in class every single day. Once he did it so hard, I fell and hit my head."

Yusuf put down his orange juice. "You never told me this before."

Danial shrugged, chewing slowly on a cheese stick. "It wasn't a big deal."

Yusuf wanted to shout that it was definitely a big deal when a bully made you fall out of your chair. Then he remembered that Danial still didn't know the full story about the notes in the locker. So he drank the rest of his orange juice in silence, still stewing over the incident in the hallway that morning.

Danial wasn't done. "You better stay away from Ethan," he warned. "He's one of the Coyotes now, not someone you can mess with."

Yusuf was hardly listening. "Coyotes?"

"The football team? Weren't you listening to the morning announcements? They announced all the team members' names."

Yusuf stared at his half-eaten lunch. Growing a foot over the summer wasn't bad enough, this guy was also on the football team? "Ugh. Some people have all the luck."

Danial grinned a little. "And some people don't have any," he said, pointing at Yusuf.

Yusuf wanted to say "Shut up," but Amma always told him that was rude. He stuck his tongue out at Danial instead, and went back to his juice.

Mr. Parker sat on his desk, legs crossed at the ankles. "Welcome to robotics club," he solemnly told the kids assembled in the science lab.

There weren't many of them. Yusuf looked around. There was Danial, of course, sitting right next to Yusuf with a huge smile on his face. There was a boy who looked older, with an easy grin and dark hair. Madison Ensley from science class sat in the far corner, looking bored. He wondered why she was there. He'd never met a girl who was interested in robotics.

"Thank you, Mr. Parker." Danial continued to beam, as if he'd won the TRC already. Yusuf nudged him to tone it down a bit.

"Alrighty," Mr. Parker continued, reviewing the

signed forms on his desk. "We have four students so far. Danial, Yusuf, and Madison from sixth grade, and Tony Rivera from seventh grade."

"That's it?" Yusuf blurted out.

Mr. Parker nodded. "That's it. Told you, son. Robotics isn't too popular around here." He looked a little sad, as if this fact pained deep inside him. He turned to write something on the whiteboard.

Danial leaned into Yusuf's side. "I knew Cameron wasn't going to show. He's a liar."

Yusuf jumped as the door opened slowly. "Maybe that's him now."

But it wasn't. The door opened all the way and Jared entered slowly. "Is it too late to join the club?"

Mr. Parker turned back to face the class. "Not at all, Jared. Come in and find a seat. There are plenty to choose from."

Jared sat on Yusuf's other side. They nodded at each other, then looked away.

They settled in and got to work. Mr. Parker had written *Welcome to Middle School Robotics* on the board in slanted handwriting that looked like it was dozing off with boredom. "What's she doing here?" Danial whispered behind Mr. Parker's back.

Mr. Parker turned and frowned. "Really, Danial . . ."

Madison leaned back and crossed her arms over her

chest. "I have four brothers," she said loudly, arching her eyebrows. "I've always loved playing LEGOs with them. My mom used to buy me dolls when I was younger, but I never played with them."

"Dolls are fun," Danial replied in a normal voice, making everyone laugh. But it was a kind laughter, and Yusuf found himself relaxing despite everything that had happened that day.

And despite knowing they didn't have enough team members to enter the TRC competition.

"Robots are machines that can be programmed to carry on a series of actions automatically, even make decisions based on their environment," Mr. Parker continued. "We use them in conjunction with computers, which act as their . . . what?"

"Brain!" Yusuf answered quickly. This was easier than the alphabet.

"Correct." Mr. Parker grinned. He seemed to be different from science class Mr. Parker, more relaxed. "Give me some examples of robots in the real world."

"The assembly line for car manufacturers," Yusuf replied, remembering the documentary from last week.

"Yup. What else?"

They all thought about this. Finally Tony the seventh grader raised his hand. "Bionic legs for disabled people."

Jared said very quietly, "Vacuum cleaners? Like

Roomba or something. My grandmother would give her right arm for one of those."

Then Madison raised hers. "Oooh, I know! Amazon uses robots in their warehouses. For packaging orders and stuff."

They were on a roll. The ideas came fast and furious. Yusuf couldn't stop grinning at Danial. This wasn't TRC, but it was robotics. It was something.

Journal entry 3

September 11, 2001

Something happened today that I don't think I'll ever forget, even if I live to be a hundred years old. My hands are shaking as I write, but Mrs. Clifton tells us that journaling helps process emotions, whatever that means.

So here goes. Our country has been attacked by terrorists. It seems so weird to write this, like I'm playing a part in a movie. But it's true. Also awful and horrifying and scary.

We were doing history lessons in first period when an announcement came over the PA system. "Planes have hit the Twin Towers in New York City. Planes have hit the Twin Towers in New York City."

I knew that voice—it was Mrs. Jahangir, our vice principal. She kept repeating the announcement over and over, and her voice sounded shaky, like she was crying. The kids kept looking at one another, puzzled, but I knew something serious had happened. Mrs. Jahangir is the strictest person at school. Nothing but the worst could make her cry.

It was definitely the worst. Mr. Jasper stopped teaching history and switched on the television in the corner of the room. It's a big one—thirty-two inches—that we take out only for special occasions like watching a history video. Today is history in the making, Mr. Jasper whispered as he stared at the screen in horror.

We watched the news the entire morning. Nobody switched classes like we usually do; nobody even stirred from their chairs. My eyes ached, but they were glued to the TV. The Twin Towers are—were—two tall buildings in New York, and they'd been hit by airplanes. Not by accident as I first thought, but on purpose. We watched as the smoke poured out from one tower, and flames from the other. Red, angry flames licked the windows and concrete. The class next door came into our room at some point, because they didn't have a television. Our teachers stood like statues, their faces full of horror and worry.

Finally Mr. Jasper switched the television off and made us go back to our textbook. But his hands kept trembling and finally he excused himself. I think he *went to the bathroom to cry. That's okay. Sometimes when things are really bad, I lock myself in the bathroom and cry too.*

They decided to let us go home early. In the school bus, everyone was quiet. Confused. I couldn't get the pictures out of my mind. The flames and smoke. The stunned faces of people covered in white ash.

Amma and Abba were watching the news when I got home. Sarah and Farrah baji were both crying, holding hands. They saw me and opened up their arms for a hug. I haven't ever hugged anyone tighter than that, not even Abba when he gave me Silky as a birthday present last year.

We watched the replays of the morning together. I realized something even worse had happened after Mr. Jasper had turned the TV off in our classroom. The burning buildings had collapsed. "Like they were made of paper," Sarah said, staring at the screen.

How is that even possible? Don't they make buildings out of really strong concrete?

"I don't understand what's happening," I whispered in Farrah baji's ear.

She hugged me again and whispered, "I don't either."

We just have to take one day at a time.

10

"What do you mean 9/11 was terrible? Of course, I know. The whole world knows." Danial kicked a pebble with his shoe as they walked to school. There were lots of kids on the sidewalk around them, some with parents, others without. "That's like saying spinach tastes gross. Talk about stating the obvious."

Yusuf shrugged. "I guess you're right. But there's still a big difference, because nobody really wants to talk about it. If you ask anybody about spinach, they'll be happy to give you their opinion. But ask them about 9/11 and they get all quiet."

"Maybe that's how adults deal with tragedy. Our neighbor's son was killed in Iraq and she never talks about it. If you ask her, she shakes her head and a vein pops in her forehead."

Yusuf imagined a gigantic blue vein throbbing in the center of a white forehead. "My abba loves talking about the shooting in his store."

"There wasn't really any shooting," Danial pointed out. "Only a guy waving his hands around. Who knows if there even *was* a gun in his pocket?"

Yusuf glared at Danial. "You better not say that in front of my parents. Abba will be heartbroken."

They were almost at the gates of the school, on a little stretch of El Paso Street where an old, abandoned warehouse stood. "Why are you talking about 9/11 anyway? It happened two whole decades ago."

Yusuf didn't want to tell him about the journal. Not yet. He finally replied, "Rahman mamoo said history informs our present and affects our future."

"What does that mean?"

Yusuf looked around, then stopped. He pointed to the old building in the distance. One crumbling white wall carried the words NEVER FORGET in deep black graffiti. "Look, that wasn't there yesterday. It's new."

They stopped and inspected the graffiti. It was so fresh the paint glistened in the early sunlight. Many kids around them were pointing to it, murmuring loudly. Mayor Chesterton was very strict about graffiti. He'd called it a sign of the devil in a news conference last year, when graffiti had appeared overnight next to the courthouse. "That will be gone by tomorrow," Danial offered in a small voice. "It always is."

"Yeah, sure."

It seemed as if the whole school had seen the graffiti message. Kids were whispering about it in the hallways.

A few kids pointed to Yusuf and Danial as they passed under the black banner that still hung over their heads. "Terrorists!" someone called out, hard and sharp.

A flash of plaid moved past, bumping into Danial. "Hey!" Danial shouted, but Yusuf saw Ethan Grant's tall frame and put a hand on Danial's arm.

"Just . . . don't say anything."

Miss Terrance was ready for a discussion in social studies class. She stood with hands on her hips, legs spread slightly apart so that they looked like two tall buildings teetering on the spindly foundations of her heels. "All right, everyone saw the words on the warehouse outside school this morning, so let's talk about it and get it off our chests before we work on today's lessons. Okay?"

Nobody said anything. Yusuf's throat was dry. Uncle Rahman's journal entry about the Twin Towers tumbling down in a pile of ash and stone echoed in his mind. Did anyone even know what "Never Forget" really meant?

Had anyone ever really thought about it, the way he hadn't been able to stop thinking all night long?

"We learned about it in fifth grade," Madison finally said. "It was a bunch of terrorist attacks a long time ago, when my mom was a teenager."

"Yes," said Miss Terrance, writing *9/11* on the whiteboard with a bright red Expo marker. Then she wrote *Never Forget* under it.

A boy with wispy red hair raised his hand. "It was Arab terrorists. Like him."

Yusuf felt the hair on his neck rise in protest. "Like me?" he squeaked. Why did people think all Muslims were Arab? His family was from South Asia, not that anyone in the class cared.

Miss Terrance scowled heavily. "How old do you think Yusuf Azeem is, fifty? How could he have anything to do with 9/11?"

There was an awkward laughter, but the red-haired boy persisted. "It was his folks. They said that on the news last night."

Miss Terrance's scowl got even darker. "Okay, seems like you kids need some education. I don't want anyone pointing fingers at one of their classmates." She turned away and wrote on the whiteboard: *ASSIGNMENT!!!*

"I want you to research 9/11 and present a report two weeks from now. And it better be good, because I might choose you to read it out loud. Got it?"

They all grumbled, but Yusuf relaxed. Two weeks. He had some time to convince his classmates he wasn't a terrorist. Uncle Rahman's journal would probably have some great tips. Perfect.

At lunch, Danial talked nonstop about his morning. "Everyone was so mean, you can't even believe it. They were chanting 'Never forget!' like it was a fight song or something."

"In class?" Yusuf looked skeptical.

"Our homeroom teacher was late." Danial stared at his uneaten sandwich. "It was the worst five minutes of my life."

"All because of a line of graffiti."

Danial shook his head. "My dad says it's always just below the surface, waiting to boil over."

"The graffiti was just the catalyst," Yusuf whispered.

"Trust you to bring science into bullying."

"Science is in everything."

Danial looked mildly annoyed. "No wonder they call you a nerd." But he picked up his sandwich and took a bite.

They sat in silence for a while. Then a plaid wall planted itself in front of them. "Hey, terrorists."

Yusuf looked up. Ethan and the redheaded boy

from Miss Terrance's class. No surprise that they were friends. "What do you want?" Yusuf wanted to shout, but it came out in a whisper. The lettuce in his mouth turned to dust and tried to choke him.

"Seems like you guys aren't getting the message."

Danial seemed frozen next to him. "What message?"

"Never forget. Duh." Ethan and his friend laughed like it was a joke. Was it? Yusuf couldn't tell why everyone was suddenly making such a big deal about 9/11. They hadn't had this sort of reaction last year, or the year before. Just a few days of angry looks, and a big assembly in their elementary school with a lot of tearful adults. Then life moved on.

Maybe Danial was right. Middle school was bad. Sorrowfully bad.

Ethan leaned forward until his nose was almost touching Danial's. "We hate you guys. You should leave Frey." He said it as if it was something small. Normal. Ordinary. He had freckles on his nose and cheeks, little dots of brown dusted over his pink skin like wildflowers after the first spring showers.

Yusuf and Danial stopped breathing.

"Hey, dude, come on, leave them alone. Nobody cares about them."

All four of them jumped. Yusuf saw Cameron walking toward them casually, hands in pockets. Ethan leaned back, away from Yusuf and Danial. He gave them a serious look, then said, "Catch you later," and sauntered away to join Cameron. The red-haired boy scurried after him.

Yusuf started breathing again. Beside him, Danial let out a shaky whoosh of air, like a deflating balloon. "What. Was. That?" Danial finally said.

"I guess 9/11 is different this year."

"Why?"

"Good question." Yusuf watched Cameron and Ethan high-five each other. Then the two boys turned away, but Cameron looked back with a serious, almost sad look on his face. Yusuf met his eyes for a full five seconds, then he looked down again.

After school, in the robotics club, Mr. Parker handed out snack-sized bags of barbecue chips and cans of Sprite, then gave them blank sheets of paper to create flowcharts. Madison yawned so loudly her jaw cracked. "Flowcharts? Are you serious? After-school clubs are supposed to be fun."

Mr. Parker ignored her. "Flowcharts help in the decision-making process a robot must follow. I want you to get comfortable with this, so that when we actually begin to do some programming you aren't clueless."

Danial said, "We've been programming since we were

eight years old," putting a hand on Yusuf's shoulder to include him in the "we."

Yusuf shifted in his seat. "Not real programming, just basic stuff."

Mr. Parker looked at Yusuf. "Give me an example."

Yusuf wasn't sure he wanted to. "Sometimes I make games for my baby sister on Scratch."

"He's being too modest," protested Danial. "He once created a robot that brought us juice boxes from my mom's fridge while we watched TV."

Yusuf didn't know where to look. Everyone was staring at him as if he'd grown a horn in the middle of his forehead like Aleena's unicorn. "It wasn't a big deal," he told them, touching his glasses. "It was just a moving arm with wheels, and it kept dropping the juice halfway."

Tony Rivera clapped his hands together loudly. "That's awesome, dude! Sounds a lot better than the thing I tried to make last summer. It was supposed to mow the lawn for me, but it ended up cutting down my mom's hedges."

The others laughed, and again it was a nice laugh. A kind one. Yusuf felt his face cool down, his chest relax. These were his kind of people.

Mr. Parker made them practice flowcharts for the next thirty minutes. Yusuf didn't mind. A flowchart was basically a visual algorithm, and he could never get enough of those. He bent his head down and worked.

At four twenty-five, Mr. Parker passed around a trash bag for the empty chip bags and cans, saying, "All right, pack up now. And remember to get those snack sign-ups back to me by the next class. I'm not going to keep on feeding you like this."

"Will we actually get to work on machines in the next class?" Madison asked.

"Maybe," Mr. Parker replied.

The door smashed open, startling them all. Cameron sauntered in, hands in pockets, a lopsided grin on his face. "Perfect timing!" he remarked. "I'm here to join the club."

11

Friday was a half day because of school staff trainings. Amma was waiting for Yusuf in her old Chevy outside school on Friday afternoon. "Early dismissal means we can pray Jummah!" she said cheerfully as he climbed into the passenger seat.

Yusuf would rather have gone home with Danial to play Mindstorms. He clipped his seat belt and leaned back to ruffle Aleena's hair. She sat with a crumby mess of French fries on her lap and around her seat. "You have ketchup on your chin," he told her.

She licked her lips. "We go pray now?"

Amma started the car. "Yes, we go pray now." She looked sideways at Yusuf. "I was thinking, we can hand her over to your abba after Jummah, and then we can go do something on our own."

Yusuf brightened. "Can we go to Conroe? I want to go to Best Buy to look at their electronics section."

Amma smiled. "We'll see."

Friday prayers were offered in congregation in the trailer behind Abba's dollar store, as always. It was sweltering hot, but Abba insisted they stay inside. "I don't want anybody to complain about us to the mayor again," he said.

A few men grumbled loudly. "I'll be glad when the construction is finished and we can have a good space to pray," someone said.

Danial's father gave a short sermon about Prophet Abraham, the father of the three monotheistic religions. Yusuf sat in the back with a few kids from school, all shuffling their feet and fanning themselves with the palms of their hands. Danial was pretending to be asleep, his eyelids fluttering as if he was having a wild nightmare. The women were on one side behind a white curtain hung from the ceiling, and he could hear Aleena protesting over and over, "Hot, Amma, hot," until Amma took her outside. Yusuf looked longingly at the closed trailer door and blinked back the sweat from his eyes.

Mr. Khan droned on. "And the Holy Quran calls Prophet Abraham an upright man. When the disbelievers thrust him into a fire to punish him for preaching, he was unshaken in his faith. He prayed to God Almighty, and lo! God cooled the fire before it could reach him."

"That's impossible," Yusuf whispered to Danial. "Fire can't just . . . cool down."

Danial shrugged without opening his eyes. "Your problem is that you take everything literally. Maybe God sent down rain or something. Lots of things in the Quran are metaphorical."

"Then why wouldn't the text say God sent down rain?"

Danial poked an elbow into his side. "Maybe to make you think."

Yusuf spent the rest of the sermon thinking about Abraham, tied up in the midst of a fire, praying for help. Maybe he should try that with Ethan. He was almost positive praying wouldn't help with the problem of locker notes or unexpectedly tall bullies, but he was willing to try.

After Jummah, Amma dropped a sleeping Aleena at Abba's store, and they drove off. Once they got on the highway, Yusuf leaned against the seat and heaved a sigh. The breeze from the open window was refreshing, even though the temperature was 98 degrees. "Where are we going?" he asked.

Amma adjusted the rearview mirror. "I need to pick up some supplies for your father, and then we're free. We can do whatever we like."

"Can we eat burgers from Whataburger?"

"Sure."

"Can we stop at a 7-Eleven and get cherry Slurpees?"

"Only after five o'clock, when they're buy one get one free."

"Can I go to Saturday club?"

Amma looked at him sideways. "I thought we already discussed it?"

"I know, but I never thought we'd actually get six members on the robotics team, which means we can actually compete in the TRC, which has been my dream since third grade, and by the way, you need to sign up for snacks, otherwise everyone will be very mad, and Saturday school doesn't even make any sense because it's been Sunday school since forever."

Yusuf stopped talking when he ran out of breath. Amma didn't reply. She kept her eyes on the road, as if Yusuf hadn't said a single word. Yusuf waited for a long minute, breathing deeply, then slumped back in his seat again. Danial had been right. His mother would never yield.

"Do you think we should stop the classes altogether?" Amma suddenly asked. "Do any of the students actually get any benefit from them? From all the hard work I do preparing and creating lesson plans?"

Yusuf sat up again. "Amma, your classes are so fun. I still remember that Jeopardy! game you created with all the articles of faith. And you tell amazing stories."

"But?"

"But . . . can't we do it any other day? Like on Sunday, when the kids are hanging out at the construction site playing in the mud and annoying each other?"

Amma chewed on her bottom lip. "You know, that's not a bad idea. Once we get done with making lunch, many of the women and children are just sitting around. Sameena was complaining about it to me just last week. She wanted me to put all the kids to work at building, with the men!"

"Ugh, Sameena Aunty is so weird."

"Don't be disrespectful," Amma warned.

"So you'll think about it?" Yusuf asked, trying to squelch the hope that was rising in his chest.

"I'll think about it."

After getting Abba's supplies from Sam's Club, they stopped at the first Whataburger they found. It was just off the highway, with the famous orange W on the front entrance and a long line of cars in the drive-through lane.

They sat in the back of the restaurant near the

windows, eating burgers and fries with milkshakes. "This is nice, just the two of us." Amma smiled at him. "Remember we couldn't do this for the longest time, because of Covid?"

Yusuf took a big bite of his cheeseburger and wiped the sauce off his chin. He hated talking about Covid. Nothing much had changed in Frey, but the virus had hurt a lot of people in Houston, where their family lived. He racked his brain for a different subject. "Amma, how old were you when 9/11 happened?" he asked.

She paused with a hand holding a fry halfway to her mouth. "Uh, seventeen, I think?" she said casually, as if she couldn't even remember the exact year. "Why?"

He remembered Uncle Rahman telling him the journal was their secret. He'd never lied to Amma before, so he said, "My social studies teacher has given us an assignment, to write a report about 9/11." He left out the part about the kids in school using the T word, or the hurtful notes in his locker. The one that morning had been, predictably, *WE WON'T FORGET.*

Amma ate some more fries, chewing on them thoughtfully. Her face was dark, her eyes downcast. "It was a difficult time for me. For all of us. I was in high school when it happened. I remember watching the news on the television in our teachers' lounge. Some of my friends were crying. A boy in the cafeteria started howling and smashed a tray on the wall. It was tough."

Yusuf tried to imagine his mother at seventeen, young and scared. "What did you do?"

"What could I do? Nothing."

"Nothing?" Yusuf couldn't imagine facing a national tragedy and doing nothing.

Amma put down her fries. "I cried a lot. All the time, as I remember. Your Sarah khala would come into my room at night and crawl into bed with me, and we'd look at the airplanes in the sky. Wondering if another one would crash into a building. Maybe close to us. Maybe it would be our house next time."

"Wow." Yusuf didn't know what to say. "That's seriously messed up."

Amma waved a hand, like she was brushing away an insect from her face. "It was a long time ago. It was bad, but slowly it got better. We just went on the best we could. One day at a time."

"One day at a time," Yusuf echoed. Uncle Rahman had written the same thing in his journal. Maybe that could be the title of his report.

Amma wiped her hands with a napkin and smiled at him brightly. "Forget about 9/11. Are you looking forward to the football game tonight? I bet some of your friends will be playing!"

12

They got back to Frey at five thirty, the back seat of the car full of boxes for Abba. Mr. Khan was waiting for them at the dollar store with Danial. "Can't believe we have to spectate such a violent sport," Danial said to him dismally.

"Can't believe we have to watch any sport," Yusuf replied, thinking of his unfinished projects on Scratch.

"We have to support the school team," Amma told them severely, taking Aleena into her arms. "No complaining."

"First practice game of the season!" Abba said, clapping Mr. Khan on the back. "I can't wait to see those boys in action!"

Mr. Khan grinned back. "The new team is supposed

to be very quick on their feet. That Grant boy got picked, I hear."

"Impressive for a sixth grader. He must have amazing skills."

Yusuf shivered. Watching Ethan plow into other kids who were much smaller than him wasn't his idea of fun. "Why do we have to go? I'm tired."

"We're going because we're part of Frey," Mr. Khan said, very seriously. "We need to participate in all the town activities."

There was a little silence. Then Amma said quietly, "We've been proving ourselves for the last twenty years."

Mr. Khan's eyebrows shot up. Abba looked at Amma sharply. "What are you talking about? What's brought this on?"

Yusuf knew it was their conversation at Whataburger. Amma had been unusually quiet on the ride home. "Nothing," Amma said, and turned away with Aleena. "Let's go."

They walked to the big field behind the middle school, the adults in front, Danial and Yusuf behind. Aleena was on Abba's shoulders now, singing the ABC song loudly. "You sing too, bhai," she commanded Yusuf from her perch.

"No thanks." Yusuf shook his head. He'd eaten too much at Whataburger, and his stomach was hurting.

There was already a medium-sized crowd at the football field. This was the first practice game of the season, the evening Coach Henderson was going to officially reveal his brand-new team. "Don't any of these people have anything to do on a Friday evening?" Danial whispered, glaring at the crowd.

"Probably not," Yusuf whispered back.

Sameena Aunty was waving frantically from the bleachers in the back. They made their way to her single file, smiling politely. Aleena waved and grinned at everyone, enjoying her height. "What took you so long? The game has almost started!" Sameena Aunty reprimanded them, patting a hand over her bright pink hijab.

Mr. Khan and Abba settled down with several other Muslim men. Amma sat next to Sameena Aunty with Aleena in her lap. Yusuf noticed that Amma was leaning slightly away from the other woman, her back straight. "Did you come alone today?" Amma asked politely.

Sameena Aunty opened a tote bag at her feet and passed out bags of snacks and juice boxes to everyone. "Yes, Mujeeb wasn't feeling too well. He decided to stay home."

"I'm sorry to hear that."

"You're lucky your husband goes with you to these events. It's dangerous for a woman to be out alone these days."

Yusuf wondered what she meant. Amma didn't reply, just busied herself with opening a bag of Cheetos for Aleena as if it was the most complicated task of the century. Sameena Aunty continued, "I feel comfortable because I wear the hijab. I feel sorry for women who don't. It's such a big protection."

Amma's lips tightened. "The hijab doesn't stop something bad from happening," she finally said, her voice so low Yusuf had to strain to hear over the noise around them. "I can promise you that."

Sameena Aunty's forehead crumpled into a frown. "Well. I don't know what to say," she muttered.

"How about just watching the game?"

The practice game started at exactly six thirty, when the sun had descended enough in the sky for the heat to lessen. Yusuf and Danial took their snacks and sat on the next step. A few kids from their class were sitting close by, but nobody spoke to them. Madison from robotics club gave them a big smile, then turned back to her friends.

Coach Henderson was big and stocky, his dark hair and skin shining with sweat. "Welcome to the first practice game of the season, everyone!" he boomed into the microphone. "I'm so happy to see our town come out to support the Frey Coyotes!"

The crowd clapped and hooted as the team ran onto the field in a line. Ethan's tall, menacing frame was unmistakable. He led the team proudly, holding his helmet under his right arm.

"Go, buddy!" came a shout from the other side of the bleachers. Yusuf craned his neck to see who it was. A tall man, with shaggy blond hair and a matching beard, stood clapping. His claps were so loud they cracked in the air like gunshots.

"Who's that?" asked Yusuf, even though it was obvious. This was what Ethan would look like when he grew up.

"Mr. Trevor Grant," answered Danial. "He's even meaner than his son."

"Really?" Yusuf felt his heart beat faster.

"Yeah, he cut off my mom on the highway leading out of Frey the other day, and he rolled down his window to scream at her. Called her a stupid foreigner. She came home almost crying."

Yusuf digested this in silence, thinking of Mrs. Khan, always so composed and well dressed, crying in the middle of her gigantic open kitchen. A movement beside him made him jump a little. It was Jared. "Ethan's not that bad," he said, sitting down next to Yusuf.

"How do you know?"

Jared hesitated, then answered, "He's my cousin."

"No way." Danial's eyes almost popped out of his head. "You guys are so . . . different."

Jared shrugged uncomfortably. "He means the hair," Yusuf explained, kicking Danial's leg.

Jared relaxed. "We used to live in West Virginia, a bunch of our families. Ethan's parents got divorced and he moved here last year with Uncle Trevor. To be near Grandma, you know."

Yusuf thought of Mrs. Raymond's sweet smile as she chatted with Abba about roses. "That's nice," he murmured, but he really didn't think so. Nothing about Ethan or his father seemed nice. They both had a simmering quality about them, like pots of water quietly boiling on the stove.

"Meet this year's team, everyone!" Coach Henderson was back at the microphone, blowing his whistle loudly enough to make everyone cover their ears. He slowly introduced the team, smiling like a proud papa bear. One by one the Coyotes came up to the microphone to say "Hi" or "Howdy" while everyone clapped and hooted.

Then the game began. It was only practice, but there were enough players to form two teams. Yusuf tried to understand what was going on; he'd been attending these Friday night games ever since he could remember, and they still confused him.

"Just follow the ball," Danial told him, leaning forward.

Yusuf tried, but it was too fast. His eyes kept returning to Ethan, watching in fascination as he pushed the other boys with his entire body and ran with the ball toward the end zone. "Wow, he's a monster," Danial said, almost admiringly, as Ethan tore headfirst into a seventh grader.

"He's not that bad," Jared repeated.

The other boy fell to the ground like a ton of bricks. The coach blew his whistle at Ethan, which made Mr. Grant jump up from the bleachers and run down to shout. Soon there was a crowd of angry parents surrounding the Coyotes, while the coach blew his whistle over and over. The seventh grader lay down armadillo style on the grass, his arms around his stomach, rolling around as if he was in pain.

By the time the game ended, the sun was setting, and it was time for maghrib prayers. Jared waved at Yusuf with a quick "See you on Monday," and walked away. Mr. Khan led the prayers in the parking lot, behind a wall of cars, far away from the crowd. The men in the front, the women at the back, all turned toward Mecca. Yusuf tried to concentrate, but the noise from the crowd still lingering around the bleachers kept drowning out most of Mr. Khan's words. Abba kept glancing nervously at the bleachers the whole time they prayed.

As they were walking home, Sameena Aunty called out to Amma, "Try wearing the hijab next time; it'll be such a nice change."

Amma didn't reply, but Yusuf saw her roll her eyes like a teenager.

Journal entry 4

September 12, 2001

I know I'm only supposed to write weekly entries, but I don't really care. Everything in my life—everyone's lives—has changed since yesterday, and I don't think Mrs. Clifton is going to mind if I write down what I'm feeling.

What am I feeling? I don't really know. Numb, like someone froze me in a human-sized freezer and now I just can't get my body to start moving again.

The news keeps repeating that the evil men who carried out the attacks yesterday were Muslim. I asked Abba about it this morning. Demanded it, trying to keep my voice from shaking. He looked like he hadn't slept all night. But he stared into my eyes and said, "Yes, son, they were Muslim, all nineteen of them."

Nineteen? Where were they from? Why did they do this? How can they be Muslim when our religion teaches peace and love? I had so many questions, but

Abba didn't look like he had any answers. His back was bent like an old man's, and he turned away from me with a deep sigh.

Amma's been to New York a few times, so I asked her about it. What's it like? What are the Twin Towers? Her face crumples, and I remember that the towers don't even exist anymore. I swallow hard, wondering how it would feel if the buildings I saw every day in Houston suddenly disappeared in flames.

The only good thing that happened today was that I didn't go to school. Amma said it was better if we all stayed at home. Even Farrah baji, who loves school, didn't protest. Her eyes were red, and she lay in her room, bundled up in her blanket even though it wasn't cold. Sarah told me that some kids in school had pushed her and yelled at her yesterday as she walked home from school. I wanted to hug her, but she'd locked her door.

I spent the day outside on the street, watching, listening. Most of our neighbors are South Asians, from Bangladesh, India, and Pakistan. Abba calls them his special friends, and our street Desi Street.

Today, everyone was outside on Desi Street, it seemed. They kept talking and shaking their heads, drinking tea and telling stories of how nice New Yorkers are, and how bravely they're handling things.

"What will happen to us Muslims?" an uncle asked.

Another uncle replied, "Nothing, it's not our fault." But everybody looked scared, which was weird. I've never seen adults look so scared before. They passed around a copy of the Houston Chronicle. "Assault on America" was the headline in red. Then a picture of the Twin Towers, still standing, smoke billowing out. The next line was even more sinister: "Terror Hits Home."

My home. They were talking about my country. My home. I still can't believe this happened. A cruel catastrophe. I got a chill down my spine as I read the words again. The pictures on the front page showed people holding each other and crying. Their faces were frozen in horror. Abba said, "All of America is crying right now."

I finally got up and left. I couldn't stand everyone's grief anymore. I wish we could go back to how things used to be, when the adults didn't look sad one minute and angry the next. I called Jonathan on the kitchen phone, wanting to hear one of his corny jokes, but nobody picked up.

13

"The soil is finally here," Abba told Yusuf on Saturday. Then he stopped as if Yusuf should know what he was talking about.

"What soil?" Yusuf asked. He was sitting in a corner of the dollar store, attaching a cleaning brush to a piece of metal he'd found in the storage room in the back. Rusty sat licking her paw next to him, tail flapping lazily.

"The soil for Mrs. Raymond, of course." Abba came closer. "What exactly are you doing?"

Yusuf was trying to make a small cleaning robot, but it was just a jumble of ideas right now, so he gathered all the parts into his arms and stood up. "Nothing, just fixing something. What's all this about soil?"

Abba sighed dramatically. "If only you'd pay attention.

Mrs. Raymond needs her soil delivered to her right away. You will be the one to deliver it. Samjhe?"

"Yes, I understand."

"Good. Now go."

There were two standard delivery methods for the A to Z Dollar Store. For longer distances, or when an adult was available and willing, Abba's old car was used. But when Yusuf made the delivery by himself—within a half-mile radius—he had to use a red wagon with a long black handle. Yusuf felt like a little boy carrying around his toys whenever he was sent on delivery errands. But he gulped down his embarrassment and always did as he was told.

He piled three bags of flower soil into the wagon and with a grunt pulled it to the front of the store. "Look carefully before crossing the road," Abba reminded him. "If the soil spills, I'll have to replace it for free."

Yusuf nodded and took the paper with Mrs. Raymond's address. "I'll be careful."

Rusty uncurled from the floor and rubbed herself around Yusuf's leg, making him stumble a little.

"I don't want to replace three bags of soil for free," Abba repeated, looking as if he was regretting the decision to send Yusuf.

"Abba. I'll be fine."

"It's not you I'm worried about. It's my money."

The walk wasn't too bad, except it was already hot enough to wilt the weeds that peeked from the cracks in the sidewalk. Rusty meowed as she crept alongside Yusuf, blinking in the sunlight. "You don't have to come with me, you know," Yusuf told her.

She meowed back, but kept walking.

Mrs. Raymond's flower shop was on Travis Street, parallel to the street that Abba's store was on. Yusuf took a shortcut through the Dairy Queen parking lot, where cars were double-parked even though it was past lunchtime. A few big motorcycles stood in the back, and Yusuf looked at them enviously as he walked by. It would be so much fun to ride a motorbike someday. He imagined the wind rushing through his hair, the handlebars cool under his fingers.

Rusty leaped ahead of him and disappeared into the alley with the trash cans. Yusuf waited for a few seconds before deciding to leave her behind. She knew her way home. In fact, she probably knew her way through every inch of Frey.

"Hey, delivery boy, let's see what's in your wagon!" someone called out from the Dairy Queen entrance, but he kept his head down and pulled the wagon even harder behind him. The person laughed, but nobody followed him. Next time he'd take the longer route, he told himself.

Soon the laughter grew fainter, and Yusuf was alone again. A car passed him slowly, then the road was empty. Still, he walked all the way to the stop sign to cross the street.

You could smell Mrs. Raymond's garden before you ever got to it. Today the smell of roses was the strongest, followed by something else Yusuf couldn't place. Lilies, maybe? The rickety old gate hung open, and he let himself in with his wagon saying, "Mrs. Raymond? Hello?" loudly all the while.

"Hello, young man! Your father called to let me know you were on your way." Mrs. Raymond appeared, all smiles and outstretched arms, out of nowhere. She was wearing muddy overalls and muddy gloves and her face was smudged with mud, but she seemed delighted that her soil was finally here.

Yusuf helped her unload the wagon, then turned to leave, but she would have none of it. "Nonsense, come drink some soda or eat some cookies. My grandson is here to keep you company while I write out a check for your father."

The grandson, of course, was Jared. He sat on a bench in the corner, working on a canvas. "Hello," he offered weakly.

"You paint?" asked Yusuf, surprised.

"Sometimes." Jared shrugged. The canvas was filled

with the colors of the flowers around them. They were mostly red, but also purple, and one yellow with dots of brown. "It's sort of my therapy."

Yusuf came closer and sat down on the bench. "Why do you need therapy?"

Jared picked up a paintbrush and dabbed some more brown dots around the red splotches. "After my mom was deployed overseas, and I moved in with Grandma, the doctor said I should try painting. For my nightmares."

Yusuf digested this slowly. Jared's mom was in the army? He had nightmares? He looked so . . . ordinary. "Where's your dad?" he finally asked.

Another shrug. "I don't know. Never met him."

Yusuf couldn't imagine never having met Abba. He also couldn't imagine a day without Amma. He stared at the painting, trying to say something that would match the enormity of Jared's losses. But he couldn't, so he stayed quiet.

Meow! They both jumped a little, then Yusuf looked down and said, "It's just Rusty."

Jared leaned over and petted Rusty on the head. "She's pretty. I wish I had a cat. My therapist said if I had a pet I wouldn't need to paint."

"Why don't you get one? We didn't pay anything for Rusty; she just showed up in my dad's store one day."

"Grandma says she's too old to care for another living

thing. She already has the garden. And me."

Yusuf racked his brains to offer something to Jared. "You can come by my dad's store and play with Rusty whenever you feel like it," he finally said.

A little smile peeked out from behind Jared's sad eyes, like the first hint of sunlight after a summer rain. "Thanks," he whispered. "That would be . . . nice."

Mrs. Raymond bustled up to them, beaming. She had a porcelain plate full of oatmeal cookies in her hand. "So glad to see Jared's found a friend," she said, putting the plate down on the table. "Clear away your paints now, young man."

Jared stood up and grabbed a cookie. "Can Yusuf stay for a while, Grandma? I want to show him my paintings."

Mrs. Raymond beamed even wider. "Of course, that's a great idea. I'll call Azeem and let him know where you are, Yusuf."

Yusuf looked at the cookies. They smelled delicious. "My mom also takes out the nice china for guests," he murmured.

Mrs. Raymond pushed the plate toward him. "Guests are a blessing, as I'm sure your mother will tell you. Take some, boy!"

Yusuf had never thought of himself as a guest. He smiled at Mrs. Raymond, then took a cookie and followed Jared to the back of the garden. They walked through pathways lined with plants of all sizes, past shelves full of all kinds of flowerpots. They ducked through a doorway that connected to a little house on the other side, old and ramshackle but neat as a pin. Jared's room was not much bigger than a closet, with a narrow bed and a small wooden desk. "I'm on my seventeenth painting," Jared remarked. He dug under his bed and drew out a handful of canvases. "One for each week my mom's been gone."

Yusuf stared at the paintings. They were all abstract slashes, some in pastels, others in dark angry colors. In a few, he could make out distorted faces. "These are . . . amazing," he finally breathed.

Jared didn't reply. He was looking at the paintings as if he'd never seen them before. "Want to play cards?" he finally asked.

Yusuf almost said cards were the devil's game, but there was no way on earth he was going to repeat Danial's words, so he just nodded and shrugged. Jared slid the paintings back under the bed. He took out a worn pack of cards from a drawer in his desk and sat down on the floor to deal them out. "Sorry they're in such bad condition. I play a lot of solitaire."

Yusuf had heard of solitaire. Abba's computer had

that game. Surely it couldn't be haram if Abba kept it on his computer? He relaxed and sat down on the floor next to Jared. "Can you teach me? I think I'm a solitaire kind of person too."

An hour later, Yusuf headed back alone to the garden. Mrs. Raymond handed him a check, saying, "Tell your father I need two more bags of soil. My roses need to bloom!"

Yusuf looked around him, trying not to choke under the heavy fragrance. "That's a lot of roses," he said.

"Ha! There better be a lot. I'm the only supplier of flowers for the parade this year."

This was not the first time the parade had been mentioned. Yusuf frowned. The 9/11 parade was always a small event organized by Frey's churches. Hardly anybody showed up unless 9/11 fell on a weekend. Last year, they didn't even have a parade because of Covid. "They need so many roses for that little parade?"

Mrs. Raymond chuckled. "Oh, it's gonna be a big one this year. It's the twentieth anniversary, you know. Plus this year my son's in charge, and he likes to do things big."

Yusuf's head was starting to throb from the rose smells around him. He fiddled with his glasses and asked, "Who's your son?"

"Why, you must have seen him around town, tall as a lamppost. His son goes to your school."

Yusuf had a sudden image of Jared in the bleachers, telling him about his cousin. "Mr. Grant?" he squeaked with a dry throat. "In charge of the parade?"

"Yup, that one."

14

The following week's Saturday club was everything Yusuf had imagined it would be. The area outside the school was deserted, and the air was crisp and fresh. Their team of six, plus Mr. Parker, assembled inside the school gym, their shoes squeaking in the silence. A big box marked LEGO EV KITS stood in the corner. Cameron looked half asleep, but everyone else was ready to get to work.

"Well, I can't believe we finally have a shot at TRC," Mr. Parker said as he passed out a sheaf of papers, grinning. "Gather around, kids. Let's get started."

Yusuf looked at the papers. *Welcome to the Texas Robotics Competition 2021–22.* There was so much to go through. Contest rules. Release forms. FAQs. He sat down on the gym floor and started reading, his head bent and lips moving. This was important. He didn't want to miss a word.

"Too early for robots!" Cameron groaned as he sank down beside Yusuf.

Tony Rivera sat on the other side. "That's why we have Yusuf."

"Shhh!" Yusuf held up a commanding finger.

There was silence as the team sat on the floor, digesting the TRC papers. Registration deadline was November 29, 2021. Regional contest in Conroe on January 15, 2022. State contest in Austin on April 9, 2022. Yusuf wrote the dates down in a notebook. They were more important than the birthdays of all his family members combined.

Madison raised her hand. "It says we need a team name."

"How about Cam Bots?" Cameron suggested. "You know, since y'all needed me to complete the team?"

"Ugh, Cameron." Madison rolled her eyes at him. "Your ego needs to take a seat."

Yusuf expected Cameron to argue, but he kept quiet. He looked almost subdued, like he wasn't sure what he was doing with a group of self-professed nerds on school property on a Saturday morning. Finally he yawned at Madison and closed his eyes. "Whatever."

"No names," Danial said firmly.

Mr. Parker's grin was back. "You mean you kids won't even consider Team Parker?"

Danial looked at him, alarmed. "Wait, do we have to name our teams after our coaches? Is it a rule or something?"

"Don't worry, I'm only joking."

Madison laughed out loud, followed more uncertainly by Danial. Jared looked from one to the other in confusion. Yusuf ignored them all. "How about the Freybots?" he said slowly. It was a game he and Danial had made up when they were little. They'd dress up Amma's brooms to look like robotic gladiators, with kitchen-cloth bandannas, stick arms, and googly eyes, and fight in her kitchen until she'd shoo them away.

Madison replied, "I like that. Show some Frey pride in front of those big-city kids."

Jared nodded. Tony reluctantly followed. Soon they were all grinning, all except Cameron. "It's a stupid name," he spat.

"No, it's not," Danial spat back.

Mr. Parker raised a hand in warning. "Let's take a vote, shall we? All in favor say aye!"

"AYE!" five of the six team members shouted.

Cameron bowed mockingly at them. "Whatever," he muttered. "I don't care."

"Freybots, here we come!" Yusuf and Danial yelled together.

Mr. Parker reached over, opened up his box in the corner, and began taking out LEGO parts. "You know you'll have to come up with a fight song now, don't you? It's not every day we get to compete in the TRC."

Madison started humming under her breath.

"What if we win, guys?" Tony suddenly said, his face comically shocked at the idea.

Danial began lining up LEGO parts on the gym floor carefully, as if they were made of his mom's best china from Dubai. "Let's not kid ourselves," he said nervously. "The chance of winning is, like, minuscule. You'd need to create an amazing machine, then win three out of three eligibility matches in the regionals, and then be one of the top five in the regionals. And the final state contest is huge. That's where the other contestants are, like, robotics gods or something. Those guys probably drink gallons of coffee and work with robots all day long."

Mr. Parker put a firm hand on his shoulder. "Calm down, son. Let's take one step at a time."

Danial took a deep breath. "Y-yes, sir."

The team gathered around their teacher. "Okay, step one," Mr. Parker said. "Finding out this year's challenge. This team has at least one seventh grader—that's you, Tony—so we can compete in the advanced level."

Tony raised his arms above his head and said, "Whoop!" But he looked a bit scared. Yusuf swallowed. The advanced level was a big deal. It meant making a robot from scratch to solve a real-world problem. In 2020, the winning team had made a machine that collected plastic from oceans. The year before, they'd created a robot that saved children from fires. Theoretically, of course, with the trash—and children—being clunky obstacles on a gigantic course. Still, the advanced level was a very big deal.

"Are . . . are you sure we're ready?" Jared squeaked.

Mr. Parker nodded. "Yup."

Yusuf relaxed. If Mr. Parker thought they were ready, then they definitely were. "Yup," he repeated firmly. Cheerfully.

Tony threw an arm around Yusuf's shoulder. "We got this robot golden child on our team. You bet we're ready!"

Yusuf and Danial walked home from Saturday club with light steps and eager eyes. "Man, this is going to be epic!" Yusuf sang. "I can't wait for next week."

For once, Danial didn't have anything negative to say. "TRC is pretty awesome," he agreed. "I can't wait to get to the regional contest, see the arena where teams compete, hear all the coaches yelling."

"I don't think Mr. Parker would yell at us," Yusuf protested.

"The competitions can get intense," Danial told him darkly. "Wait and see. Parker will be a nervous wreck by January."

There was no use arguing with Danial. He thought his powers of prediction were unmatched.

They walked in silence until they reached Main Street. The clock on the front of city hall said one o'clock, and Yusuf suddenly realized he hadn't eaten anything since the very quick breakfast Abba had made before leaving for his store. "Don't wake your mother," he'd warned, whispering. "She was up last night with Aleena."

Yusuf had nodded and swallowed his half-burnt toast quietly. Aleena's asthma got worse in the fall, and sometimes she couldn't breathe at night. Yusuf could hear her coughing and wheezing most nights, and when it got bad, Amma spent the night with her.

Yusuf turned to Danial. "Do you want to get some lunch?" He could smell the aroma of tacos and Mexican rice, maybe even fajitas, from the food trucks around the town square. "I got my allowance yesterday."

Danial looked around doubtfully. "You know it's not going to be halal."

Yusuf was already striding toward Wicks Avenue on

the far-right corner of city hall. He was sure to find some food trucks there. "It's okay," he called over his shoulder. "You can eat the rice."

Danial followed him, and Yusuf could almost feel the scowl aimed at his back. "I don't want to eat the rice. I'm starving!"

Yusuf increased his pace. He wasn't in the mood to hear his grumpy friend complain about food options. "If you want to eat chicken, then eat chicken!" he yelled back. "Just don't tell your parents . . ."

Yusuf stopped short as he rounded the corner to Wicks Avenue. It led to the back of city hall and right to a big park full of benches and a playground. As expected, there was a line of food trucks on the street, but there were also other things he hadn't seen before. A low wooden platform stood in the middle of the street, with a gigantic American flag stretched across it. A small utility trailer with its sides uncovered and the top part filled with tall blocks stood to one side.

Yusuf stared at the utility trailer. He knew what it was, because the wheels were peeking out from under the metal parts. Abba was always looking at pictures of utility trailers on his computer and wishing he owned one to deliver supplies. On the trailer bed were a bunch of rectangle structures, like big building blocks made of white plastic. Some were short, but two were equally long and straight, and towered over the other structures in the trailer bed like proud beacons.

"Is that supposed to be a float?" Danial whispered behind him.

Of course, a parade float. The sides hadn't been decorated yet, but that's surely what it was. Yusuf looked at the white structures again. The two tall ones were like a distant memory, a shape he'd seen somewhere before. "Are those models of . . . buildings?" he breathed.

Danial clicked his tongue. "The Twin Towers. You know, from 9/11?"

Never forget. Of course. Next week was the anniversary of 9/11, and the local news had been reminding them of the "bigger, better parade" on Main Street for weeks now. That's why Jared's grandmother needed so much soil. She'd been right: they'd require a lot more flowers than usual this year. That was a big float to cover.

"What're you kids doing here?"

At the rough voice just behind them, Yusuf turned so quickly he elbowed Danial in the ribs with force. "Ow!" whispered Danial, but without much steam.

He should apologize, but Yusuf was transfixed at the sight of Ethan's dad—Mr. Grant—standing way too close to them. His hands were on his hips, and his face looked like it had twisted into an ugly mask. His sleeves were rolled up, and Yusuf couldn't stop looking at those beefy forearms full of tattoos. "Why. Are. You. Here?" repeated Mr. Grant from clenched lips.

"Er, for some lunch?" squeaked Danial, pointing to the food trucks.

Yusuf's stomach rumbled, but not from hunger. He had a feeling Mr. Grant wasn't just talking about Wicks Avenue.

Yusuf was right. Mr. Grant leaned closer until they could smell his breath, a mix of tobacco and meat. "Your kind has been here in Frey long enough. We Patriot Sons are about to take this town back. This country back."

Danial's gulp was so loud Yusuf could hear his throat move up and down. "Patriot . . . Sons?" Yusuf whispered.

Mr. Grant leaned back with a grin that would be perfect on a hungry coyote's face. He was looking at something behind them. Yusuf turned without wanting to. In the distance, right near the entrance to the park, stood a group of motorcycles, with men and women just like Mr. Grant sitting on them. Arms crossed on massive chests. Eyes glinting in the sunlight.

"Time to leave Frey, Mooz-lim," Mr. Grant whispered behind them.

15

A week later, on the morning of September 11, 2021, Yusuf and Danial headed with their families back to the town square. It was a Saturday, but Mr. Parker had canceled the Saturday club due to "the nature of the holiday."

Yusuf wasn't sure a memorial event for an awful terrorist act counted as a holiday, but he was glad they weren't having the club meeting. The sick feeling hadn't left his stomach since the week before, when they'd run into Mr. Grant near city hall. The robotics after-school meeting on Tuesday had been difficult enough, with the other team members chattering about TRC regulations and planning matching T-shirts with FREYBOTS on the front like babies. How could anyone focus on robotics when Mr. Grant was stomping around the town square throwing threats about like they were candy?

The morning was overcast, as if a storm they couldn't see yet loomed on the horizon. Danial and Yusuf walked behind the adults, Aleena swinging her arms between them. "Where we going?" she asked cheerfully. "Nother foo-ball game?"

Danial shook his head sadly. "Nope. Just a parade, with floats and things."

Her smile brightened. "Floats? With princesses?"

Yusuf took a deep breath and exchanged looks with Danial. "I don't think so."

They reached the town square and searched the crowd for familiar faces. It looked like everyone in Frey had shown up for the parade. Main Street was decorated with little flags and streamers hanging from streetlights. Popcorn vendors scurried about, waving their arms to attract attention. City hall had a giant flag and a wreath of roses on its big wooden doorway. Signs that read NEVER FORGET and TWENTY YEARS hung from the roof of the public library, edged with red and white ribbon. On the sidewalk was a small stage with blue carpeting and a white plastic podium.

"It's so . . . festive," Amma murmured sadly.

Aleena pulled on Yusuf's hand. "Where the floats?" she whined.

Yusuf looked toward Wicks Avenue, where the high school marching band waited with their instruments. Mr. Grant was nowhere to be seen, nor was his group of motorcycle friends. "The floats will come out from right there," he pointed, trying not to shiver.

He was being silly, he told himself. It was just an annual parade, even if it was way bigger and more elaborate than ever before. He'd been to one each year since he could remember, except when he was seven and stayed home with a fever. This was Frey. His hometown. His birthplace. How bad could the parade be? Then he turned to the post office and saw the other Muslim families clustered together with grim looks on their faces.

Okay. Maybe it was different this year.

Abba and Mr. Khan led them toward the others. Yusuf counted. Everyone had shown up, even Razia Begum, wrapped in a black shawl and leaning on her grandson. "Assalamo Alaikum," they all greeted one another, minus the usual smiles.

"You're late again," Sameera Aunty said accusingly. "We've all been here since eight thirty."

"We couldn't find Aleena's inhaler," Amma replied with gritted teeth. Then she whispered under her breath, "Not that it's any of your business."

Yusuf looked at Amma in surprise. She never said anything mean to anybody. "Amma . . . ," he began, but the crashing of drums drowned him out. The high school band. The parade was starting.

They all stood with hands on hearts for "The Star-Spangled Banner." Then Mayor Chesterton walked slowly onto the stage and gave a speech about loyalty and being true Americans. "Give me a break!" Amma grumbled, louder this time.

Abba, standing on the other side of her, whispered, "Shush, this is important stuff," as if the mayor was the most riveting old man on earth.

Danial and Yusuf stood side by side, waiting, waiting. The crowd around them was clapping and cheering, and faint country music streamed from speakers on the streetlights. After the mayor left the stage, the band began to march, instruments waving in the air, music blaring.

When it passed them, Aleena cheered so loudly she started coughing, and Amma had to pat her back. Then a boy carrying a huge American flag more than twice his height staggered along. Behind him were the floats: a small one with Miss Frey (also known as Jodie Garrison, a twelfth grader) dressed in a white gown and a tiara with fake rubies, waving both her arms. A medium-sized one from the local grocery store, full of employees dressed as giant cans of corn and beets. Another small one with an adult-sized Mickey Mouse throwing candy at the crowd.

And then the next float rounded the corner from Wicks Avenue and came into full view. It was the Twin Towers float Yusuf had seen the week before, only now it was complete with a skirt of roses, probably straight from Mrs. Raymond's garden. The crowd quieted down. The music changed to "The Star-Spangled Banner" again. Mr. Grant walked alongside, dressed in a cowboy outfit, his tattooed arms glinting in the sunlight.

The float passed the Muslim families, and they all clapped respectfully, just like everyone else. Yusuf felt a tug in his chest thinking about everything he'd read in Uncle Rahman's journal. The pain, the grief in his uncle's words as he described what Americans had gone through twenty years ago. Maybe the signs were right. Maybe they shouldn't ever forget what happened.

Mr. Grant stepped onto the stage and cleared his throat. He stared straight at the Muslim families as he roared into the microphone. "It's been twenty years since we were attacked. Twenty years of tolerating the enemy that lives right among us, in our cities and towns and neighborhoods. No more. The Patriot Sons are here, and we will rid our nation of the enemy!"

They all met at Urooj Diner for brunch. Owned by a Lebanese Christian family, the diner had been a staple in Frey since 1968. After the parade, every table was packed, every seat taken. A loud buzz of chatter hung in the air. It looked like every single person in the restaurant was talking about the parade.

"That Trevor Grant is a real tool," Mr. Khan said, digging a pita chip into his hummus with such force that it snapped. "Hasn't even lived in Frey a year, and already thinks he owns the place."

"What are the Patriot Sons, anyway?" Abba asked. "I've never even heard of them before."

Another uncle shook his head. "They're hooligans, that's what they are. Going around calling us the enemy . . . how dare they? My grandfather was the first doctor this town ever had. Built the clinic I practice in every day."

Yusuf sat with Danial, Cameron, and a couple of other boys at a back table. A platter of chicken shawarma lay steaming over a bed of rice. Cameron scooped up some chicken with a piece of bread and rolled his eyes at the uncle table. "They're overreacting. How do they know Mr. Grant was talking about . . . us?"

Yusuf and Danial exchanged looks. Danial cleared his throat and told the others how they'd met Mr. Grant the week before, how he'd told them Muslims should leave Frey. "Leave?" a boy named Asif squeaked. He was in fourth grade and sometimes came over to play video games. "Leave our home? Why?"

"My mom always says Frey is full of ignorant folks," Danial said. "She says we're gonna move to Houston or Austin; they're much more friendly over there."

Yusuf had been hearing this talk of moving for years. He shook his head at Danial. "Come on, you're not going anywhere."

"Says the guy who gets notes in his locker."

They all turned to look at him, alarmed. "What notes?" Asif whispered, looking like he was about to faint.

Yusuf gave Danial a dirty look and said brightly, "Listen!" He motioned toward the uncle table to distract them before they started asking questions.

Mr. Khan was standing up now, a grim look on his face. "I received a letter yesterday that I need to share with you all. I was waiting for the right time, and I suppose this is . . . perfect."

Everyone in the diner leaned forward to hear. Even the table of teenage girls was unusually quiet. Mr. Khan was the unofficial leader of their little community, and the one who dealt with business matters relating to the new mosque. He reached into his jacket pocket and took out a letter. "Please don't go out to the construction site tomorrow. We've received an order of temporary stay from the judge. There's been a petition against us, and we've been called to a zoning meeting with the city council to decide things."

Yusuf blinked rapidly. Decide things? What things? This was getting really serious.

Mr. Khan continued, his face dark as the midnight sky over a gloomy forest. "Guess who the main petitioner is? The Patriot Sons."

Journal entry 5

September 18, 2001

The last week has been dreadful. There's a sadness inside me, tight and crushing. I can't stop thinking of the thousands of people—thousands!—who died for no reason except that they were in the wrong place at the wrong time. The people who worked in the Twin Towers. The firefighters who went to save them. The people on the planes. When I think of them all, my throat begins to ache, and my chest feels like someone is sitting on it.

But sadness isn't the only thing I feel. I also feel anger, a deep, vicious anger that makes me want to hit things and howl like a wounded wolf. School has turned into a nightmare place. Everyone's always quiet, like they don't know where to look or what to say. Some kids scowl at me in the hallway as I walk past. Once a kid turned around and pointed to me. "It was his people!" he shouted, his face red.

I know what he means by "my people." Muslims.

I'm a Muslim, so somehow all the other Muslims in the world must be connected to me, and I to them. Is that even possible? I don't know.

I don't know anything anymore.

Mrs. Clifton says giving names to our emotions is healthy, but I hate to tell her that it's not working. She's been urging us every day in class to write in our journals, and I wonder if anyone else besides me does this. The kid who shouted at me in the hallway? Does he write bad words for the feelings he has for me and other Muslims? Jonathan, my best friend, who's hardly spoken to me since that day? He walks around with a clenched jaw and narrow eyes.

I watch the news every evening with Abba. Amma says it's bad for me, but Abba doesn't agree. "The boy needs to know what sort of world he's growing up in," he tells her with a grim look.

"What sort of world is that?" I want to shout. A world where hijackers and murderers are called "my people"?

Every day I sit at my desk, pretending to do my homework, but actually staring at the poster of Muhammad Ali that hangs from the wall in front of me. I got that poster after I watched a TV show about the Vietnam War. Muhammad Ali's got a stubborn look on his face, and both his hands are clenched in boxing

gloves, like he's saying, "Come fight me." Like he's
sick and tired of the whole world too.

One day at a time, I remind myself. Abba and I
watched President Bush's speech last night. He talked
about Muslims like me, about Islam being a religion of
peace. He reminded Americans—us—that our fellow
Muslims shouldn't feel scared about walking on the
streets or going about our business. That we should be
treated with respect. But what can a speech do against
people's ugly, scared feelings?

Somebody called Amma a terrorist in the shopping
center two days ago. I was with her, and I wanted
to punch the person who said it. But he was big and
angry, and he looked like he hadn't slept in a week.
Amma wrapped her dupatta tightly around her head
and continued shopping like nothing had happened.
"He's just upset," she said.

Yesterday, Sarah said her science teacher refused to
teach the Muslim kids in her class. She's in ninth grade
and almost a quarter of her classmates are Muslim.

I'm guessing speeches don't really make a difference.
Even those made by the president of the United States.

"It will get better with time," Abba tells me. "We
just need to heal." But a wound this big . . . how long
will it take to heal?

16

Nobody seemed to have heard Mr. Khan's instruction about halting the construction at the mosque. Yusuf tried protesting, but Amma and Abba still went the next morning. He tagged along because of Sunday school. He'd been the one to insist on the change of day, so he couldn't very well refuse to attend. Plus, he was curious about the other Muslims. Would anyone else show up to build the mosque even though a judge had told them not to?

They all did. The uncles continued to haul wooden planks and hammer nails as if no letter had been sent to them via certified mail. "We can't afford to stop working just because of this foolishness," an older man grumbled. Yusuf didn't remember his name, but he owned a little computer store near Main Street where Abba had bought Yusuf's laptop.

Abba agreed. "We're so behind anyway. The mayor wants us out of the trailer before the end of the year."

Yusuf wondered about Mayor Chesterton as he walked toward the train tracks. The mayor always had a kind smile on his face when he came to Abba's store. "We're so grateful to you and your family, Azeem," he often said. "We're happy you're a part of Frey."

Lately, though, the mayor was coming by less, and smiling less. At the parade the day before, he had looked exhausted, and his mouth was a thin, straight line on his face. And he'd avoided looking at Abba or any of the other Muslims. Things were definitely changing in Frey, and not in a good way.

"Hey." Cameron joined him as he passed the big tree. "I need to talk to you."

Yusuf gritted his teeth and continued to walk. "I don't want to hear one of your stupid jokes about desi people."

"What? They're hilarious. How many desi uncles does it take to change a light bulb? That one's a classic."

"Sorry. Not interested."

Cameron pulled at his shoulder. "Wait. It's not a joke. I wanted to ask about what you said yesterday at the diner."

"What did I say?"

Cameron made an impatient sound in his throat. "About your locker. About someone sending you notes."

Yusuf stopped. They were almost at the train tracks, where Amma and Sameena Aunty were spreading out king-sized bedsheets for the kids to sit on and study. He turned to face Cameron slowly. "It's none of your business."

Cameron's face was hard. "I'm making it my business. Tell me about it."

"Why?" Yusuf's brain was working overtime. Cameron hadn't shown an interest in Yusuf's life for years. He never even stopped to talk to Yusuf or wave hello. Why was he suddenly asking all these questions, unless . . . "Did *you* send me those notes?"

Cameron gave a short laugh, more like a bark. "Me? Why on earth . . ?"

Yusuf turned completely until he was facing Cameron. They stood close together, scowling at each other. "I don't know. You seem to hate Muslims just as much as Ethan Grant and his father."

There was a shocked little silence as Cameron digested this. Then his face grew blank and he stepped back. "Whatever, dude. I was just trying to help."

Yusuf watched as Cameron walked away. He chewed his lip. Cameron was his TRC teammate; maybe he'd been too harsh on him. But the notes in his locker were not something Yusuf liked to talk about. They'd stopped for now, and maybe it was because he'd prayed them away. There was no point in talking about them.

"Yusuf, we're starting!" Amma called out, and he reluctantly turned back to her.

Sameena Aunty waited as Yusuf settled down on the bedsheet. "You need to stick with the good kids, Yusuf," she suddenly said. "There are some bad seeds among us, unfortunately."

Yusuf looked up. "Cameron?"

She sighed as if someone had died. "I don't know what happened to him. He used to be such a good boy."

Yusuf wasn't sure Cameron was a bad person. Apart from being rude and uncaring about traditions, he seemed okay. He opened his mouth to say so, but Aunty was looking at him with a clear message in her eyes: don't argue with your elders.

"Yes, Aunty," he said meekly. Cameron Abdullah wasn't worth a lecture.

Sameena Aunty was clearly in charge of the classes today. She made Saba, a seventh grader in Yusuf's school, read aloud a passage from the Quran three times. "Make the *kh* sound harder, from the back of your throat!" Sameena Aunty snapped again and again.

Saba's voice was low as she tried to say *kh*. Yusuf felt

bad for her. She was dressed in jeans and a University of Houston sweatshirt, with a plain black hijab on her head. Yusuf had seen her in school a few times, always alone, always reading a book as she walked the hallways. She looked up, and he gave her a reassuring smile.

"What are you laughing at, boy?" Sameena Aunty snapped.

The other kids giggled. Yusuf's smile vanished. "Er, nothing. I was just—"

"Have you done your homework?" she interrupted.

Yusuf wasn't sure what she was referring to. Homework was usually memorization of a verse from the Quran, or a hadith. "Yes?" he ventured.

She glared at him as if his nose was longer than Pinocchio's. "Okay, then. Tell me the story of the Migration. When did it happen and why?"

Yusuf gulped. The Migration, or hijrah, was the most important aspect of Islamic history. So important that Muslims began their calendar with that date. There was no way he could do justice to the story with Sameena Aunty breathing down his neck like a wounded dragon. Best to distract her. "There were actually two migrations," he began. "The first was around the year 613, when the early followers of the Prophet fled to Abyssinia in Africa. A kind king gave them refuge there."

"Why did they run away?" a little boy asked. Technically he was in Amma's class, learning the Arabic alphabet, but they were all sitting together on the bedsheet, too close to really be separated. Yusuf had to admit, stories were much more interesting than a foreign language.

Sameena Aunty sighed again, even louder. "The people of Mecca didn't like the Muslims. They saw the brand-new religion of Islam as something very different, something against their traditions. They feared the Muslims because they didn't understand this new faith. That's why the Prophet Muhammad gave them permission to leave."

Another girl raised her hand. It was Sameena Aunty's nine-year-old niece, Rehana. "That's not fair," she protested. "Why should anyone have to leave their home? They had a right to stay."

The kids nodded. Next to Yusuf, Amma gave a little sniff. She'd been deathly quiet since the parade the day before, and Yusuf thought she looked ill as she sat cross-legged with an Arabic book in her lap. Their eyes met, and Yusuf suddenly knew exactly what she was thinking. The people of Frey also thought the Muslims were different. Would Yusuf and his friends have to migrate too? Or would they stay in their rightful home?

✱ ✱ ✱

The church bells sounded just as Sunday school was ending. Yusuf helped Amma fold the bedsheets and put them away. The aunties got lunch ready as the stream of churchgoers walked by, some saying hello, others silent. "Come eat with us," Abba invited them with a smile, but they all shook their heads. Nobody smiled back.

The adults sat on chairs to eat. Plates were passed around and water was poured into cups. "Falafel!" Aleena cried. "My favorite!"

Yusuf fixed plates for both of them and sat down on the roots of the big tree. Danial and his parents hadn't come today, so he was stuck with Aleena for company. She'd been coughing much more lately, and Amma had made her wear a thick scarf around her neck. "This itch," she complained to Yusuf, pulling at the scarf.

"Never mind, eat your food," he replied, looking toward the church. Maybe he'd see Jared again.

"Did someone say falafel?" came a voice from across the street. Yusuf and the others turned. It was the pastor, a tall, well-built young man with silky brown hair and smiling eyes. Behind him stood a silent, wide-eyed Jared.

Abba was ecstatic. He invited the visitors over and plied them with food. "Please, eat with us! Farrah, bring some Coke! What will you have, young man? I've seen you before in my store, haven't I? Welcome, welcome!"

Jared nodded shyly and edged toward Yusuf. "Hello."

"Hey." Yusuf tried to think of something clever to say. It was weird to see a school friend in an unusual location. Once he'd seen his fourth-grade music teacher in a Walmart in Conroe and had almost run away in distress. "How are you?"

Jared shrugged. "Okay. My painting's almost finished."

"Cool. Maybe I'll come by to check it out."

"That would be nice."

The pastor was already sitting down with the uncles, digging into falafel. After a few minutes, he put down his plate and looked at Abba. "Oh, I forgot to introduce myself! My name is John Nielson. I'm the new pastor of the New Horizons Church down the street. I wanted to tell you how sorry I was about the . . . the things that happened yesterday at the parade."

Abba waved a hand. "What things? Nothing happened. It was a very good memorial service. Very emotional."

The pastor nodded. "Yes, it was. But I want to assure you that the members of my church don't see you as the enemy. You're our neighbors. Our friends."

Everyone was quiet. Then Amma spoke up. "Apparently everyone in Frey doesn't feel the same way."

Abba glared at her before turning back to the pastor.

"No, no! We all love this town. We know it's our home. . . ."

The pastor leaned over and put a hand over Abba's arm. "Yes, it is your home. I promise."

Yusuf couldn't stay silent anymore. "But the Patriot Sons . . . ," he began loudly, his heart beating so fast he could hardly hear his own words. Abba always told him not to interrupt when adults were talking. But what had happened the day before at the parade didn't concern just the adults. It concerned everybody. Especially those who got mean notes in their lockers at school.

Yusuf was tired of staying quiet. He was tired of being scared and feeling foolish. "Everyone here is worried about the Patriot Sons," he finished quickly, before he lost his nerve. Abba gave him a hard look, but the others all nodded.

The pastor turned his kind, smiling eyes toward Yusuf. "The Patriot Sons don't represent us, young man. We're as worried about them as you are."

Yusuf gulped. Somehow the pastor's words didn't give him any comfort.

17

On Monday morning in Miss Terrance's class, the students were all talking about the parade. "The floats were so good this year," Madison marveled. "I took dozens of pics on my mom's phone."

"I think the band was the best part," someone else replied. "My sister was in it."

Miss Terrance went to the whiteboard and wrote *9/11* in big letters with her dry-erase marker. Yusuf focused on his desk, gritting his teeth. It was already September 13—why couldn't the town move on to another topic now?

Never Forget.

Miss Terrance tapped a knuckle on the whiteboard. "The parade wasn't just about the floats and the band, was it?" she asked. "There was a greater purpose, a bigger commemoration."

Yusuf looked up as she wrote *Commemoration* on the board. It was their vocabulary word of the day, apparently. Yusuf stared at it. *Commemoration.* He liked how it felt inside his brain.

Madison shifted in her seat. "I don't get it. Why do we . . . uh . . . commemorate . . . things so much? It's all history, isn't it?"

Yusuf remembered again what Uncle Rahman had told him about history affecting the future. Miss Terrance turned to the class and passed around a handout. Yusuf glanced at the title: *America's War on Terror.*

"Good question, Madison! We have a reading comprehension package today, and it ties very neatly into what we're talking about. How many of us know somebody in the military?"

A few kids nodded. Jared raised his hand slowly, as if worried someone would bite it. Miss Terrance gave him a sympathetic smile. "This passage is about the wars our country fought—is still fighting—as a result of 9/11. Because of events that happened twenty years ago, we are still going through . . . something. Feeling something. If Jared's mom or Damien's uncle is in the military, that means it's very much current affairs, not history. Right?"

Madison nodded. "I guess."

Yusuf began to read the handout. It was all about how the U.S. declared war on Iraq and Afghanistan to get revenge on the people who'd attacked America on 9/11. There was nothing in Uncle Rahman's journal about war. At least not yet.

He thought of Aleena and her asthma. When she couldn't get enough oxygen into her lungs, she flapped her arms and legs about in panic, not caring who or what she hurt. Is that what countries also do when something terrible happens on their soil? Just hit out in panic?

He finished reading the handout and looked up. Miss Terrance was staring straight at him. "Yusuf, what did you think of the memorial on Saturday?"

He almost dropped his paper. "Me?"

"Yes, you."

The whole class became silent. The kids in the front turned to stare at him like he was a specimen in a petri dish. Yusuf wanted to demand why Miss Terrance had singled him out, of all people. But he knew the answer. Because he was different. Muslim. The enemy. He gulped again, and thought of Prophet Moses, who prayed to God to help him speak. Of Prophet Abraham, who prayed to God to cool the fire he was trapped in. The problem was, Yusuf was no prophet, and at that moment he couldn't even remember the simplest of prayers. "Um, it was nice," he finally stuttered. "Nice . . . commemoration . . . for those who lost their lives."

Miss Terrance beamed at his use of the vocabulary word. "I thought so too." She turned toward the rest of the class. "All right, get to work on the assignment. You have twenty minutes left. And don't forget. Today's the day to turn in your 9/11 reports. Please put them on my desk as you leave the class."

Yusuf groaned under his breath. He'd completely forgotten about the report. Why did they have to write it at all? Wasn't it enough that they were suffering the effects of Never Forget in real time? He waited until the bell rang, and all the other students filed out of the classroom, laughing and talking. Then he approached Miss Terrance. She was sitting at her desk, reading a newspaper. "Ma'am . . . ?"

She looked up with a smile. "Yes, Yusuf? Are you doing okay?"

Of course. Why wouldn't he be? "Um, about the assignment . . ."

"Let me guess. You haven't finished it yet."

Yusuf nodded miserably. "Uh, yes. I'm sorry."

She didn't seem mad. "Sure, no problem. Take your time." She smiled at him. "It's not a graded assignment, just something I thought would be helpful to the class."

He blinked at her. Danial always said people who were too nice had something to hide. He wondered if Miss Terrance was hiding something. Her hair was pink today, and she wore a matching pink blouse over gray slacks. She looked completely normal, as if she'd never held a secret in her life. "Do you think it will make a difference?" he asked her boldly. "The report, I mean."

Her smile widened until she looked like the cat in *Alice in Wonderland*. "Of course. Knowledge is power, Yusuf. Remember that."

The door slammed open, and a stream of kids started walking in. The next class was already here, which meant Yusuf was late for math. He nodded at Miss Terrance as he left. "I'll remember."

At lunch, Cameron came over with his cafeteria tray and sat next to Yusuf. Danial was so shocked his mouth fell open and bits of peas from his samosa dropped onto his shirt. "What are you doing here?" he sputtered, wiping his chin. "We don't associate with the likes of you."

Cameron ignored him and looked at Yusuf. "So, are we going to discuss robotics or what? I have some great ideas about the competition."

Yusuf thought about their little argument on Sunday. "Yeah, sure. Listen, I'm sorry—"

Cameron slapped his shoulder lightly. "No need to

apologize. We're friends, aren't we?"

Yusuf hadn't known this, but he nodded anyway. For some reason, being friends with Cameron wasn't as scary as he'd thought. Danial's sputtering grew louder. "What is going on?" he whispered furiously. "Why is he apologizing? Why does he think we're friends?"

Yusuf patted Danial on the back. "Come on, we're TRC mates. We can be friends."

"Absolutely not. He's a Muslim hater and a poser. He runs with the wrong crowd." Danial took a deep breath and whispered into Yusuf's ear. "My dad thinks he may even be in a gang."

Yusuf rolled his eyes a little at that. Cameron might be a tough guy, but there weren't any gangs in Frey. It was such a small town, any gang activity would stand out like a dinosaur's tail. Yusuf looked again at Cameron and his pierced ear. The Patriot Sons were almost definitely a gang. Maybe there were more. Maybe Frey had hidden secrets too.

Cameron took a bite of his beef taco and closed his eyes. "Yum, this is good stuff."

"My mom says they mix pork meat into the beef," Danial told him in a nasty tone.

Cameron chewed slowly and winked. "I guess that's why it tastes so delicious, right, Yusuf?"

"Ugh, disgusting!"

Yusuf was almost positive Danial was joking about the pork. Still, he put down his own taco and wished he'd brought lunch from home. "What did you want to tell me about the competition?" he asked.

Cameron didn't reply. He was looking intently toward the cafeteria door. "Incoming," he said in a low voice.

Yusuf and Danial turned. Ethan Grant and his friend Sammy had entered the cafeteria. Their faces wore identical hard looks and ugly scowls. Before Yusuf could steel himself, they were looming over his table like predatory birds over frozen mice. "Hope you heard loud and clear what my dad said at the parade."

Yusuf couldn't say anything even if he wanted to. Which he didn't.

Sammy grinned at them—a cold, small grin. "Loud and clear. We all heard it."

Cameron held up his palms. "Hey, guys, come on. Chill."

Ethan growled. For a minute it seemed like he would hit someone or something. Then his face relaxed. "Hey, Cam, haven't seen you in a while. Why're you sitting with these pathetic losers? Let's roll."

Cam nodded like he totally agreed with that character judgment. He pushed back his chair and stood up. "Yeah, let's roll."

The three strolled away with casual steps, Cameron's

earring glinting in the harsh cafeteria lights.

Danial's hand trembled as he closed his lunch box with a half-eaten samosa still inside. "Is this what sixth grade is going to be like from now on? Lunchtime bullies, with a side of Cameron?"

Yusuf was still staring at Cameron's back. "I don't know," he replied slowly. "I think he sat with us to . . . protect us?"

Danial looked at him as if he'd grown horns. "You're out of your mind. The day Kamran Abdullah does something good and kind will be the day I eat my own shoe."

18

Miss Terrance had said that knowledge was power. Yusuf decided that writing the 9/11 report might help him figure out Ethan and his father. Why he wanted to do this wasn't very clear to him, except that he kept remembering the topic of persecution from the previous Sunday school class. The disbelievers of Mecca had made the lives of the early Muslims miserable because they didn't understand or trust the new religion being practiced. Hatred grew among them, even though the Meccans all used to be family and friends.

Just like Frey. Only this was not seventh-century Arabia, and the Patriot Sons were like no friends or family Yusuf had ever seen. He figured that maybe understanding the Patriot Sons could prevent the

Muslims of Frey from being kicked out of town, or at the very least, let them finish their mosque.

Luckily he had library on Tuesday. He spent the period researching 9/11 and the war on terror. Uncle Rahman had written one boy's story, as it was happening, in real time. But Yusuf needed to see the big picture: what an entire nation had gone through twenty years ago. Mrs. Levy, the librarian, showed him how to search archive databases on the library computer. "These are connected to the best libraries in Texas," she told him proudly. "You can find anything you need in here."

His search came up with hundreds of news stories, and he copied and pasted them into his Google Drive for reading later. He looked through hundreds of images. Of the Twin Towers with smoke pouring from the top floors. Of firefighters looking exhausted and people crying with mouths wide open. The pictures were twenty years old, but the grief and pain came through like it was happening right now. This was what Uncle Rahman had written about. What he'd felt.

Then other words caught his attention. Terrible words. The Patriot Act. The War on Terror. Islamic terrorism. Enemies.

"Need some help?"

Yusuf looked up, startled. It was Madison. She slid

into the seat next to him and peered at his computer screen. "Secret surveillance. Ooh, are you writing a crime novel or something?"

He stared at her. "Yeah, that's definitely what I'm doing."

She gave a little laugh. "Might be fun. I love writing stories. I could help you."

Yusuf wished she'd go away. He wasn't used to girls who sat too close and laughed too much. "No thanks. I'm just working on my 9/11 report."

She stopped smiling and leaned back. "Oh, yeah? I learned so much doing that report. Like, did you know 2,996 people died in the attacks? I thought it was only a few hundred."

Yusuf thought of Uncle Rahman's journal. He nodded and whispered: "The deadliest attack on U.S. soil."

"Yup." Madison nodded back slowly. "That's messed up. Like, why would anyone do such a terrible thing?"

Yusuf didn't know what to say. She was looking at him as if he knew the answer, and he felt a sudden rush of hot anger in his chest. "Why're you asking me?" he demanded. "Just because I'm Muslim, I'm supposed to know what other Muslims feel or think?"

Madison's eyebrows rose to reach her bangs. "What? No, that's not what I meant! I didn't even know you're Muz-lim or whatever."

His chest squeezed some more. "It's not Muz-lim. It's Muslim. And Islam means peace. Like, literally. So whatever those attackers were, they weren't Muslim."

They stared at each other for a few seconds, then Madison nodded. "I get it. Sorry."

Yusuf went back to his computer screen, breathing like a marathon runner. He quickly closed all the windows on the computer. "Whatever." He opened up the search engine and typed "Muhammad Ali." A list of items came up. Heavyweight champion. Muslim. Vietnam War.

Soon he was reading again. He could feel Madison sitting beside him, tapping her foot, but he refused to turn.

The bell rang, and she got up. As she walked past him, he heard her mutter, "Sorry again, okay?"

In robotics club after school, Mr. Parker passed around chocolate chip cookies Jared's grandmother had sent, along with the instructions for the TRC competition. "This year's problem is to remove clutter from a trash site," he told them, waving a thick booklet over his head. "Here's the scenario: A garbage truck has collapsed in the middle of the road, spilling trash of various sizes into oncoming traffic. You have to build a robot that will clean up the trash and pile it into containers, all the while dodging cars and pedestrians. The garbage is of different sizes and has to be sorted before being put into the containers."

The students began talking excitedly. Tony Rivera asked, "What's the duration of the challenge?"

"Three minutes," replied Mr. Parker, and the chatter increased. Yusuf tapped his right foot nervously on the floor. Three minutes? That seemed too short for an elaborate challenge that included sorting.

Cameron was sitting next to him again. He had a toothpick in his hand and was using it to pick between his teeth like a farmer. "So, what're you thinking, Yusuf?" he asked in a lazy voice. "A robot built for speed or quick movements? Or both?"

They all stopped talking and looked at Yusuf. Without taking a vote, they'd somehow selected him to be the team captain. He returned their stares nervously. Danial was sitting on his other side, pouting because of Cameron. Jared and Tony were on the floor, looking through their box of LEGO parts. Madison sat slouched in the far corner near the window. She hadn't made eye contact with him since the club started.

"Uh, I think we need both," Yusuf finally replied. "Small and lightweight, so that it can move around the traffic and avoid people. But also strong enough to hold trash items and take them across the road."

Jared raised his head. "I can make some sketches for the early design."

"Excellent idea." Mr. Parker began writing on the whiteboard. "It's best to organize every team member's job. That way, each of you has a function within the team." He wrote *designer, builder, programmer, note taker.*

"Who's going to do what?" Danial asked anxiously.

Mr. Parker pointed to Yusuf. "The team captain gets to assign tasks."

Yusuf took a deep breath. This was going to be easy. "Tony and Jared can design the bot. Danial and I will program it. Cameron is the builder—he's always been really fast at building LEGOs—but we'll all help."

Madison scoffed from her seat near the window. "That leaves the girl to take notes. Like a secretary or something. Perfect!"

Yusuf willed himself to be patient. He was still mad about what had happened in the library earlier, but she had a point. The TRC instructions said that the job of the team captain was to realize every member's potential. He faced Madison squarely and said, "You told me in the library you loved writing. Note taker isn't just a secretary. You have to keep a big binder with every detail about the project. Our progress. Our **mistakes. Pictures. It's like historian and reporter and** record keeper all rolled into one. And probably artist too. You'll be great at it."

Madison lost her angry face. "Oh. Okay, then. I guess I'll do it."

He relaxed. He couldn't stay mad at anyone for too long. She'd apologized twice, hadn't she? He gave her a ghost of a smile, and after a pause she gave one back to him.

Tony raised his hand. "I can make a practice arena in shop class," he offered. "Our teacher's okay with us doing extra projects."

Mr. Parker clapped his hands once. "It's decided. Now please get to work reading the project details. We'll get started with design on Saturday."

The hour passed quickly. After the club, Mr. Parker caught up with Yusuf in the parking lot. "Walking home alone?" he asked. "Where's Danial?"

Yusuf shrugged, his hands in his pockets. "His mom picked him up."

"And Cameron?"

"I don't know." Yusuf turned to Mr. Parker. "Danial says he's a bad kid, like a gangster or something. Is that true?"

Mr. Parker let out a short laugh. "Just because he's got an earring and a tough attitude? It takes more than that to be a bad kid, Yusuf. You should know better."

Yusuf felt his cheeks go warm. "I guess. But it's not only Danial who says that about him. It's Danial's dad too. And other people I know, like my Sunday school teacher."

Mr. Parker stopped in front of a small white Volkswagen. "What's your own gut feeling? What do you think Cameron's like inside?"

Did he think Yusuf was a mind reader? "I don't know."

"I think you do." Mr. Parker got into his car and closed the door. He rolled down the window and stuck his face out. "I don't care how Cameron dresses, but I see how attentive he is in my class, and how good his ideas are. Mark my words, Yusuf, he's going to be an asset to your TRC team. They all are."

Journal entry 6
September 25, 2001
Jonathan is acting strange, there's no question about it. At first I thought he was just sad about the attacks, like me. Like everyone else in school. But our sadness is different. I have Amma to hug me, and my sisters to distract me. Abba is only teaching two classes at the university this semester, so he's at home most of the time. Apart from watching the news, he also spends a lot of time out on our street, talking to the neighbors, making sure everyone is okay. We've

been here longer than the other immigrants, and they look at Abba as their leader.

That's another thing that's happened after the eleventh. A lot of our Muslim neighbors have started praying together. The mosque is many miles away, and it's safer to meet at someone's house for the five daily prayers. That's our house, I guess. Abba says the neighbors need comfort at a time like this, and Amma's okay with it. So we have neighbors in the house all the time.

I think that's why my sadness isn't so huge and scary—I don't feel alone. When someone tells a story about what happened to them that day, like a person shouting, "Go home, loser!" in the street, or "Hey, Osama's cousin!" in the mall, we can all laugh about it and tell each other it will be okay. One day, we will learn to respect each other and be neighbors again.

Abba gives Friday sermons about forgiveness and mercy, and how our hearts bleed for our fellow Americans. His voice is always soft and unwavering. I'm sure I'm not the only person who finds calmness from his words.

Jonathan doesn't have that. He told me yesterday after school that his uncle is still missing, the one who worked in New York City near the Twin Towers. My heart jumped when I heard that. His whole family must be so worried. "I'm sorry," I told him. He moved away quickly.

"Are you?" he asked in a loud voice. "You sure you're not glad?"

I stared at him in shock. Why on earth would I be glad his uncle was missing? How can he really be my best friend if he thinks like that? But as he turned away from me, I realized he was thinking the same thing about me: How can Rahman be my best friend if he's one of THEM?

I couldn't stay silent. I could see he was hurting, from the slump of his shoulders. "I hope they find him," I whispered. "I hope things can be okay again soon."

Jonathan turned back and pushed me in the chest with the full force of his hand. "Why don't you just go back where you came from?" he screamed at me. The other kids looked at us, but nobody said anything. My hands trembled, and I made them into fists so nobody would see.

"Back where?" I asked, my voice low. "I was born here, in the same year as you, in the same city as you."

He shook his head violently. "No," he said. "You're not American like me. Go back to where you belong."

My chest hurt, but it wasn't from his fist. I couldn't believe what I was hearing. But in a weird way, I could totally believe it too. Jonathan ran away as if *he couldn't stand to be near me another second. I tried to call his name but couldn't. My throat was tight, and my eyes were full of tears.*

When I went home, Abba was getting ready to lead the prayers for our neighbors. "Let's pray for our country," he told them. "For our friends and neighbors." I thought of Jonathan and choked, but I prayed with them. Please bring Mr. O'Reilly's brother back to him, God. Then maybe Jonathan will forget everything, and we can go back to normal again.

19

"Why are you lugging all those books around all the time?" Amma asked as Yusuf left for school on Thursday. "Don't you have a locker at school to put them in?"

Yusuf tried to pretend he wasn't holding five textbooks and two notebooks in his arms, plus a lunch bag that was dangling from the crook of his elbow. "What books? They're just a few things I need for school."

Amma narrowed her eyes at him. She'd left store-bought croissants on the table and disappeared into her garage office before Aleena woke up, but now she was back again in the kitchen, watching him like a hawk as he got ready for school. Ugh. Two more minutes and he'd have been out of here without anybody noticing his load of textbooks. "No, your school definitely has lockers. Mrs. Khan was telling me about how Danial doesn't bring his books home anymore."

Yusuf groaned loudly. "Okay, fine. I'll leave them in my locker today. Happy?"

She smiled and kissed him on the top of his head. "Yes, darling, I'm happy. I don't want to see my son bent down under the load of all these books."

He smiled back as he left. "Stop calling me darling!"

"Never!" she replied as she closed the front door after him.

Yusuf was still smiling as he met Danial on the corner of the street. He was still smiling as they walked to Frey Middle and entered the building a good twelve minutes before the bell rang. He waved goodbye to Danial as they parted in the hallway. It was only when he reached his locker, which he had been avoiding like the plague for three weeks now, that his smile slipped. He stood in front of the locker, staring at it. Should he open it? Should he dump his books on the floor in front of it and run away? Both options seemed equally impossible.

Man up, Yusuf, he told himself. *You're not a baby. If your dad can handle a robber, you can definitely handle a few notes.*

With a surprisingly steady hand, he reached up to the lock. Seven zero two zero. As he dialed the numbers, he suddenly realized he'd never changed the combination like the school had advised. What if the person who put those notes inside knew his combination? The thought of somebody else walking up to his locker and opening it, putting mean notes with tilted almost-cursive handwriting inside, made him want to puke.

The lock clicked, and the door swung open slowly like something out of a horror movie. He peered inside carefully.

Nothing. There was no new note.

Yusuf's chest heaved. Thank God. Maybe the note writer had forgotten all about Yusuf. Maybe he'd moved on to another victim. Yusuf could feel relief running like a cool hand over his forehead. It was going to be okay. He didn't have to be scared anymore.

He dumped his textbooks in the locker and swung the door shut again. Before it closed, he caught sight of lined paper sticking out from the top shelf. The old notes. Why in the world had he kept them?

He reached for them and stuffed them in his pants pocket. He'd wait until he got home to get rid of them.

After lunch, the combined classes of sixth grade had PE. Coach Boston was a tall, muscular man with thighs like pillars and a blond ponytail that swished around like a whip. "Change into your gym shorts and get out here in five minutes!" he yelled as they filed into the gym on their way to the changing rooms.

Yusuf hated the changing rooms. Amma and Abba had written a letter to the school in August requesting that Yusuf, along with all the other Muslim students at Frey Middle, be allowed to change in private for PE. The response from Principal Williamson was swift. No special accommodations for students. Everyone hated changing in public, but they did it anyway. The Muslims weren't any different.

In other words: get used to it.

He and Danial were together, at least. Danial held up a towel and looked away as Yusuf wiggled out of his pants and into his shorts. Then Yusuf did the same for Danial. It took all of five minutes. The other kids were laughing and joking. Ethan Grant was swatting the behind of another boy with his towel, and the other boy was yelling "Hey!" over and over.

Yusuf glared at Ethan, a tight feeling rising in his chest. "I don't think you should do that." It took a second before he realized he'd said it out loud. Loud enough for Ethan to hear.

"What. Are. You. Doing?" whispered Danial furiously. "Stop trying to be a hero."

Ethan turned to Yusuf. "What's your problem, dirty Mooz-lim?"

Yusuf's stomach turned to jelly, but he clenched his fists at his sides like Uncle Rahman had done. He was never going to be a hero, but he was definitely a decent person. He took a deep, deep breath, and said, "You need to stop hitting people. It's not funny even if it's with a towel."

Danial made a faint noise in his throat. His eyes looked as if they would bulge right out of his face. He walked backward until he was away from Yusuf.

Yusuf hardly noticed. What was Ethan going to do? Hit him with a towel too?

Ethan blinked and leaned forward. "How dare you. . . ."

"What?" Yusuf said quietly. He looked around. The other boys had crept closer until they formed a circle around Yusuf and Ethan. Danial was nowhere to be seen, but Sammy, Ethan's red-haired friend, stood nearby, watching with fascinated eyes. "How dare I tell you to stop being a bully? I dare, because I'm Muslim, and that's what we do."

The crowd oohed as if they'd heard something scandalous. Yusuf knew his statement was cheesy, but also accurate. The residents of Frey—some of them, at least—thought of Muslims as terrorists. As bad people. It was time they learned what being a Muslim was actually all about. He remembered what Amma had taught him the first year of Sunday school, when he was six or seven. *"We have a responsibility to spread kindness and help others. To serve and protect God's creatures, not hurt them."*

Ethan put up his fists and brought them close to Yusuf's face. They were like mini versions of the hams Yusuf had seen on the butcher's counter next door to Abba's dollar store. "I guess you want to fight," said Ethan with a sneer.

Yusuf shook his head. "No, I don't," he said quietly. Sadly. *"You* do."

The door to the changing room slammed open, and Coach Boston strode in. Danial scurried behind him, his face pale. "What's going on here?" Coach demanded.

The crowd broke up and everyone backed away, leaving Yusuf and Ethan standing before each other like wrestlers. Ethan put down his fists. "He was threatening me."

"No, I wasn't," Yusuf protested.

"No, he wasn't," agreed Danial breathlessly. "Ethan was—"

Coach Boston put up an angry hand. "Quiet! Explain it to the principal."

★ ★ ★

Principal Williamson wasn't happy at being disturbed. She sat on her leather chair and stared at Yusuf and Ethan with cold black eyes. "So, fighting in the locker room, eh? That's original."

Ethan scoffed lightly. "We weren't fighting. Right, Yoo-soof? It was all a big misunderstanding."

Yusuf's eyes widened. Ethan's tone was almost . . . friendly? The tightness around his mouth was gone, and he was smiling like an innocent child who had zero idea of who had eaten all the cookies. "Are you joking?" Yusuf asked him.

Ethan turned to the principal. "It's true. We're best friends, aren't we?"

Principal Williamson looked from one boy to the other. "Are you? What's Yusuf's last name?"

Yusuf waited with bated breath. Did Ethan know his last name? They didn't share any classes except PE.

Ethan shrugged. "Ahhhh . . . I forgot . . . maybe Osama or something?"

Principal Williamson turned to Yusuf with a sigh. "What really happened in the gym, young man? I know your father. I know how he raised you. You're going to tell me the truth, aren't you?"

Yusuf gulped. Telling the truth would only land him in deeper trouble with Ethan and Sammy. But lying was really not an option either, was it? Amma and Abba would be devastated if he lied. "He was hitting another kid with a towel. Sort of like a joke," Yusuf finally replied. "I told him to stop. It wasn't a big deal though, really."

The principal didn't seem to agree with the last part. She gave Ethan a glare and said, "You can go now. I'm going to call your father this evening."

Ethan blushed so brightly his face looked like a red neon sign. "Please, ma'am . . ."

She put up a hand. "Go now."

He shuffled out, but not before giving Yusuf the nastiest look a boy could give another. Yusuf squashed his fear. This was not over.

Principal Williamson turned her attention to him. She made a steeple with the fingers of both her hands and looked at him from above it. "So, how's it going, Yusuf? Middle school is tough, eh?"

He nodded, still on edge. "Definitely."

"Mr. Parker says you're the guy giving us a shot at winning TRC this year." She smiled, the hard look in her eyes gone as if it had never been there. "That man's been trying to get to TRC for years. You have a big task ahead of you."

Yusuf was surprised his science teacher thought they

had a chance at winning. His shoulders relaxed. "We'll try our best, ma'am."

"That's good enough for me." She stood up, still smiling. "You can go now. And stay away from Ethan Grant. And his father."

20

Saturday club was like a party for nerds. The Freybots sat cross-legged on the floor of the gym, with their LEGO Mindstorms parts scattered around them like candy wrappers. Mr. Parker watched the team from his perch on a bleacher, smiling slightly. Since the first task at hand was to design their robot, all eyes were on Tony and Jared. The others crowded around Tony as he slowly made sketches on pieces of paper and then crumpled them up in frustration. Jared watched him with intense eyes. "Don't you all have something better to do?" Tony finally yelled.

Madison waved a binder and pencil in the air. "I'm recording all your mistakes," she told him, grinning.

Danial was busy uncrumpling the papers and smoothing them open. "Why are you throwing these away? We may use one of these for the design later."

Yusuf groaned. Loudly. As captain, he was aching to get started. But he also knew the design process was crucial. A flaw in the design could mean the difference between winning and losing. If Principal Williamson was right about Mr. Parker's hopes for TRC, Team Freybots really needed to win the regionals in January.

The added pressure didn't help.

Tony threw another piece of paper across the floor. It landed on Jared's lap, and he yelped.

Mr. Parker clapped his hands once. "Okay, kids. Give these guys some space. Go play with the LEGOs while he works."

The others moved away. Yusuf and Danial hunched over their laptops reading the TRC contest guidelines they'd downloaded. Cameron took an armful of LEGO pieces into a corner and began to assemble them into little bot babies. His hands were a blur as he worked, his eyes focused like laser beams on the LEGOs. For once, his mocking grin was completely absent. Yusuf elbowed Danial. "See, told you he's going to be great at building our robot."

"And I told you: ugh."

Mr. Parker ended the club just before noon. Yusuf stopped Jared as they were leaving. "How's the design going?"

"Okay, I guess," Jared replied uncertainly. "Tony thinks he's got a good design, but there's no way of knowing until I make some decent sketches over the weekend."

Mr. Parker led them out and locked the school. "See you on Monday, kids!" He waved as he walked toward his Volkswagen. "I've got tickets to a play in Houston tonight!"

"Sounds cool," Yusuf called out. He'd been to a few Christmas plays in the public library, but nothing too exciting. He could just imagine the theaters in Houston, the actors dressed in fine clothes. To be honest, everything in Houston sounded way more fun than Frey.

Jared was fiddling with his backpack. "Can you help me?" he burst out. "With the sketches, I mean. This is my first real robotics club. I have no idea what I'm doing."

Yusuf slapped him lightly on the shoulder. "Of course. Want to come over to my house now? You can call your grandmother from there."

Yusuf's house was quiet when they arrived. Amma met them at the front door with a finger to her lips.

"Shhh, Aleena just fell asleep. She was having trouble breathing."

Yusuf and Jared tiptoed inside, but not before Yusuf pointed to a neat row of shoes in the hallway. "Can you take your shoes off, please? It's a rule in my house."

Jared did as he was told. Yusuf relaxed. He didn't like inviting kids from school because they asked questions about things like these. Why do you take your shoes off in the house? What is that language your dad is speaking on the phone? Why do you eat such spicy foods? But Jared was okay. He didn't ask unnecessary questions.

They made a detour to the kitchen to devour Amma's aloo parathas, still warm from the stove. Then Jared called Mrs. Raymond to tell her where he was. Yusuf could hear her excited voice through the phone. "She says I'm welcome to stay as long as I want," Jared told him after hanging up.

"Perfect."

In Yusuf's bedroom, they flopped on the floor and took out Tony's papers. There were a lot of them, full of pencil markings and lines and circles. Yusuf pored over them, relieved to see that they made a lot of sense. "Tony's got a good eye," he remarked. One design was the classic arm robot with a single wheel. Another was a flat wagon-shaped robot with smaller arms and four wheels. A third was a big arm and a

174

little arm on each side of a pillar robot.

Yusuf could see the benefits and difficulties of each design. An arm robot was probably going to be the fastest, but its single wheel made it more prone to falling. A wagon robot was stable but also slower and bulkier. "None of these are the right one," he murmured.

Jared peered over his shoulder. "We could try combining them."

They spent more than an hour perfecting Tony's designs. Jared took notes as Yusuf talked, his words so rapid they bumped into each other as they left his mouth. The afternoon was hot, and he wished he had a fan in his room. Halfway through, he remembered Madison and began recording his notes in his laptop to send to her.

At three o'clock, Amma knocked on the door and peeked in. "Snacks, anyone?" she asked.

Yusuf's forehead was beaded with sweat. "Do we have any ice cream?"

Amma shook her head, then her face brightened. "Aleena's awake now, so I could take you kiddos to Dairy Queen."

Everybody knew DQ had the best ice cream in the northern hemisphere. Jared and Yusuf said together, "We'll be right there."

Before they left, Yusuf had something for Jared.

"You'll never guess what came in the delivery truck for my dad's store last week."

"Dollar store items?"

Yusuf picked up his pants and dug through a pocket. He came up with a handful of papers. The notes from his locker! He hastily put them on his dresser and searched the other pocket. "Here, since you play solitaire so much."

Jared looked at the playing cards Yusuf was holding out. "These are for me?"

"Yeah. My dad doesn't really sell a lot of them. He was going to return them, but I took one pack. Aren't they nice?"

Jared nodded. The cards had the Statue of Liberty on the box. "I've never been to New York," he whispered.

Yusuf nodded. "Me neither. But I like this statue. Lady Liberty. She welcomes all the immigrants who come to our country."

Jared stared. "Our country? Uncle Trevor says it's not your country. It's ours. White people's."

Yusuf's face burned. "Since when have you started listening to Ethan's dad?"

"He's my uncle, remember? He comes over for Sunday dinner every week."

"Well, tell your uncle I was born here, just like him. So was my mom. So that makes this our country too."

Amma knocked on the door again. "Are you two coming? I want to swing over to St. Mary's pumpkin patch first. Aleena's been begging to go."

Yusuf knew better than to complain. Aleena was the baby, and she had asthma. That meant if she begged for something, she usually got it. Plus, the pumpkin patch might be fun. Sometimes they had games like dunk the pastor.

Jared was silent in the car. Was he thinking of what Yusuf had said? Or about what Ethan's dad was saying every week at Sunday dinner? Yusuf gave him a little smile to show he wasn't mad. Jared was a good, kindhearted person. It wasn't his fault he was related to an adult bully.

The pumpkin patch turned out to be very fun indeed. St. Mary's was a big Catholic church on several acres of wooded grounds, and their pumpkins were the best in Frey. Yusuf and Jared stood in a long line to dunk Father Robbins, an elderly fellow with bushy white hair and an easy grin. They ran like little kids around a big play fort and jumped on a giant trampoline until they were exhausted. Aleena's favorite was the tractor hayride, and she made the boys ride with her three times. By the time Amma drove them to Dairy Queen, everyone was starving.

"Forget just ice cream, I'm going to eat a burger

and fries too," Yusuf announced as he collapsed next to Jared in the booth.

Amma took out her phone. "I guess you better call your grandmother again, Jared."

Jared grinned at Yusuf. "She's going to be so happy I've made a friend."

21

Yusuf stayed up late to work on his 9/11 report. He read articles from 2001 about each of the terrorists, staring at their faces and wondering why they'd done what they'd done. He questioned what kind of Islam they practiced, which was so different from his own. He wanted to scream at them, "Thanks for ruining everyone's lives, you evil men!"

The next day he went to the mosque construction site with bleary eyes. The half-built structure was cold and empty. The uncles clustered in a group on plastic chairs drinking chai and looking wistfully at their tools. "My dad reminded them they can't build until the zoning meeting," Danial told him as they walked toward the Sunday school area.

"I don't even know what a zoning meeting is, exactly," Yusuf grumbled. He didn't like not knowing things. He should have looked it up when Mr. Khan mentioned it in Urooj Diner.

"It's where they decide petitions about parking and roads and things like that," Danial answered helpfully. "Like what you can build in a school zone versus a residential zone."

Yusuf didn't answer. He took off his glasses to rub his burning eyes.

"What's wrong with you?" Danial asked. "I bet you stayed up all night planning our robot design."

Yusuf felt a pang of guilt. He shook his head. "Not really."

Danial raised his eyebrows. "What else could you be doing?"

Cameron strolled toward them, his usual mocking grin fixed on his face. "Collecting pumpkins with his new friend, more likely."

Danial's mouth dropped open. "Pumpkins?" he wailed. "You went to St. Mary's without me?"

Yusuf felt his cheeks grow warm. "Aleena was begging," he said. "You know how she is."

Danial calmed down a little. "I told you younger siblings are a pain."

"Yes, you did," Yusuf agreed, hoping Cameron would go away.

No such luck. Cameron was openly laughing at him now. "You sure, Yusuf? It wasn't because your new friend Jared begged you? You guys were really having a great time."

Yusuf jammed his glasses up his nose. "What? No . . . yes . . . uh."

"Your new friend? What am I, then? Old news?" Danial's voice was shrill. "Jared is Ethan's cousin, or don't you care?"

"Come on, that's not his fault!" Yusuf protested.

There was a rumble underneath their feet, and then an earsplitting whistle announcing the ten o'clock train. Yusuf waited while the train shrieked and crashed and hurtled through. It took less than a minute but felt like twenty. When the train was gone, he looked for Danial.

His best friend was stalking away toward the Sunday school kids like a boy on a mission. Yusuf swung around to face Cameron. "What's the matter with you? Why did you say that? Were you spying on me?"

"I was there with my parents," Cameron replied, shrugging. "I actually waved at you several times. You were too busy having fun to notice me."

Yusuf ran after Danial. Cameron followed. "What's

the big deal anyway? Aren't you allowed to have other friends?"

"Yes, I am." Yusuf stopped. "No, I'm not. Wait . . ."

Cameron's laughter was like a big gust of wind across the construction site. The aunties looked at him in disapproval. "Whatever. This drama is too childish for me."

Yusuf gritted his teeth. "You can't just say things like that and walk away. You made this mess. You clean it up."

Cameron's face hardened. "Look who's talking."

"What do you mean?"

"The whole thing with Ethan in the changing room last week. What business did you have confronting him? He wasn't hitting *your* behind with a towel. Why didn't you just leave it alone? You're not a hero like your dad, you know."

Yusuf stood in shock. Cameron had completely lost his mocking, easy grin. He looked almost like the kid they'd been friends with in elementary school. Earnest. Serious. A little mad at everything around him. Yusuf put a trembling hand to his glasses. "I wasn't being a hero! I *had* to do that. It was my duty as a Muslim."

"Are you serious? Your duty?" Cameron's whisper was furious. "Listen, just keep your head down and don't make waves. Like your parents and my parents, and everyone else around here. Since when did you start to challenge things? Dangerous things?"

Yusuf swallowed. Was he really challenging things that could end up being dangerous? He thought of Ethan's ham fists and narrowed eyes. No! Ethan was just a big bully. He'd never really hurt Yusuf.

Ethan's father was another matter, though. Yusuf remembered how twisted his face had been as he stood on the 9/11 memorial stage, shouting about the enemy.

"Everything's okay," Yusuf finally said shakily, even though he didn't really believe it.

Cameron shook his head in disgust and turned away. "You're not as smart as they all say, dude."

After Sunday school, Amma handed the kids big trash bags and told them to clean up the street outside the construction site. "The people from the church should have a clean path to walk on as they leave," she told them. "It's the neighborly thing to do."

Danial took a bag and joined Saba and Rehana with his head held high. Yusuf sighed and walked beside Amma, holding a big bag for both of them. "I thought you didn't care what people thought about Muslims," he said after a while.

Amma wrinkled her brow. "When did I say that?"

Yusuf shrugged. It wasn't anything she'd said, really.

"Abba's always saying we have to present this perfect picture of how we are, but you don't always agree with that."

She bent to pick up a Coke can. "Your abba comes from a different background, Yusuf. He didn't grow up here. He still feels like an outsider, even after fifteen years in this country."

Yusuf frowned. "So that's why he's always trying to be perfect?"

"Exactly. He feels the need to prove himself." She gave Yusuf a little smile. "Not me. I was born here; I belong here. I'm not going to apologize for being Muslim or try to do things exactly like everyone else. If I don't like those violent football games on Friday nights, I shouldn't have to attend them, right?"

He nodded. He didn't want to watch football either, especially if Ethan Grant was the captain of the Coyotes. "Is it because of 9/11? All this hatred of Muslims?"

Amma stopped so suddenly that he almost bumped into her. "What do you mean?"

He stopped too. "I've been researching 9/11 for my school report, and it's all about the wars and everything. It's very confusing."

Her sigh was so loud a few kids around them turned to see what was happening. "Suspicion of those unlike us is common human behavior. We don't trust who we don't know. But yes, 9/11 was terrible, and it really fueled the fire of hatred in this country."

Yusuf chewed his lip, wondering if he should tell her about Ethan and the incident in the gym. Principal Williamson hadn't called Amma and Abba about it, but if they ever found out on their own, they'd be devastated. Especially Abba. Maybe it was better to tell them.

He opened his mouth to speak, but a shout from nearby interrupted him. Everyone turned to see what was happening.

A group of men with picket signs stood on the corner, closer to the church than the construction site, but walking toward them. They weren't many, but they were big and bulky. Yusuf looked closer and recognized the motorcycle crew from Wicks Avenue—Mr. Grant's friends. But wait, there were others too. People he recognized. A young man who worked at the grocery store downtown, and the lady from the post office near Abba's store. And Mr. Thomas, a substitute teacher at his old elementary school. They all looked serious. And sort of mad.

The Patriot Sons.

The group got closer, and he could see what the signs said now.

STOP BUILDING.

GO AWAY.

THIS IS OUR TOWN.

Mr. Khan and Abba came outside to see what the commotion was. The other uncles and aunties joined them too. They stood with their arms crossed and their mouths in straight lines, silently watching the Patriot Sons grow closer. "Don't say anything," Mr. Khan warned. "We stopped building already. We don't have to respond to their taunts."

The church doors opened and a stream of people came out. Yusuf hoped the Patriot Sons would leave, now that others were watching them. Abba always said bad guys weren't so brave when they had witnesses. Yusuf got ready to wave at Jared, or Pastor Nielson, or anyone else he recognized.

There was no one. He didn't see familiar faces in the crowd. Not a single smile. They avoided the construction site and walked on the other side of the street. In a few minutes, they were all gone. All except the Patriot Sons, who were now only a few feet away, holding up their signs and shouting, "GO AWAY!"

Yusuf shivered, even though the breeze was warm and humid.

Journal entry 7

October 9, 2001

I can't believe it's been almost a month since the 9/11 attacks. I feel like a totally different person, like someone took away all my happy thoughts and replaced them with dark, alien ones. I know I'm supposed to write in this journal every week, but it's been so hard to find words that make sense. Jonathan doesn't even speak to me anymore. He just turns away when he sees me, his lips tightly shut and his eyes fixed on a point on the floor. I want to tell him a corny joke, but he doesn't look like he's ever going to laugh again in his life.

I miss him. I don't have anyone else to hang out with in school, unless you count the two other Muslim kids in my class, Sami and Farhan. Nobody talks to them either. A few kids push against us in the hallways, or throw a ball hard and fast at us in the gym. Small things that tell us we're not wanted.

I want to scream that it's not my fault. None of this is. But nobody's listening.

Amma says things will get better with time, they always do. "When my father died," she told me once, "I felt like the world had ended. I loved him so much. But after a while it became easier to breathe, easier to go on with life."

I'm not sure this will ever happen to us. It's not like we have to get over one person dying. There was so much destruction on 9/11, so many deaths. How do you ever forget that?

America declared war on Afghanistan a few weeks ago, like it was no big deal to kill innocent people thousands of miles away. "We need to take revenge," a news reporter said on TV. "Root out the mastermind behind the 9/11 attacks."

I felt sick when I heard that. The people in Afghanistan aren't responsible for 9/11 any more than I am. Why should we be dropping bombs on them?

Our neighbors are from Afghanistan, and they walk around like half-dead ghosts these days. "What will happen to our family?" they ask when they come to our house for prayers. Abba doesn't have a reply, but we pray for their family, and their country, just like we pray for ours.

Maybe that's why I stopped journaling. Because there are too many questions without answers. Nothing to report except the worry that keeps following my family around like a black cloud. But now I'm back because I have something to write about. Two things, actually.

It was Mrs. Jahangir's last day at the school today. She was crying as she put all her things in a box. I've started sitting in her office at recess instead of going outside for a repeat encounter with Jonathan.

"Why are you leaving?" I asked her. "Where will you work now?"

"I can't work here anymore," she replied. "Everyone is horrible to me."

I stare at her, wondering who this "everyone" is. Her boss, the principal, is the kindest man. He'd been on vacation on the eleventh, but had come back the next day and called an assembly. He'd told all of us to take care of each other. No bullying, he'd warned. But then I remembered President Bush's speech, and how it didn't really matter.

I hugged Mrs. Jahangir and told her I'd miss her. She kept crying and didn't reply.

The second thing that happened was that Abba's contract wasn't renewed for next semester. His boss at the university told him they didn't need his kind there. Abba told Amma as they drank chai after dinner. It was past my bedtime, and I wasn't supposed to hear, but I did. My chest squeezed and my eyes hurt, but I kept quiet. Abba went on a job interview to Atlanta the next day, and when he got back, he said everyone on the plane was staring at him throughout the flight. Two men came and sat next to him. "In case I tried anything," Abba said in a bitter voice.

I've never heard him speak like that.

22

The zoning meeting was scheduled for Friday, October 8, at six thirty p.m. Abba made Yusuf stay home from school because he said everyone needed to attend Jummah and pray very hard about the outcome of the meeting. "But I don't even know what's being discussed," Yusuf protested.

Amma was making French toast in the kitchen. She banged the skillet so hard on the counter, the angry sound echoed around them. "The Patriot Sons don't want us to build our mosque, that's all. Nothing out of the ordinary. So many cities in America go through the same thing every day. Zoning laws get violated all the time."

Yusuf watched as she poured milk and sugar into a

bowl and whisked furiously. He didn't think it was a good idea to tell her she had forgotten the eggs. And the cinnamon. "So, it's our fault?"

"Honestly, I don't know," Amma snapped. "Stop asking questions."

Abba reached over and put a hand on Amma's shoulder. "Don't worry, jaan," he said to her in a low voice.

Amma looked at him, then Yusuf. When she spoke, her voice was quiet. "No, it's not our fault. Mr. Khan got permission from the city council before we started to build."

Yusuf relaxed. "Okay, then," he announced cheerfully. "The meeting will be fine."

His parents exchanged glances. "I'm sure," Abba agreed, nodding firmly.

Yusuf poured some orange juice in his glass and went to wake Aleena. "Oh, by the way, Amma," he called out from the hallway. "You forgot to add eggs to that mixture."

At Jummah, the trailer was crowded. Everyone had kept their kids home from school in the hopes of a massive prayer marathon. The middle schoolers stood in Abba's parking lot under the sun. Saba, the hijab-clad seventh grader, nervously paced up and down. "I heard the city council is really mean," she whispered, clutching her little purse to her chest.

Danial nodded morosely. "My dad said it'll be the toughest meeting he's ever been in. He's not a lawyer, you know. He's in IT."

"Yeah, dude, we know," Cameron scoffed.

Danial scowled. "I'm just saying . . ."

Yusuf could tell that the kids were all nervous. "It'll be okay. It's not our fault," he told everyone, trying to smile.

Danial rolled his eyes at him. "Do you eat some special breakfast every morning that makes you so disgustingly cheery?"

Yusuf managed a small grin. "Just my mom's French toast!"

Sameena Aunty peered from the trailer door and gestured sternly. "Come on, children. The sermon is starting."

With a groan, they went inside and stuffed themselves into the back row. Mr. Khan gave a long lecture about prayer and perseverance, quoting verses from the Quran in Arabic and English. Yusuf almost dozed off, but Danial kept pinching him awake. "Pray for the meeting," Danial hissed in his ear more than once.

The rest of the day passed slowly. At six fifteen, they all gathered on the sidewalk outside the Frey Public Courthouse. "Ready?" Mr. Khan asked grimly.

Nobody replied.

The courthouse was an old red-stone building, almost as old as Frey itself. It used to be the home of the Frey brothers and their families, with rooms and kitchens added as time went on. Some of the original parts had been destroyed in a fire in the early 1900s, and three restoration projects had kept the rest of the structure alive. Now it contained not only the courthouse, but also a small museum about the Freys.

Yusuf and Danial had visited the museum section of the building on field trips every single year in elementary school. They'd never entered the courthouse before.

Officer Strickland stood at the wide, curving entryway. He had light brown hair in a buzz-cut army style. "Azeem, how are you?" he hollered. "Attacked any more bad guys recently?"

Abba came forward to shake his hand. "No, no. Everything's been quiet. Brother, how are you?"

They shook hands like old friends. Yusuf supposed that's what they were. They'd first met on the day of the attempted robbery of the A to Z Dollar Store in 2011. Officer Strickland had responded to Abba's 911 call and helped all the customers inside the store get outside to safety while Abba stood over the robber's unconscious body. After that, Officer Strickland came over to the dollar store several times a year, just to say hello. Sometimes he brought little presents for Yusuf and Aleena, like toy cars or plastic bracelets.

"Big crowd with you tonight," he murmured as he waved all the Muslim families inside.

Abba shook his head, his smile gone. "Zoning meeting."

Officer Strickland nodded sympathetically and pointed down the small hallway. "First door on the left."

The Muslim families all crowded into the room. It was the first time Yusuf had been inside a courtroom. To his disappointment, it looked nothing like Judge Judy's courtroom. Instead of a judge's bench, there was a long table at which sat five people Yusuf didn't know—two women and three men. Almost all of them were white, and all looked very serious. A plaque in the center of the table read FREY CITY COUNCIL. Mayor Chesterton was the sixth person at the table, and he was the only one who even tried to smile.

Yusuf looked around the room. Many of the seats were already taken. Yusuf recognized their next-door neighbors, Mr. and Mrs. Oliver, and Jared's grandmother, Mrs. Raymond. Jared sat next to her, staring down at his shoes. Miss Terrance and Principal Williamson were also there, and so was Pastor Nielson.

Yusuf and his group settled in the front together, like a pack of sheep not sure exactly where to go. It was six twenty, and people kept streaming into the room in twos and threes, until not a single seat was left empty. When the clock on the wall struck six thirty exactly, Officer Strickland closed the door with a firm bang. Yusuf tried not to gulp.

Mr. Khan and Abba sat in the front of the room directly facing the city council members. Next to them in the aisle was a microphone stand. Pastor Nielson came forward to give a prayer, looking apologetically toward the Muslims. "Amen," he murmured, and the entire room echoed with "Amen."

A woman from the city council stood up from her seat and began. "Good afternoon, ladies and gentlemen. I'm Carla Busby. We've called this meeting today in response to a complaint filed by the Patriot Sons regarding the construction of a religious building in Frey." She looked around, her forehead wrinkled. "Where are . . . the Patriot Sons?"

"Here!"

Yusuf turned to look at the back of the room, where Mr. Grant sat with arms folded across his chest, his face dark. He was surrounded by men and women Yusuf had seen before: mostly the motorcycle group on Wicks Avenue, but also a few people from the neighborhood. The eighth-grade math teacher Mr. Hobson was also in that group, arms folded the same way as Mr. Grant's.

"Okay, then," Mrs. Busby continued. "And the Islamic Center of Frey is represented by Mr. Khan, correct?"

Danial's father looked as if he'd rather be anywhere other than in the courthouse right now. "Yes," he answered miserably.

"Now I'd like to invite the mayor's assistant, Jorge Diaz, to come up here and tell us about the paperwork that was filed by the Islamic Center."

A man came up to the microphone with a big file folder in his arms. "Ahem, yes, thank you. I'm Jorge Diaz, assistant to Mayor Chesterton. I've been working in this capacity for six years, and since then we've received eleven permit requests to build places of worship in Frey. Of those, five were approved, and the rest denied due to various reasons. The Islamic Center's petition was one of those five that were approved. But so were many others, like the new Methodist church over on Darby Street—"

"Nobody asked about the other churches!" Mr. Grant shouted from the back.

The crowd started whispering like a swarm of angry bees. Yusuf gulped again. Was this how the entire proceeding would go? Mr. Grant intimidating everyone from his seat?

Mrs. Busby didn't like the interruption. She stood up again and glared in Mr. Grant's direction. "Please don't talk out of turn, sir."

Mr. Grant uttered an "ugh" loud enough for everyone to hear. Then he was quiet.

Mr. Diaz continued, his voice trembling. "The Islamic Center had all their paperwork in order. They had all the correct permissions, and they had gotten the required seed funding for the initial year. They also submitted architectural plans and met all the zoning requirements."

A man on the city council raised his finger. "What are those requirements, Mr. Diaz?"

Mr. Diaz looked at the mayor and then at the file in his hands. "Well, ordinarily there would be lots of requirements, such as parking lots and building height and other things. But the center is being built near the train tracks, which isn't a residential zone, so most of those didn't really apply."

The crowd started whispering again. Yusuf frowned. If none of the zoning requirements even applied to their mosque, why were they all there? What exactly was the Patriot Sons protesting?

23

Mrs. Busby called Mr. Grant to the microphone. He glared angrily at everyone as he spoke. "I'm the leader of the Southeast Texas chapter of the Patriot Sons. We are the group protesting the building of this Iz-lamic church, or whatever they call it."

Yusuf wanted to shout that it was called a mosque. How could an adult not know such a simple thing? But then he remembered what Miss Terrance had said. *"Knowledge is power."* Maybe Mr. Grant was showing his power by pretending *not* to know something?

A man from the city council asked the next question. "The mayor's office says everything is in order with the permits, and the city has given them permission to build. The construction is fifty percent complete, as I understand. Is that correct, Mr. Khan?"

Mr. Khan stood up and nodded. Then he added, "Yes, that's correct," in a too-loud voice.

Mr. Grant scowled even more. "The mayor's office did all this in secret. They didn't give any of the residents the opportunity to protest."

There was a small silence in the room. Jorge Diaz raised his hand from his seat near the mayor. "We followed the same procedure for all religious buildings. We don't generally allow citizens to protest or give input on any of the buildings being constructed."

The city council man offered a little smile. "Imagine the chaos if that were to happen. Would we protest at every gas station or every school being built? Every home? Why is this case special, Mr. Grant?"

Mr. Grant's mouth opened and closed like a fish's. He cleared his throat and scowled some more. Danial leaned toward Yusuf and whispered in his ear, "Because we're Muslim, of course."

Yusuf elbowed him. Danial loved to state the obvious.

Mr. Grant was looking at some papers. "The Patriot Sons are objecting to zoning regulations in particular."

"Yes, but Mr. Diaz already explained . . ."

Mr. Grant went on as if nobody had interrupted him. "The Mooz-lims are building their temple in an area which is a mix of commercial and residential. New homes are being built on Cypress Road, just down the road from the train tracks. And there's also the New Horizons Church to consider. It's next door to the construction site, and members are worried that the traffic congestion will block their side of the road."

Yusuf turned to look at Pastor Nielson. Did his church really worry about the traffic? Most of the Muslims either walked or shared rides anyway. Frey was pretty small, but Mr. Grant was making the traffic situation sound like that of Houston or Dallas.

The clock said seven o'clock. Yusuf shuffled his feet. He hadn't been hungry at lunch, but now his stomach was rumbling. "Do you have any snacks?" he whispered to Danial.

"Do I look like a baby?"

Amma tapped Yusuf's shoulder from Aleena's other side. "You can have Aleena's Goldfish."

He gratefully took a few orange crackers. Aleena was watching a cartoon on Amma's phone, wearing pink cat-ear headphones and staring intently at the screen. "Thank you," he told her, even though she couldn't hear him. At least her cough was better today; otherwise Amma would have stayed outside the courtroom with her.

The city council was discussing something quietly. "What's happening?" Yusuf asked Danial.

"Shhh!"

Mrs. Busby stood up again. "We have decided to agree somewhat to the Patriot Sons' request and allow for public opinions. The microphone is open, so if you'd like to say something in favor or against this construction project, please come forward. We will take the comments into consideration when we make a decision."

Yusuf realized he shouldn't have eaten the crackers. He looked around desperately at the other Muslims in the room. What did this mean? Public opinion? If they got a lot of people against their mosque, would they be forced to knock down what they had built?

"How is this fair?" he burst out, louder than he'd intended. The people around him turned to stare at him, but they didn't look too angry. A few were nodding. Principal Williamson gave him a reassuring smile, and he tried to relax. Maybe public opinion would be in their favor? All Yusuf could do was wait and see.

Mr. Parker was the first in line. "I'm a teacher at Frey Middle, and in my many years at the school I've had the pleasure of teaching quite a few Muslim students. They've always been good in their studies, and their parents are involved. Last year one of these kids won the state science fair and made me proud. This year, they're taking us to a regional robotics competition. It's my honor to call these people my neighbors, and they deserve to have a place to pray, just like I do."

Yusuf wanted to clap, but nobody else did, so he made do with a little high five with Danial. Mr. Parker gave a nod to the city council and walked back to his seat.

Next was Miss Terrance. Her lips were pursed as if she had a lot of feelings bottled up inside her. "This whole proceeding is ridiculous, in my opinion! We've got churches being constructed left and right in this town, but nobody protests against them. I have no problem with anybody building a house of worship, as long as they preach good things and don't hurt anybody."

Several people in the room clapped at that. Then someone shouted from the back, "That's the problem. These people don't preach good things."

"Yeah," someone else called out. "They're terrorists, all of them."

Yusuf gripped the seat of his chair with both hands, wishing he was somewhere else. This was much worse than what had happened with Ethan and Sammy. These were adults. They were supposed to know better.

After Miss Terrance left, a woman came up to the microphone—Mrs. Geller, one of Abba's most frequent customers. "I never trusted these people," she almost shouted. "Azeem has these Arabic writings on his walls, like he's going to hex us all. They don't belong here with regular folks. They should just . . . leave."

Yusuf froze. Leave? How could anyone say that so . . . callously? He turned and saw that Danial's face was white. Yusuf gave his hand a little squeeze. A few seats down, one of Amma's friends from the mosque was crying quietly, a tissue held to her eyes.

Amma leaned forward and whispered over Aleena's head, "Don't listen to these people, darling. They're just repeating the hate they hear on TV."

For once, Yusuf didn't mind that she had called him darling. He felt bad for Abba, sitting in the front with Mr. Khan, hearing such terrible things about his shop. Yusuf bent his head and stared at Aleena's cartoon. Even without the sound, he was able to follow along: a bear and a little girl went on silly little adventures together.

At least twenty other people stood up and said things at the microphone. Some for the mosque, some against. Pastor Nielson went up and called Abba and Mr. Khan the best neighbors he'd ever had.

Yusuf couldn't listen anymore. He kept his head bent and focused on Aleena's screen. At one point she put her head on his shoulder and dozed off. He kept watching.

A movement on his right brought him out of his trance. Amma was leaving her seat and walking toward the microphone. He sat up straight. What was she doing?

"My friends and neighbors, I thought it was time you heard from an actual Muslim." Amma's voice was strong and sure, like all the times Yusuf had been sick and needed reassurance that he'd be okay. "I've lived in this town for thirteen years. I volunteered as lunch monitor when my son was in elementary school. I worked with my husband to set up his store, which you all shop at. Before this, I lived in Houston. My siblings and I were born there.

"We are Americans just like you. In all the time you've known me, have you ever seen me do anything bad? The families who are building a mosque here have always been model citizens of this town. This country. It hurts my heart to hear my neighbors protest my right to worship God, as if I am less than them. It's the principle this great nation was founded on. It hurts my heart to see us all so divided, so angry."

Amma's voice trembled, but she walked back to her seat with her head high. Several people in the room clapped, and some said, "Hear hear!"

"Good job, Amma," Yusuf whispered when she sat down again. She didn't reply.

Finally the clock struck eight, and the city council took an informal vote. "All those in favor, raise your hands, please," Mrs. Busby ordered. Yusuf held up his hand, high up so that everyone could see. Then the people against the mosque got to vote, and Yusuf tried not to notice how many of his neighbors and teachers were holding up their hands.

"Thank you," Mrs. Busby said, sighing, as the rest of the city council packed up their files. "We will review the meeting notes and send a formal notice with our decision next week. Thank you to all of you who took time to come here today and give your input."

Mr. Grant refused to sit down. "As you can see, most people are against this church being built."

Mrs. Busby stared at him. "Actually, only twenty-one out of sixty-seven were against the construction of this mosque. That's not most people."

Mr. Grant made a deep, angry sound in his throat. To Yusuf, it sounded like a train right before it roared off into the distance.

The crowd dispersed slowly. Mr. Khan and Abba looked relieved as they came back to their families. "Thank God that's over," Mr. Khan said, wiping his forehead.

Mr. Grant turned to look at him. "Oh, no," he said loudly, his words spitting fire. "It's just beginning."

24

On Saturday morning, Abba rose early. "I need to swing by the shop first. I forgot to put out food for Rusty last night."

Yusuf was already packing his backpack. He had the designs for their TRC robot ready, thanks to the sketches Jared had made. "Can't you do that later? Rusty can catch one of the rats in the garbage out back."

Abba gave him a horrified look. "What rats? There are no rats in my garbage."

Yusuf grinned as they left. "That's what you think."

Abba's car was old and creaky, but unlike Amma, he let Yusuf roll down the window and stick his head out as they drove. "Doughnuts?" Abba asked as they passed a row of shops.

"Only if we can get some for my robotics club."

Abba parked the car and took out his wallet. "Sure. Why not? Buy doughnuts for all your friends. They should see how generous we are."

Yusuf came back from the shop holding a box of jelly doughnuts, still thinking about what Abba had said. "Why do you care so much about what others think?"

"What's that?"

"I mean, like buying doughnuts so that my friends will think you're generous. It's . . . weird."

Abba was silent, and Yusuf bit his lip. He didn't want Abba to get angry or hurt. "Sorry, I didn't mean . . ."

"That's okay." Abba sighed as he started the car again and began driving toward the dollar store. "I understand what you're saying. Sometimes I worry too much about how people are viewing me. Us. But you see, it's also important that the values we learn from childhood are actually visible to others. Being good and kind and generous are all important, and your friends should see those parts of you all the time."

Yusuf took out a doughnut from the box and gave Abba a smile. "Nothing wrong with that, I guess."

"But weird if it gets too much, eh?" Abba grinned. He seemed to be in good spirits today.

"Why are you smiling?" Yusuf asked.

"You have jelly on your cheeks, just like you used to when you were little."

Yusuf wiped his cheeks. "I thought you'd be worried about the zoning meeting yesterday. Amma looked wiped out."

Abba shook his head. "No, not worried. Didn't you see how many people came out to support us yesterday? So many of our neighbors and friends. So many of your teachers. Even your principal was there."

"There were also Mr. Grant's friends," Yusuf pointed out sadly.

Abba shook his head again. "Good always overpowers bad, that is God's promise to believers. You must remember that, Yusuf. No matter how bad things get, we have to have faith that God will help us."

Yusuf finished his doughnut and started another. "But Amma was really different last night. I've never seen her so . . . sad."

"She'll be okay soon, inshallah. It's hard to accept that everyone doesn't like us. But we cannot let that bring us down, can we, son? Things will work out, you'll see."

Abba slowed down. They were at the intersection of Broad and Marbury Streets, with the dollar store straight ahead. A few people were already gathered out front. "Look at those shoppers. It's still almost an hour to opening time, but they line up outside because they like my shop. They prefer to spend their money here, because they trust me."

Yusuf leaned forward. "That's strange. They don't usually start lining up this early."

Abba drove forward and reached the store. Yusuf's stomach gave a big lurch. "Oh . . . no," they both whispered together.

The storefront was a mess. Someone had broken the glass on the door and thrown all sorts of trash— broken bottles, empty cans—across the main steps. The streetlight outside had been smashed to bits. On the store wall, right under the sign with Abba's name, were the words GO HOME, MUSLIM SCUM in white spray paint.

Abba got out of the car with slow steps, as if he was an old man. The people gathered outside came toward him, talking at the same time. One of them—Mrs. Cordoba, who owned the taco place across the street— hugged Abba. He stood awkwardly in her embrace, his shoulders heaving.

Yusuf slumped back in his seat, his eyes hurting so much he had to close them. He wrapped his arms tightly against his stomach. *I'm not going to cry*, he told himself fiercely.

But his self wasn't really listening.

Amma arrived half an hour later, along with Mr. Khan and Danial. Officer Strickland was already there, taking pictures of the damage. "Seems like your average delinquents, trying to intimidate you," he told them.

Abba's face was haggard. "This is awful. We've never had this sort of trouble in Frey before. Who could have done this?"

Amma tightened her lips. "The Patriot Sons, who else? This is retaliation for yesterday, obviously."

Officer Strickland held out a hand. "Now, ma'am, let's not start accusing anyone."

"Why not?" she argued. "They're accusing us of things that aren't true. Saying we're bad people, that we preach hate and put hexes on others. The whole town is accusing us—"

Abba cleared his throat. "Farrah, stop."

Amma sobbed in her throat and walked away.

"Please ignore my wife, she's just upset," Abba told Officer Strickland. "Did you get any fingerprints or anything?"

The officer shook his head. "Not really. It's difficult to get any prints on this scene."

Mr. Khan asked suddenly, "What about your security camera?"

Abba groaned. "It only captures footage inside the store."

"Too bad." Officer Strickland took a deep breath. "I actually agree with your wife. It probably was the Patriot Sons, even if we can't prove it. They've been giving us trouble for several months now. Ever since that Trevor Grant moved back home and got everybody riled up."

"I don't even understand what the group wants." Abba sounded bewildered. "What Trevor wants."

"Some people . . . are just troublemakers," Officer Strickland replied. "They want things to remain the same, like it was hundreds of years ago. They don't want change, especially if that means they lose their place in life."

"That makes no sense."

"Tell me about it. Change is the best part of life, my wife always says."

The men went into the store, still talking. Yusuf sat on the sidewalk with Danial, trying to breathe. Rusty wove in and out of their legs, meowing. For once, Danial said nothing. He kept staring at the paint on the wall, his lips moving soundlessly. "Say something," Yusuf finally begged.

"What is there to say?" Danial pointed to the wall. "That says it all, doesn't it?"

"Do they really feel this way about us?" Yusuf whispered. "I thought this was our home."

Danial patted him on the shoulder. "Sorry, dude. The truth hurts."

By the afternoon, the entire town had heard about the incident. A reporter from the *Frey Weekly* asked Amma and Abba questions. Amma answered tersely, while Abba stood at her side. "Do you have any enemies, Mr. Azeem?" the reporter asked.

Abba looked up, bewildered. "Enemies? Everybody loves Azeem from A to Z, don't you know that?"

Amma looked straight at the reporter with a grim face. "Yes, we do have enemies, unfortunately. People who want to divide us. Who want to spread bigotry and prejudice."

Abba just sighed. It was like his positive attitude had been crushed along with the bottles and cans at the front of his store.

Cameron, Madison, and Jared came by at lunchtime. They sat on the sidewalk with Yusuf and Danial, watching Officer Strickland and his team taking photographs of the spray paint like it was a clue in a murder investigation. "You guys are famous again." Cameron grinned. "First the robber with the gun, now this."

"Shut up," Madison told him.

"Don't let my parents hear you say that," Yusuf warned her.

"You okay?" Jared asked Yusuf quietly. "We missed you at TRC club today."

Danial gave him a dirty look. "He's been busy."

Madison discovered the box of cold doughnuts on the sidewalk and passed it around. She said: "Since you didn't bring the robotics design, Mr. Parker made us watch videos of past TRC events instead."

Yusuf had forgotten all about the robotics club. Funny how he'd been obsessed with TRC for years, but now he couldn't stand to think about it, with everything else going on. "Sorry," he told Madison. "I'll bring the design next time."

She shrugged and ate a doughnut. Yusuf watched his parents. They were now standing alone, leaning against the car, holding hands silently. The image brought tears to Yusuf's eyes again. He blinked rapidly before anyone saw.

Jared whispered in his ear, "It's okay to be sad."

"Thanks," Yusuf whispered back, and stopped blinking so hard.

Journal entry 8
October 26, 2001
We watch the news together as a family now,

something we've started doing every evening. Most days it's news of the war. Words like "Taliban" and "ground offensive" are seared into my brain. I can't sleep at night anymore. I lie awake in my room, watching the shadow of the tree outside my window sway in the breeze. What if the war comes here? What if we're bombed by our enemies in the middle of the night?

Sarah says that's not possible. I bet the people of Afghanistan also thought the same.

Today, there was something else in the news. President Bush signed a new law called the Patriot Act. It's supposed to help stop people from doing bad things, but I don't really understand how. Abba had a worried look on his face as he watched the news, and then later, when the neighbors all gathered in our living room for prayers, they discussed it. Secret surveillance. Wiretapping. Search warrants. It all sounded very confusing to me.

Abba said, "This is going to be misused by the police. Anybody can be arrested, even if they did nothing wrong. Anybody can be secretly recorded."

The neighbors agreed. "Whatever happened to innocent until proven guilty?" they asked each other sadly. "What is happening to our nation of laws?"

Later, I asked Farrah baji about the Patriot Act. She's been so quiet since 9/11, hardly going out or talking to her friends on the phone like she used to before. She shrugged and said, "It means Muslims can be treated like the worst scum on earth and nobody will care."

I was shocked. Farrah baji has never talked like this before, all hard and angry.

In the evening, after dinner, Abba and I went for a walk. Silky followed us for a little while, then meowed and jumped into some bushes. I wasn't worried. She always went for adventures, but she always came back.

Abba and I walked some more, not talking. We left our subdivision and reached the little shopping center near our house, the one with the day care and the dentist. Everything was closed now, and the parking lot was empty.

"Isn't this nice?" Abba sighed. "I like being alone sometimes."

I sat down on the curb and looked up. The stars twinkled like little gems on black velvet. Yes, definitely nice.

Next thing I knew, a police officer was standing right in Abba's face, shouting, "What are you doing here? Do you have any identification? What are you planning?" My heart thumped in my chest like a big rock rattling about, but Abba calmly took out his wallet and told him we lived just down the road.

"I'm just taking a walk with my son, Officer," he said.

The officer returned Abba's wallet and told him, "We know that neighborhood; we're watching it carefully."

We walked back home as silently as we'd come. I came up to my room and I'm at my desk with my journal, and Muhammad Ali is looking down at me from my wall. From the window I could see Abba sitting on the front steps for a long time, his head bowed, his shoulders heaving.

25

October 2021 was the longest month in the history of Yusuf Azeem's life. Things slowed down until they resembled sugar-laden molasses on a hot summer day. Every day felt like ten, and every week felt like twenty. He'd put up a calendar on his wall with the TRC dates, reminding himself that this was the Build Month, as Madison called it. The team worked hard, meeting almost every day after school in Mr. Parker's science lab to build their robot.

Cameron was in his element with the LEGO Mindstorms parts. Slowly the robot took shape, with big wheels, a compact squarish body, and an arm for picking up trash.

"What're you kids going to call her?" Mr. Parker asked.

Madison made a list of names in her binder, and the team voted on Miss Trashy. "Perfect." Madison grinned.

Yusuf's sadness weighed him down; he just couldn't share the team's excitement. He stayed in the background while the others took turns admiring Miss Trashy. Mr. Parker gave him some sharp glances but didn't ask questions.

It was strange how everyone else in Frey went about their business without any worries. The pumpkin patch at St. Mary's got daily visitors who took hayrides and dunked Father Robbins until he was blue in the face. The library on Wicks offered countless story times attended by all the little boys and girls of the town, including Aleena Azeem. Hordes of parents and siblings crowded the bleachers on Friday nights to cheer on the Coyotes as they played against other local teams. It was a typical fall in Frey, Texas.

Yusuf, though, felt like Coraline after she went through the door in the wall. Things felt strange and unusual. *He* felt strange and unusual. Every night he had the same dream: of a masked man with tattooed arms, bearing down on him with spray paint in both hands.

Jared nodded wisely when he told him. "Yup. You're

going through some emotions. You need to paint it out. Or get a pet."

Yusuf wasn't interested in painting, but the pet was a good idea. Rusty was always up for a snuggle and a hug, as long as you fed her. He began spending more time at A to Z, going there after school to keep Abba and Rusty company.

At least Abba was doing well. Not completely back to his cheery self, but with straight shoulders and the smile back on his face. There'd been a flood of customers after the vandalism, all wanting to show their support by shopping at A to Z. "Don't you mind those delinquents," Mrs. Raymond told Abba as she bought way more soil than was necessary. "They don't scare us."

Yusuf didn't want to tell her it was probably her son who was the delinquent in question. He kept his mouth shut, because Officer Strickland had come by the day after the incident and told them they had zero evidence of who the perpetrators were. "Sorry we couldn't be of more help, old pal," he'd said. "Maybe expand your security system to the outside too, eh?"

Abba had just nodded. What else was there to say?

A week after the vandalism, the city council sent a formal letter to Mr. Khan saying that the Patriot Sons' petition had been denied, and that they were free to continue building their mosque as planned. "We were always free to build it," an old uncle grumbled as they sat around on chairs near the construction site. "Last I checked, this was America."

Mr. Khan was also smiling again. His reputation rested on the mosque being built. "Back to work, then," he told everyone, slapping the old uncle on the back.

The construction resumed as if it had never stopped. So did Sunday school. On the last day of October—Halloween—Sameena Aunty talked about perseverance. "The Quran says that God doesn't burden any human being beyond their capacity," she told them. "What does that mean?"

The kids thought about this. "That we're strong?" a boy guessed, flexing his muscles.

She gave him a withering glance. "What else?"

Saba tapped a pencil to her hijab-covered head. "Maybe it means that we are stronger than we think? That we can do things we didn't think we were capable of?"

"Very good." Sameena Aunty looked around with hawklike eyes. "Yusuf, you're being very quiet these days. We know your family's been through a lot. Do you agree with this statement?"

Yusuf gulped. Everyone was looking at him now.

"Um, not really. Sometimes God gives us more than we can bear."

He'd whispered, but everyone heard him. Sameena Aunty's mouth dropped open. "How dare you question God's word!"

"But . . ."

"Stop it!" Amma interrupted loudly. "Sameena, this isn't the right way to teach kids."

The two women eyed each other, and then looked away. After class ended, and the kids left, Amma approached Sameena Aunty with Yusuf behind her dragging his feet. "Don't say anything, please!" he begged.

Amma's mouth was an obstinate line. "It's about time someone said something to her."

The women argued for a while. "You have to let the kids say what they're feeling," Amma insisted.

"Not if they're saying things that are wrong!" Sameena Aunty shot back.

"How else will they learn?"

"You can't tell me what to do! You don't even follow the commandments yourself!"

Amma's face turned red. "It's my choice whether or not to wear hijab!"

Yusuf tried to ignore them. He wished the train would show up and drown out their voices. Finally Mr. Khan came by and asked about lunch, because everyone was waiting. They gave each other dagger eyes and walked away, leaving Yusuf sadder than ever.

"Man, that's rough."

He turned to see Cameron laughing at him. "Go away," Yusuf grumbled.

Cameron put a hand on his shoulder. "Look, I know what you're going through. I've been through all this stuff as well."

"I highly doubt that."

"Whatever." Cameron paused. "I have the perfect solution to your problems. Be ready tonight at six thirty. Dress in a costume or something."

He walked away before Yusuf could ask what he was talking about.

Danial was aghast. "You're going trick-or-treating with Cameron? What is wrong with you? It's literally haram!"

Yusuf rummaged through his closet. It was past six o'clock and he had no idea what to wear. "It's not haram," he corrected. "It's frowned upon."

"So you want the whole community frowning at you?" Danial sighed. "Look, dude, I know you're upset about your dad's store, but this is ridiculous."

Yusuf didn't reply. The doorbell rang, and he went to open the door, followed by a nervous Danial. "Where are your parents, anyway?" he asked, noticing the empty living room.

"Abba's store is always busy on Halloween night," Yusuf explained. "Amma and Aleena are helping out. They'll bring dinner for us on their way back."

He swung the door open. It was Jared and Cameron, parking their bikes in the front yard. "Ready?" Cameron asked with a devilish grin.

"Um, I'm not sure what to wear?" Yusuf mumbled, suddenly scared. What if everyone found out a bunch of Muslim kids were out celebrating Halloween? Sameena Aunty would eat them alive.

Jared held up a big bag. "I have costumes!"

Danial's eyes popped. "Where did you get these?"

"Pastor Nielson's personal stash."

Thirty minutes later, four slim, nervous Santa Clauses walked out of the Azeem house and headed toward the neighboring homes. The sun had already set—Danial had insisted on offering maghrib prayers before leaving, just to beg for forgiveness for what they were about to do—but the streets were busy. A steady stream of little kids was already out, holding hands with parents.

"Guys, I think we're too old for this," Jared noted.

"Too old for Halloween?" Cameron scoffed. "Don't be silly." He led them to the end of Yusuf's neighborhood and across the street to the next one. "Nicer houses," he explained. "Better candy."

Jared and Yusuf walked side by side like quiet soldiers. Yusuf kept an eye out for familiar faces, but all he could see were shadows in the darkness. A strange sort of fear bubbled in his chest, mixed with excitement. He looked at his fellow Santas-in-disguise. Danial seemed to be a different person now that he was hidden under the costume. "Nobody will guess we're Muslim!" He laughed and did a little tap dance. "Woo hoo! This is fun!"

They knocked on door after door. Jared held out a big plastic bag that gradually filled with goodies. Almost everyone who opened their door had a big smile on their face, open and friendly. One man looked at their costumes, puzzled, and called out, "Is it Christmas already?" Then he shrugged and gave out snack-sized chocolate bars. Yusuf briefly thought about disguising his voice when he said thank you, but then he realized he didn't know these people, and they didn't know him. He was just a random kid in a Santa suit, enjoying the evening with his friends.

Back home by eight o'clock, they lounged on Yusuf's bed and ate their candy. Amma and Abba came back with a sleeping Aleena and two large cheese pizzas. "Everything okay here?" Amma asked as she peeked in, smiling.

Yusuf smiled back at her, the sadness in his heart gone for now. "Yes, everything's okay."

Danial waved at her. "We had the best time, Aunty!" he shouted, and Cameron threw a pillow at his head before he spilled the beans.

Amma's smile turned into a surprised laugh. "I'm glad," she said. "Eat pizza and go home, please. You have school tomorrow."

26

On Monday, Yusuf felt like a new man. It wasn't every day he got to sneak out of the house and masquerade as a hidden figure begging for treats. The thrill of the previous evening, along with the mystery of what would happen if his parents found out—if Sameena Aunty found out—was the perfect balm his tortured soul needed. For the first time in weeks, he'd slept the whole night through. No nightmares. No insomnia.

"What are you smiling about?" Danial grinned at him in the hallway.

Yusuf's eyes widened. "The bigger question is, why are *you* smiling?" He couldn't remember the last time Danial had looked happy on a Monday morning.

Danial shrugged happily. "Last night was *epic*!"

A few kids turned to see what the fuss was about. "Shh!" warned Yusuf, but he was nodding. "It *was* pretty awesome, wasn't it?"

"That Cameron is a cool guy." Danial seemed equal parts happy and surprised.

Yusuf stopped. "You sure about that? I seem to remember you saying you'd eat your shoe if Cameron was anything but awful."

Danial raised his leg. "That's why I'm wearing these sneakers. They're soft."

Yusuf couldn't believe it. A joke out of Danial Sourpuss? This was an even bigger miracle than Muslim Santas out on Halloween.

The day flew by as if it had wings. On Tuesday, in after-school club, Yusuf passed out Amma's homemade sugar cookies, then sat down with his teammates to work. Miss Trashy sat on a table, ready to be examined. "We still need to make minor adjustments," Cameron said. "But she's mostly ready for the challenges."

"She's beautiful," Madison breathed, making a sketch for her binder.

"Let's talk about programming today," Mr. Parker interrupted, taking out his dry-erase markers and stacking them on his desk. He scribbled on the whiteboard. "We need to figure out how to best code this thing to win the challenges."

"This thing?" Madison frowned. "She. It's a she."

"Sorry," Mr. Parker replied. "We need to figure out how to program *her*."

"Thank you."

Yusuf looked at the board. *Which coding program is the best?* He exchanged grins with Danial. This was the best part of robotics. Soon the group was talking heatedly about the various programs they'd used, and why. "Scratch is for kids," Cameron declared. "I like LEGO's brick programming better."

Danial nodded. "Yup. I agree."

"What?" Yusuf couldn't believe it. "I thought we agreed on Scratch."

Danial shrugged easily. "It doesn't have the same capabilities."

Mr. Parker pointed to Yusuf. "Would you have any trouble using the LEGO brick program for your robot?"

Yusuf couldn't remember the last time Danial hadn't backed him up. Or had taken Cameron's side over his. He shrugged. "I suppose not."

Madison made quick notes in her binder. "Copy that, Captain."

Mr. Parker motioned to their laptops. "Let's work on some practice code then, shall we?"

★ ★ ★

The week passed quickly. Yusuf watched in disbelief and slight amusement as Danial and Cameron started hanging out together. "Want to share my biryani?" Danial asked Cameron during lunch period on Friday. Everyone else was eating cafeteria pizza, but Danial had brought a big Tupperware container full of fragrant basmati rice.

"How can I say no to biryani, dude?" Cameron took an extra spoon and started eating. "I haven't eaten this in months."

Danial paused. "Come over to my place anytime. My mom cooks the best biryani."

Jared leaned over. "Didn't Danial kinda hate Cameron?" he whispered.

Yusuf was still staring. "I thought so too."

"So that means I'm next, right?" Jared grinned. "He's going to start offering me food soon too?"

Yusuf caught sight of Ethan throwing orange peels all over another kid's lunch. "Don't count on it," he muttered, ducking his head. The week had been great, and he didn't want to ruin it by having another ugly encounter with Ethan Grant.

Jared was also looking at his cousin. "His dad beat him that day, you know," he said softly.

"What? When?"

"After your argument with him in the locker room.

Principal Williamson must have called Uncle Trevor." Jared looked down at his pizza. "They were at our house when the call came. Uncle Trevor got really red and almost choked on his food. Then he hit Ethan in the face."

Yusuf's chest constricted. "Really?" he whispered. Nobody deserved to be beaten, not even Ethan.

Jared was still staring down. "Uncle Trevor told Ethan never to let anyone bully him, especially not those Muslim kids. He said you have to stand up for what's yours."

Yusuf's chest loosened, and a scowl formed on his face. "Me? I wasn't bullying him. It was literally the other way around."

Jared looked up. "That's how they think," he whispered. "That everything is theirs and you guys are taking it over."

Yusuf gulped. How could one argue with a person who believed they were right? Who believed that using violence and scare tactics to get what they wanted was okay? "But we're not taking anything over," he said slowly. "We only want to live in our home. In peace."

Jared nodded. "I see that now. My grandma says you can only make enemies with strangers. If you get to know someone, it's hard to hate them."

Yusuf liked that a lot. "Your grandma is very smart."

Jared smiled. He always smiled when he spoke about Mrs. Raymond. "She looks a lot like my mom, you know."

"She does? Then you must be so glad to be with her."

Jared finished the last of his pizza and stood up. Yusuf raised a hand to stop him. "Wait," Yusuf said. "I . . . this might be cheesy, but I want you to know that I always pray for your mom to come home soon." It was a weird thing to admit, but it was the truth.

Jared's face crumpled as if he was going to cry, but he nodded and turned away. "Thanks."

The bell rang and kids started to file out of the cafeteria. Jared and Yusuf got up and joined the crowd silently. Saba from Sunday school was just ahead of them, her red hijab standing out. She was holding a stack of books in her arms like a shield.

Yusuf thought about saying hi. He'd never seen Saba with a friend.

The next minute, somebody pushed past Yusuf. It was Ethan, followed by Sammy. The crowd was thick, but the two boys elbowed their way through. They were headed straight toward Saba. Before Yusuf could wonder why, Ethan was right next to her. "No hats allowed in the school," he growled and reached up.

Yusuf watched Ethan's hand with a strange fascination. He watched as if he was frozen in a movie, watched as Ethan took a fistful of Saba's red hijab and pulled it viciously downward. Saba screamed and put up her hands to grab the hijab, but he held on to it. They pulled in opposite directions for just a nanosecond, and then it was off.

The crowd parted as if trying to run away from Ethan. Sammy also took a few steps back, uncertain. On the ground lay the hijab, like a deep red stain. Saba, her black hair disheveled, tears on her face, stood in the middle. In that moment she looked like Aleena, her eyes wide, her mouth quivering. Yusuf realized that apart from that one scream, she hadn't said a word. The look on her face said everything.

Ethan was in front of her, hands on hips, his mouth curled in a sneer. He was probably waiting for her to say something. Yusuf unfroze with a snap and hurtled forward toward them as if somebody had pushed him from inside. Abba's words from a few months ago rushed through his mind. *"Inshallah, one day you can also be a hero like your father. I have faith in you!"*

"Hey!" he shouted. He wasn't sure what he was trying to say, but he knew he had to say something. Do something.

He almost fell on Ethan, who turned to him, shocked. "What . . . ?"

Yusuf's mouth opened and words poured out of him

like he was on fire. "How dare you touch another person? How dare you pull her hijab off? Do you have any idea what you're doing?"

Ethan took a step back. "I . . ."

Yusuf drew himself up as tall as he could. "You. Are. A. Bully," he said quietly. "You're the one who's taking over, not us. You're the one who thinks it's okay to hurt people and humiliate them, not us. How dare you?"

With a scoff, Ethan walked away. His footsteps sounded loud and sure, as if he owned the school. Yusuf let out his breath in a whoosh. He felt like his lungs had been starved, and the pizza he'd eaten at lunch sank to the bottom of his stomach. The crowd of kids around him began to talk and point at him. A few gave him a thumbs-up, and someone clapped. "Good job!" a kid from the back called out.

From the cafeteria, a teacher came running. "What's going on here?"

Yusuf wasn't ready to talk to anyone. He turned toward Saba. A few girls around her were already helping her put her hijab back on. One girl was picking up her books from the floor. "Are you okay?" he asked.

She wiped the tears from her face and straightened her spine. For a split second he wondered if this had happened to her before. "I'll be fine," she whispered.

27

Saturday club was a disaster. The Freybots tried a basic program on Miss Trashy, but she kept glitching. "Sorry," Yusuf muttered as the robot kept ramming itself into the bleachers. He'd hardly slept the night before, trying late into the night to create a simple program so that he wouldn't have to think about what happened to Saba.

It didn't work. He kept remembering the bright red of her hijab on the dirty school floor, and Saba's scared-but-resigned face. The result was a sleepless night, plus a computer program that a six-year-old wouldn't have normally messed up.

The rest of the team weren't at their best either. Danial and Cameron sat together on the bleachers, staring at

Miss Trashy as if she'd done something wrong. Madison kept taking too many notes in her binder, then erasing them and starting over. Jared and Tony studied their designs, muttering and shaking their heads.

Finally Mr. Parker clapped his hands to get their attention. "Okay, clearly nobody is ready to work today," he said, but he didn't look mad. "I know y'all are thinking about what happened yesterday. Want to talk about it?"

Yusuf frowned. "The teachers know about it?"

"Some of us do. It happened yesterday afternoon, so we haven't had an official meeting yet to discuss the incident."

Danial looked up, his face haggard. "But why isn't anyone doing anything? Why aren't the teachers punishing that horrible Ethan?"

"Wait . . . ," Jared protested. Then he stopped, his face red.

Mr. Parker sighed. "Actually, nobody's willing to say they saw Ethan Grant. I asked a few kids who were there, but they all say they're not sure what happened."

Yusuf's eyes narrowed. "I was there. I know what happened."

Mr. Parker stood up. "Will you go to the principal with me? Nobody else wants to do anything, but I will. If you want."

Yusuf stood up too. "Yes! I want!"

Cameron burst out, "What about Saba? Did anyone ask her what *she* wants?"

Everyone turned to him. "What do you mean?" Danial asked.

Cameron's voice was like shards of ice, hard and painful. "He pulled *her* hijab off, not Yusuf's. He bullied *her*. Why don't you ask *her* what she wants to have happen?"

Mr. Parker picked up Miss Trashy from the floor with slow movements. "Saba's not talking to anyone right now. She just wants to be left alone."

Cameron's shoulders sagged. "Exactly. Sometimes you don't want anyone to do anything. Sometimes you just want to be left alone."

At home, Yusuf decided to talk to Amma about Saba. Even though Amma didn't wear the hijab, she was a woman, and would probably be able to guess what Saba was feeling. "Amma, can I talk to you?"

Amma was on the phone. She held up her hand. "I'm on hold with the doctor."

"Why?"

"Aleena's been coughing nonstop and her breathing is really bad."

Abba peeked out of Aleena's room, his face haggard.

"Farrah, forget the doctor. We need to go to the urgent care right now."

Amma put down her phone quickly. "Okay, let me start my car."

Yusuf's throat was dry. Abba never came home from the store at this hour. "What's going on? Can I help?"

Amma stopped to give him a hurried kiss on his cheek. "Don't worry, jaan. She just needs some medicine. Her inhaler isn't enough for her right now."

"Will she be okay?" The thought of Aleena not being okay was . . . something he wasn't going to think about.

"Yes, of course!" Abba came out with Aleena in his arms. She was wheezing, but awake. "Say goodbye to your brother, Aleena!"

"Bye, bhai!" She waved weakly. "Take care of my dollies while I'm gone."

"Of course I will," he choked out. "I'm the best babysitter on the planet."

He went outside with them as they put Aleena in Amma's car. Amma climbed into the back seat with her, fussing with her blanket. "Wait, who's minding the store?" Yusuf asked suddenly.

Abba got into the driver's seat and started the engine. "My clueless assistant, but he's due to go home in half an hour." He paused, looking at Amma in the rearview mirror. "Maybe I shouldn't . . ."

Yusuf squared his shoulders. "No, it's okay. I can go to the store and take care of things."

Amma and Abba both stared at him in surprise. "Are you sure?"

"Of course. It's literally my second home. I even know where Abba hides his stash of secret weapons."

Abba gave a short laugh, but it sounded more like a bark. "It's only pepper spray," he said as he backed out of the driveway. "And don't touch it. You'll go blind."

Yusuf locked the house and jogged the half mile to A to Z Dollar Store. The assistant—his name was Nick and he was a senior at Frey High—was standing outside, looking worried. "Where's your dad?" he asked. "I have to leave now."

Yusuf tried to stand taller. "He sent me. You can go home."

Nick shrugged and walked away, looking at his phone. Yusuf went inside and sat on Abba's chair behind the counter. Rusty came up and rubbed her head on his leg. "Aleena's going to be okay, Rusty," he assured her. "It's not the first time she's had to go to the urgent care. Once she even went to Conroe in an ambulance, when she was a baby."

Rusty meowed her sympathies and jumped into his lap. Yusuf wanted to bury his face in her fur, but the bell over the door jingled and customers came in. "Welcome, how can I help you?" He tried to smile as he said the familiar words. His abba's words.

At two o'clock, the customers dwindled. Then Danial walked in, followed by a heavy figure wearing brightly colored clothes. Sameena Aunty. "Assalamo Alaikum," Yusuf mumbled, throwing a questioning glance at Danial.

"Um, Aunty was at my house when your mom called," Danial explained.

"Oh, dear, how are you holding up?" Sameena Aunty interrupted, looking at Yusuf with concern. "Your sister will be fine, your mother said."

"Yes, I know." Yusuf hadn't known for sure, but he wasn't going to let her see his worry. "You didn't have to come all the way here."

"Nonsense, that's what neighbors are for. And community members."

He'd never thought of her as a neighbor. She lived two miles away, at least. "Thanks."

Danial held up a brown bag with YASMIN CAFÉ on the front. It was a new place on Broad Street, full of vegetarian options. "Lunch," he announced.

Yusuf wasn't hungry, but he sat in the back room with Danial and Sameena Aunty anyway. He could see the front door easily from where he was sitting, in case a customer came by. "So, sold anything yet?" Danial asked cheekily.

Yusuf took a bite of the egg sandwich. "Diapers and some talcum powder."

Danial almost choked on his sandwich as he let out a laugh.

Sameena Aunty threw them a stern glance. "Nothing wrong with either of those things," she told them. "You boys made good use of them when you were babies."

Danial stopped laughing. "How . . . ?"

"Oh, no need to be embarrassed, child. I used to take care of all the babies when your mothers were working."

Yusuf knew Amma had worked briefly in a newspaper office in downtown Frey when he was a baby. He hadn't known Sameena Aunty had babysat him. "All the babies?" he asked. "Even Saba?"

Danial gave him a startled look, but Yusuf ignored it. He took off his glasses and put them back on again, trying to clear his head. It was no use. He couldn't get Saba out of his thoughts.

Sameena Aunty's expression had changed. She looked at her sandwich as if it made her nauseous. "That poor girl. Her mother is my best friend. She's in a terrible state, she is. Can't stop crying."

"The mother or the daughter?" asked Danial.

Sameena Aunty looked at him sharply, her face set in

stone. "Both, of course. Why wouldn't they be? Pulling off a girl's hijab is . . . violence, almost."

Yusuf's breath eased a little. So, this was what he'd been feeling since Friday. He'd witnessed violence, but he hadn't been able to name it. He just knew that what had happened had been awful. Painful. Hurtful. "Violence," he whispered.

Sameena Aunty nodded slowly. "It's not the first time it's happened, and it won't be the last. These people, they know what they fear, and they want to get rid of it. Who cares if anyone gets hurt in the process?"

Yusuf was astonished. He'd never heard Sameena Aunty say anything like that before. He had a sudden thought. "Has it . . . ever happened to you?"

She focused on her sandwich again. Yusuf thought she wouldn't answer. Then she replied, "Yes, when I was fifteen. It was my first day wearing the hijab in high school. Someone called me a terrorist and pulled it off me."

Danial's eyes were round as saucers. "Who?"

Yusuf spoke at the same time. His question was different. "When?"

Sameena Aunty stared at her food, but Yusuf knew she wasn't really seeing it. "It was my best friend, actually," she whispered. "New York City, September 12, 2001."

Journal entry 9

November 23, 2001

Silky is missing. She's been missing for two weeks now. I've put up flyers I made in art class, and pasted them everywhere with Sarah's help. "Don't worry, Silky will be back," Amma keeps saying. But she hasn't come back yet, and I keep wondering if she's lost, and is lying somewhere hurt. Then those thoughts make me choke up, so I think of something else. Anything else.

I sat at my desk this morning and stared at my poster of Muhammad Ali and tried not to think of all the horrible things going on in my life right now.

"Float like a butterfly, sting like a bee," Muhammad Ali used to say. Maybe if I pretend I'm floating in the air, everything—9/11 and the terrorists and Jonathan not being my friend anymore—will all disappear.

I try all morning to float in my mind, but it doesn't help. Muhammad Ali keeps looking at me from the wall, as if he knows I can't do it.

Thanksgiving was okay. Abba made barbecued turkey and chicken, plus a few kebab, and all our neighbors showed up. They also brought their own foods, like daal and biryani and sweet potatoes for the barbecue. The kids played in our backyard and out on the street, while the adults sat around on plastic chairs and discussed politics (what else?). Before eating, we prayed for the Afghan family's relatives to be safe, and for terrorists to stay away from our country, and for the war to be over. One aunty told us her son had been arrested. She didn't know why. They hadn't seen him in weeks. We prayed for him too. Farrah baji said he used to be in her class, a straight-A student who never got in trouble. "You stay inside as much as possible, Rahman," she told me bitterly. "Or you may disappear one day too."

I think she was joking.

After Thanksgiving dinner, Abba took the three of us out in his car. Just to do something good for someone else, he told us. Farrah baji rolled her eyes, but Sarah and I were ready for anything. Turns out, we were going to a church three streets over, to serve food to the homeless. Sacred Heart, it was called, with a statue of Mary holding the baby Jesus in her arms at the entrance. "I saw a notice in the paper the other day," Abba told us. "They need volunteers."

The pastor of the church came to greet us. He had gray hair and the kindest smile I ever saw. Abba and he became immediate friends, and they talked nonstop while we served food. I ignored them and focused on the people we were serving. Adults, mostly, but a few kids too. They all held out their plates politely, like they were in some fancy restaurant. My sisters stood on either side of me, ladling soup and handing out garlic bread, while I piled a big heap of turkey on each plate. With every movement, I felt some small part of my anger and sadness melt away and be replaced with a little bit of warmth.

By the time we finished and headed back home, all four of us were grinning. "I found a new friend," Abba said. It was nice to see him happy after such a long time. Maybe this is what floating like a butterfly really means.

28

Aleena came home at night, breathing deeply and smiling. "I got a new inhaler, see?" She showed Yusuf proudly.

Yusuf hugged her over and over. "I'm so glad you're okay," he told her.

"Of course I okay!"

He didn't want to tell her that Danial had spent the entire afternoon after lunch reading asthma information from his laptop. Symptoms, warning signs, worst cases. "Your dollies missed you," he finally replied.

She settled into her bed with her blankets and dolls. "Can you make me a new game?" she asked.

"You look exhausted," he protested.

"What's that?"

"Tired, but like a million times."

She yawned and shook her head stubbornly. "Not tired."

He lay down with her and snuggled under her covers. "How about I tell you a story instead?"

"Dragons?"

"Yeah, sure. There was once a dragon named Ethan. . . ."

Amma peeked into the room when Yusuf was almost finished. "She's asleep now," Amma whispered.

His eyes were closing too. "Can I just sleep here?"

She paused and thought about it. "Okay, just for tonight." She turned to leave. "Hey, Yusuf, she's fine, okay? No need to worry."

Yusuf tried to smile. "Yes, I know."

At school, everyone was still talking about Saba. "Serves her right," a kid named Jake said in social studies class. "Why does she wear that thing anyway?"

Yusuf looked down at his desk, blinking rapidly.

"Poor girl, I hope she's okay," Madison murmured.

Miss Terrance had heard the rumors, of course. "I'm very disappointed in all of you," she said loudly, her hands on her hips. "Nobody has any right to pull someone's clothing off."

"Maybe it was . . . a joke?" Jared said in a low voice.

The rest of the class erupted in noisy laughing. "A joke?" Yusuf couldn't believe what Jared was saying. "Pulling off someone's hijab is a joke to you?"

"Why not? It's just a hat, right?" a girl asked. "I pull off my brother's cap all the time."

Miss Terrance rapped on her desk for silence. "Yusuf," she called. "That's an excellent point. Please explain to the class what the hee-jab is."

Yusuf felt like a rat trapped by a hunter. "Uh . . ."

She beckoned him to the front of the class with sharp red nails. "Come here and tell everyone. I feel like we should hear this from someone who knows about it."

Yusuf wanted to shout that he really didn't know much about the hijab. Amma hardly ever wore it, and she was always fighting about it with Sameena Aunty. And people like Ethan hated it enough to make it a symbol of something bad. The hijab was a mystery to Yusuf as well, so what could he say to the class? And why?

Why did he suddenly have to be the spokesperson for every single thing relating to Muslims?

Miss Terrance was looking at him with a bright smile and an encouraging nod. Slowly he walked up to her desk and cleared his throat. Was this what Aleena felt like during an asthma attack, not being able to breathe? He cleared his throat several times.

"Muslim women sometimes cover their head, out of respect to God," he began, pushing his glasses up his nose. "Not everyone wears it, like my mom doesn't. But the ones who do wear it, they believe that their hair shouldn't be seen by outsiders. People who aren't their family."

Miss Terrance nodded her head slowly. "So, when someone pulls the hijab off . . . ?"

Yusuf had a sudden image of Sameena Aunty as a teenager, wearing her hijab for the first time in high school. Her own best friend had ripped it off. Uncle Rahman's journal was clear: after 9/11, friends became enemies, and families broke apart. "It's part of your dress. If someone pulls it off, it's just like pulling off your shirt or your pants. Leaving you naked."

Nobody in the class giggled at that. Yusuf was glad. They looked serious. They needed to. Maybe now Ethan would be punished.

He wasn't. A week went by, then another. Saba had come back to school after two days, wearing another hijab and holding a pile of books in her arms. She never looked up, never spoke to anyone. Yusuf tried talking to her a few times, smiling and saying hello, but she just walked past each time with a little shake of her head. It was as if she was saying, "I'm sorry, I can't talk to anyone just yet."

"It's not fair, nobody ever says anything to Ethan or to his dad," Danial complained once at lunchtime.

Cameron took a long sip from his water bottle. "What's new? Bullies never get their due."

Yusuf watched Ethan at the other table, laughing loudly. Yusuf gritted his teeth. "Someone just has to be brave enough to do something."

Danial rolled his eyes at him. "And that someone is you?"

Yusuf kept his eyes fixed on Ethan. "Why not?"

"Because of what happened to your father's store, obviously." Danial gave him a disgusted look. "You and your dad both think you're heroes, fighting against bullies. But guess what? We're few and weak, while they're strong. They will win, every time."

"I can't accept that."

"You can't . . ." Danial's indignant voice became louder and more irritated.

Cameron put his bottle down. "At least the store is good as new now," he said, obviously trying to change the subject.

Yusuf nodded without moving his head. Cameron's dad had come to the store the day following the vandalism, armed with tools and paint. "We'll have this mess fixed in no time," he'd told Abba cheerfully. That's when Yusuf knew. Cameron and his family were good, no matter what anyone said.

The bell rang, and everyone dispersed. Before Yusuf knew it, another week had passed, and Ethan was still out in the halls, laughing at everyone and everything. Terrifying people. Once Yusuf found him kicking a boy named Julio in the shins repeatedly. It was after school, and Julio was sitting on the steps outside school waiting for his ride. "Get out of the way, Julia," Ethan told him in between kicks.

Yusuf stopped right next to them. "Stop kicking him," he said loudly. Loud enough for the teachers standing outside helping with dismissal to turn around.

Ethan stopped so suddenly he almost lost his balance. He gave Yusuf a glare and walked away quickly.

"You don't know what you're getting into," Danial warned him as they walked home together that day. "You should stay away from the Patriot Sons."

Yusuf gave a small, hollow laugh. "You think I don't know that?"

Danial stopped at a red light. "Then what on earth are you doing? Don't you remember all the Islamic stories we studied? When people persecute us, we stay silent and pray to God. We don't rush into attack mode."

"I also remember the stories where the Prophet and his companions helped others who needed help. Like, constantly. Even when they had to sacrifice themselves."

Danial was quiet. The light turned green and they crossed the road. "Ethan and his dad scare me," he finally admitted.

"Yeah, me too."

Toward the end of November, Yusuf decided to take Danial's advice and focus on other things. The program for Miss Trashy was no longer glitching, which meant that it was time to code the actual sequences for the TRC challenge. He worked deep into the night, every night, writing lines of code and then deleting them. He felt like Van Gogh working on a painting, trying to still his mind of other disturbing thoughts.

He searched for Jared on Scratch and sent him a message.

Yusuf: Want to come over and help me with the code tomorrow?

Jared took forever to answer.

Jared: I don't think so.

Yusuf: Why????????

Jared: I'm not great at programming

Yusuf: Come on . . . it's not rocket science. 😄

There was silence. Jared didn't respond. Maybe his grandmother didn't allow late-night computer chats.

On the last Saturday before Thanksgiving break, Tony brought the practice arena board he'd made in shop class. It was an exact replica of the one they'd be given at the TRC regionals in Conroe. Mr. Parker asked to see Miss Trashy do a complete TRC challenge on the board. Yusuf's hands shook as he started his laptop, while the other team members set up a mini arena. Miss Trashy rumbled through, dodging obstacles, picking up garbage items and sorting them into three piles. She stumbled several times, and even rolled over once. "Nine minutes, twenty-six seconds," Mr. Parker announced when she finally stopped. "You need practice, but it's a good start."

When the club ended, Yusuf caught up with Jared sitting alone on the bleachers. "Want to come over for some coding practice?"

Jared looked up. "You have Danial, don't you?"

Yusuf told himself he was just imaging the brisk tone of Jared's voice. "Danial has forsaken me for another friend," he joked, pointing. Danial and Cameron were bent over their LEGO Mindstorms figures, their heads so close together that their hair was touching.

Jared studied the two. "Danial is always telling you not to be my friend. Because of Ethan."

Yusuf shrugged. "Forget Danial. He's a pessimist. He always thinks badly of everyone and everything."

Jared turned to Yusuf again. "And you?" This time there was no mistaking the tone.

Yusuf said, "Come on, Jared, lighten up. We're friends, you know that!"

Jared stood up. "Maybe. I guess."

"No maybe about it!" Yusuf exhaled sharply, relieved. "So, what're you doing for Thanksgiving? We're going to Houston, like always."

29

Amma drove them all to Houston on Wednesday afternoon. It wasn't a very long drive, but Aleena had to go to the bathroom halfway there, so they stopped at Buc-ee's and refilled the gas tank. Aleena was hungry, so they bought sandwiches and juices from Buc-ee's and ate in the parking lot. It was like an outdoor party, dozens of cars honking their horns and people walking about as if they had nowhere else to be.

Yusuf couldn't wait to tell everyone at Team Freybots that he'd eaten Buc-ee's famous beaver nuggets. Sweet, buttery, and perfect.

By the time they reached Nani's house in Houston, the day had turned into evening. Amma had called from the car when they were five minutes away, and

Nani stood on the porch waiting. She wore a plain white shalwar kameez and her gray hair was tied in a long, thin braid. "Welcome, welcome, how was the drive?" she cried as she hugged first Aleena, then Yusuf. "Ya Allah, how big you've both grown!"

Aleena giggled. "I'm so tall now," she boasted, stomping inside.

Yusuf followed her, looking around. "Where's Rahman mamoo?"

Amma held up a finger. "Go help your father with the bags, please."

Yusuf made a face, but he did as he was told. Uncle Rahman's blue Camry wasn't in the driveway, but maybe he'd be back later.

No such luck. Yusuf kept watching the door all evening, but Uncle Rahman never walked in. Finally Amma gave him a stern look and told him to come to the kitchen to help with dinner. As Nani took out the plates from a cabinet and handed them one by one to Yusuf, she told him all about Uncle Rahman's latest adventure. "He's gone to Seattle for a professor conference," she told him. "Went last weekend but decided to stay for a few extra days to see the sights."

Yusuf frowned. "Really? He's going to miss Thanksgiving?"

Amma was ladling chicken curry and daal into bowls.

She looked up and gave a little laugh. "I think there's some girl involved."

Nani shook her head in disapproval. "He'll be back tomorrow," she muttered.

Amma leaned over and hugged Nani from behind. "Mama, come on. It's time Rahman settled down, don't you think? I'm glad he's found a good Muslim girl, and he's doing the right thing by meeting her family."

Nani gave a grumpy little smile. "In my day, nobody made friends first. We just . . . got married. Then we met everyone."

Yusuf and Amma exchanged amused looks. Nani was always telling stories about the good old days in Pakistan. "Is that how you and Nana got married?" asked Yusuf.

There was a small silence, like he'd said something wrong. Nana had died from Covid a year and a half before, and Nani still got sad when she talked about him. "Sorry . . . ," Yusuf began.

Nani brushed a tear from her eye and smiled at him. "It's all right. That's how everyone got married. Your nana, God give him a high status in heaven, came to my father and asked for me, and it was decided."

Yusuf hugged her, then picked up a set of plates to carry to the kitchen table. They wouldn't be eating in the dining room until tomorrow, when the whole family was gathered. "Maybe that's what Rahman mamoo is doing?" he guessed. "Asking for his girlfriend's hand in front of her father."

"Hmph, 'girlfriend'! What's the world coming to?"

Sarah khala and her family arrived at ten in the morning on Thanksgiving Day, hugging everyone and exclaiming how tall all the kids had become since Eid. Aleena and Khala's daughters, Aisha and Hira, ran upstairs to play. Yusuf hung out in front of the television with their son, Saleem, who was in fifth grade. "I got all As this semester," Saleem bragged. "I'm going to be on the honor roll again."

Yusuf had forgotten how much his cousin liked to talk about himself. "Wait till you get to middle school. You'll forget all about grades."

Saleem's face fell. "Really? Is it as bad as they say?"

"It's not bad, exactly. Just . . . different."

Saleem's forehead cleared. "It's probably because you live in Texas. When I tell people my nani and cousins live here, they all look at me with pity."

"What? Why?" Yusuf asked. Saleem shrugged and fiddled with the remote. "I really don't know."

Amma called them to the kitchen to help with food preparation. "It's not fair. Do we have to?" Saleem whined.

Sarah khala pointed to Yusuf, who was already rolling up his sleeves. "See how that one's so helpful to his mom all the time? You should try to be like him."

Amma gave Yusuf a sideways hug. "It's true. He's so helpful around the house. And he helps his sister a lot too."

Saleem threw them an annoyed glance. Yusuf reddened. "Amma, stop," he whispered.

"Sorry," she whispered back, and released him.

Nani bustled into the kitchen, waving knives about. "Come on, less talking, more working!" She gave the boys a big bowl of vegetables to chop. Ginger and garlic, potatoes and shallots. Yusuf peeked into the pots on the stove. Mutton for the biryani, eggplant and potatoes for a side dish. On the counter lay a full chicken, waiting to be roasted.

Soon Aleena and the other girls wandered in, demanding to help. "I know!" Sarah khala said. "How about we make cupcakes for dessert?"

"Hooray!" Aleena shouted.

"Can we go now?" Yusuf asked. "Saleem and I want to play video games."

"Yes, go!" Amma agreed. "Just don't let Nani see you."

The boys rushed away, laughing. Abba and Ismael khaloo were in the living room, watching football. Yusuf whispered, "Better to play upstairs, or they'll give us a job to do too."

A couple of hours later, when Yusuf walked back down the hallway to get some snacks, Uncle Rahman's door was open, and a suitcase sat open on the bed. "You're back!" Yusuf shouted, spotting his uncle near the window.

Uncle Rahman turned and grinned at him, opening up his arms. "Great to see you again, kiddo!"

Yusuf hugged him tighter than usual. This wasn't just Rahman mamoo anymore. It was also Rahman from the journal in 2001—a boy just like him.

"Everything okay?" Uncle Rahman asked, letting him go.

Yusuf nodded. "I just missed you a lot."

Uncle Rahman ruffled Yusuf's hair. "I'm glad I was able to get the flight out of Seattle today. The weather wasn't too good, and I was worried."

Yusuf couldn't imagine Thanksgiving without his uncle. "Nani would have been so mad."

"I have no doubt about that!"

Yusuf looked around the room, remembering snippets from Uncle Rahman's journal. There was a desk in the corner, old and beat-up. A window above it looked onto the backyard. This had probably always been Uncle Rahman's room, even when he was a kid.

Yusuf looked at the far wall. The poster of Muhammad Ali was still there, yellow and peeling. *"Float like a butterfly, sting like a bee."* If he closed his eyes, he could imagine Uncle Rahman as a kid, sitting at this desk, writing his social studies report. He had a sudden thought. "Is this where you wrote your journal?"

Uncle Rahman looked startled, then he nodded slowly. "Yes. It's been a long time."

"It was a good idea, to write down everything that happened." Yusuf took a deep breath. "It's helped me figure out a lot of stuff."

"Do you want to talk about it?" Uncle Rahman asked. "Your amma told me what's been happening in Frey recently. I'm glad my journal is helping."

Yusuf was still staring at the poster. "Why did you like Muhammad Ali so much?" he suddenly asked. "You weren't into sports, right?"

Uncle Rahman shook his head. "It wasn't about the boxing," he replied. "Although don't get me wrong, Muhammad Ali was one of the greatest boxers of his time. No, it was about his principles."

"Principles?" Yusuf tried to remember what he'd read in the library about Muhammad Ali's life. How he'd won the world heavyweight championship in the 1960s. How he'd become famous in a time when African Americans were treated very badly. How he'd protested the Vietnam War and been banned from boxing.

Uncle Rahman nodded, his eyes sparkling. "Muhammad Ali always stood up for justice. He was willing to sacrifice everything for what he believed in, no matter the cost. That's something I will always admire."

Yusuf swallowed. "Standing up for something can be hard," he whispered, thinking of Ethan.

"Yes, it can." Uncle Rahman clapped him on the shoulder lightly. "That's why he's called the Greatest."

Yusuf grinned shyly. "Want to play video games with me and Saleem?"

"You go ahead. I'll be right there!"

At dinner time, Amma and Sarah khala talked about their childhoods like they always did at Thanksgiving. "Remember how Abba would take us to that bakery on Richmond Street and buy those little cinnamon cakes without telling Ammi?" Sarah khala giggled.

Amma laughed. "Ammi would get so mad, because we wouldn't have room for dinner!"

"And Rahman would spill the secret as soon as we got home!"

"Hey, I was little!" Uncle Rahman protested.

Nani shook her head. "Your father was never doing what he was supposed to!"

Amma patted her hand. "That's why he was such a fun dad."

There was a little silence, and Yusuf wondered if Amma was feeling sad. He couldn't imagine not having her and Abba around all the time. "What happen to your abba?" Aleena asked. She didn't really remember Nana anymore.

"He went to Allah," Nani told her firmly, and stood up. "He's waiting there for all of us."

"Can I go to Allah too?" Aleena asked.

Amma hugged her quickly. "No, not yet. Only when you are very old and wrinkled."

Aleena roared with laughter, and then everyone laughed. They began talking again, only stopping to eat more. Yusuf relaxed. Being away from Frey had never felt this good. He could feel the warmth of his family's laughter like a blanket of goose feathers around his body.

After dinner, as they sat in the living room with cupcakes for the kids and chai for the adults, Amma turned to Uncle Rahman. "Tell us about Seattle," she teased. "How's your girlfriend?"

Uncle Rahman turned beet red. "She's not . . . oof, baji! She's fine. Her family is great."

The teasing continued until Nani sternly scolded them all. "Talk about something else! All this nonsense of girlfriends is going to give your children ideas."

It was midnight before everyone went to bed, yawning and smiling. Yusuf peeked into Uncle Rahman's bedroom one more time to say good night. "Can we do a video chat sometime next week?" he asked. "I wanna show you my TRC robot. It's really cool."

"You're competing in TRC?" Uncle Rahman gave a big smile. "That's amazing, Yusuf! Congratulations!"

Yusuf's cheeks puffed. "Thank you. The contest is in January. Maybe you can come?"

"I'll try my best. Text me the date and time, okay?"

"Okay."

Uncle Rahman lowered his voice and looked intently at Yusuf. "And hey . . . don't worry about things, all right? I survived 9/11, didn't I? You can survive twenty years later."

Yusuf thought about this as he lay awake in Amma's old bedroom. Uncle Rahman was right. He could survive everything that was happening in Frey. All he had to do was stay on the sidelines, not get involved. Not try to be a hero.

30

It was easier said than done, Yusuf found, to not get involved in something. On the Monday after Thanksgiving, he came back to school to see Ethan Grant and his friend Sammy teasing a little second grader in the shared parking lot between schools. "Just walk away," he muttered under his breath, but he couldn't help but give Ethan a dark glare as he passed him.

Danial gave him a clap on the back. "Good job, you're learning!"

"Doesn't feel very good," Yusuf told him bitterly.

"But you're safe, that's the important thing."

They went their separate ways for classes, and then met up for lunch. "So, how was everybody's Thanksgiving?" Ethan boomed from the front of the cafeteria.

"All you Americans, that is. We know the Mooz-lims don't celebrate Thanksgiving."

Yusuf clenched his hands under the table. "Just ignore it," he told himself.

Cameron shook his head beside Yusuf. "He's baiting you," he whispered.

Yusuf took in a sharp breath. "Me?"

Cameron nodded. "Yes. You think he's going to forget all the times you've challenged him?"

"At least Yusuf's trying to keep his mouth shut," Danial protested.

"Won't do any good," Cameron replied darkly. "The damage is already done."

Yusuf stood up and grabbed his lunch. "I'm tired of everyone telling me how to behave," he grumbled as he walked away. "See you later."

He peeked into the quiet haven of the library. "Can I eat here, please, Mrs. Levy?" he asked the librarian.

She was sitting at her desk, reading. "Of course. Just don't get my books dirty."

"I won't."

He ate in silence, the feel of books on the shelves and colorful posters on the walls comforting him. He remembered coming in here in September to research 9/11. It seemed like a century ago.

Mrs. Levy was looking at him with warm blue eyes.

"Needed some solitude, eh?"

"I guess." He looked at his lunch, then back at her. She was clearly expecting more. "Uh, just thinking about a project I was supposed to hand in weeks ago."

She nodded. "Ah, that 9/11 one."

"Yes."

She sighed. "You know, I remember that day. September 11. We were all so shocked, it was like a silence descended on the town. People stopped laughing in the streets, stopped meeting each other for coffee or lunch. Just walked around for weeks afterward, reliving the image of the towers on fire, day after day after day."

Yusuf gulped. He'd been so involved in reading Uncle Rahman's account, he hadn't bothered to ask other people about their experiences. "I'm sorry," he whispered, not sure what he was apologizing for.

Mrs. Levy looked straight at him. "Why should you be sorry? You weren't even alive then. It's those terrorists who should be sorry, and others like them."

"I suppose."

She leaned across her desk to Yusuf. "Listen, Yusuf. Never you mind what people say about you. You're a good boy from a good family, just like all the other people living here."

His breath sounded almost like a sob. "Doesn't feel

like I'm a part of Frey right now."

"My ancestors came from Poland in the 1800s. My grandfather used to say the same thing; he never felt like he really belonged. He shortened his name and made his children speak only English, but at the end of the day they were still called dirty Jews."

Mrs. Levy glared at Yusuf with glittering eyes. "Never you mind what people call you, okay? Be proud of who you are. Because if you're not proud of yourself, how can you expect others to see you that way?"

Yusuf's eyes welled up. For some reason, Mrs. Levy reminded him of Amma. He whispered, "Everyone says to keep quiet, not get involved."

"Ah! Everybody's dead wrong!" She gave an angry wave of her hand. "Some of my grandfather's family died in the Holocaust, you know. So many people had the same attitude then too. Don't say anything. Don't get involved. And look what happened."

Yusuf had only a vague idea of what the Holocaust was. He hadn't learned about it in social studies in elementary school, but their fourth-grade teacher had taken them to the little Jewish history museum in Conroe for a field trip.

He could feel an idea forming in his mind. He pointed toward the computer in the library. "Can you show me how to do research on the Holocaust?" he asked.

★ ★ ★

That Monday after school, Amma decided to go to the park on Wicks Avenue. "We finally got good weather," she said as she made peanut butter and jelly sandwiches. "Let's not waste it."

Good weather in Frey meant anything below eighty degrees. Aleena took her dollies, and Yusuf brought his bike, their little picnic basket hanging off the handlebar. "Look, birdies!" Aleena pointed to the grass.

"Those are sparrows," Yusuf told her.

She laughed and ran toward them, and laughed some more when they scattered about. "Here, birdie!" she shouted.

Amma spread a cloth on the grass and they sat down. "Sandwiches, anyone?"

Yusuf saw some kids from school near the fountain. "I'll be right back," he told her.

Jared was sitting at the edge of the pond, throwing pebbles into the water. "Hey, Jared, how's everything?"

Jared jerked his head toward Yusuf. "Oh, it's you! You scared me."

"Sorry." Yusuf sat down next to him. "So, how's the painting going? You weren't at school today. Is everything all right?"

Jared turned away again. "My mom came back for Thanksgiving."

268

Yusuf grinned. "That's amazing! You must be so happy!"

Jared shrugged. "I guess. She's not the same mom, though. Grandma says the war changes people."

Yusuf thought of his research on the Holocaust. "Yes, it really does."

Jared went back to his pebble throwing. Yusuf watched him for a few minutes. "Wanna come over to my house again? We had fun, remember?"

Jared's back stiffened. "I can't. I'm not even supposed to be talking to you right now."

"What? Why?"

"Uncle Trevor said I can't."

Yusuf stood up so suddenly he almost pushed Jared into the pond. "That's . . . that's ridiculous! Why does he get to tell everybody in the town what to do? How to think?"

Jared straightened up but didn't reply.

"Fine, suit yourself." Yusuf gave a frustrated sound in his throat and stomped back to his family.

In social studies class on Thursday, Miss Terrance called on Yusuf with an anxious little smile. "Is your report ready, Yusuf?"

Yusuf nodded. He'd been working on the report for a while now. He handed a thin stack of papers to Miss

Terrance, but she shook her head. "I want you to read it out loud."

His breathing stopped for a second. "I can't!"

She narrowed her eyes. "Okay, not the whole report. Maybe just a summary of what you learned."

Yusuf gulped, then turned to face the class. Everyone looked bored already, which was a good thing. It meant they weren't listening and wouldn't care what he said. "I've lived in Frey since the day I was born. So has my sister, Aleena. My mom was born in Houston. My dad is an immigrant, but he got his citizenship years ago. Still, lots of people treat us like outsiders."

"What's this got to do with 9/11?" someone asked. Okay, they were listening.

"Quiet, please!" Miss Terrance frowned.

Yusuf willed his hands to stop trembling. "It's got a lot to do with 9/11, actually," he said. "We all saw the parade on September 11 to honor the fallen, but we don't realize how we treat our neighbors and friends who are still alive. We look at Muslims with suspicion, even if they've lived among us all our lives."

Madison raised her hand. "I agree with that. I've seen it with my own eyes."

Yusuf gave her a grateful look. "The worst thing is that if we see something bad happen to someone, like, say, pulling off a hijab or something else, nobody wants to say anything. We all act like we didn't even see it."

"Nobody wants to get into trouble," someone argued.

"Yeah, my mom says the bullies just want attention," someone else called out. "Best to ignore them."

Yusuf tried to calm his breathing. "That's easy to say, if it's not happening to you."

The class was quiet. Miss Terrance nodded.

Yusuf continued. "I also learned about the Holocaust. You know, the terrible thing that happened in Europe during World War Two? In the beginning, so many people just ignored how Jews were being treated. It was the little things, like name-calling and stereotyping. But here's the thing: when nobody stands up to the bullies, they get even bolder. And they think they can do whatever they want because other people just won't get involved."

> *Journal entry 10*
> *November 27, 2001*
> *The priest we met at the church on Thanksgiving Day showed up at our house today. I opened the door and stood staring at him, wondering where I'd seen him before. "Is your father home?" he asked, his eyes crinkling in the corners, and I ran to get Abba. It's not every day white people show up at our house for a visit.*
> *Abba and the priest—Father Hancock—spent the*

whole afternoon chatting in the living room. I brought them chai from the kitchen, and small chocolate crackers, and then settled in the window seat to read. I'm halfway through Harry Potter and the Goblet of Fire, and it's just as good as the previous books.

The men in the room were making reading difficult, though. Father Hancock told Abba that he was worried about his Muslim friends. It took me a minute to realize he meant us. "No need to worry, Father," Abba told him. "We are coping. We'll be fine."

"I want you to know, we are all together in this as Americans," Father Hancock insisted. Abba nodded and said thank you. I wasn't sure what they were really talking about. What are we all together in?

Then Father Hancock said something really interesting. "I wish there was a way for this neighborhood to come together 'Desi Street' and the 'African American street,' and all the other streets where the white people live. To meet each other and become friends. Remain united. We are still reeling from the shock of 9/11 and we need to be reminded that we're all one nation under God."

Abba asked, "Do you have any actual ideas, or do you just like to give speeches?"

Father Hancock laughed a little and replied that he was indeed planning something. "I have a friend who's a rabbi," he said, "and I just met a Hindu at a party last week."

Abba smiled. "So you want to start a band, then?" he joked.

Father Hancock didn't get the joke, I think. He just replied, "Maybe."

31

On December 4, Aleena danced into Yusuf's room singing the happy birthday song. "Wake up, bhai, it's your birthday!" she shouted, pulling at his covers.

Yusuf woke up, groaning. His head was splitting. "Leave me alone," he mumbled.

Aleena's face fell. "Birthday bhai!" she told him, but her smile was gone.

He groaned again. "Sorry, I'm just . . . not feeling well. Thank you for the song."

"You welcome."

"Aleena!" Amma called from the kitchen. "Leave your brother alone; let him sleep."

He stayed in bed for another thirty minutes, telling

himself what a bad big brother he was being. Finally delicious smells from the kitchen pulled him up. He washed and changed, then headed to Aleena and Amma with a bright smile.

"Happy birthday!" Aleena yelled when she saw him.

"Thank you, my darling sister!" He hugged her close. "Sorry I was being mean before."

"It's okay," she told him cheerfully. "You get dolly!"

Amma laughed. "She's insisting on giving you one of her dolls as a birthday present."

Yusuf bowed. "It will be my pleasure!"

Aleena took forever to choose the right doll. Eventually she gave him her best one: a white-skinned Barbie with red hair and a long blue gown. "Here."

Yusuf kissed the Barbie on its head. "Thank you. I will be a good mommy to her."

Aleena went into peals of laughter again. "Silly bhai!"

They sat down for breakfast. Abba had already gone to the store, but he'd left a small package for Yusuf on the counter. Yusuf waited until Amma took Aleena to the bathroom to wash her sticky hands, then opened the package. It was a slim book, with a colorful cover. *Handmade Robots from Everyday Objects.*

Yusuf smiled as he riffled through the pages. Abba had written a little note inside the front cover. *Now you can make me that robot to clean the store.* Then his smile faded. "Saturday club!" he gasped. He was already late. Very late.

Amma came back with Aleena in tow. "Not today," she said. "I already called Mr. Parker. Told him you were going to take the day off because it's your birthday."

Yusuf frowned. "What did he say?"

"He told me to tell you that they can survive one day without you."

Yusuf doubted that.

Amma began clearing the breakfast dishes from the table. "I also told your friends to come by after the club for some cake."

"You did what?" Yusuf couldn't remember the last time he'd raised his voice to his mother. "Sorry."

"What's wrong with that?" she asked, surprised.

He thought of the way Jared had turned away from him at the fountain. "Never mind," he mumbled. "Can I go work on my robotics now?"

Amma stood with hands on hips. "Absolutely not! I have a whole morning planned."

When the dishes were washed, they strapped Aleena into her umbrella stroller and walked downtown. Amma had errands to run, but she stopped at Olde Oaks Emporium to buy new shirts and pants for Yusuf. "You seem to be growing at the speed of light," she told him.

"Consider this your birthday present."

"Clothes aren't presents," Yusuf grumbled, but he stood still as she held up shirt after shirt in front of his body. "Thanks anyway."

"Go try these out. There's a good boy!"

They reached downtown just before noon. Aleena was whining by now, so they ate lunch at a little café with a blue-and-white-striped awning and wooden chairs on the pavement outside. "This is nothing like DQ," Yusuf remarked, examining the triangular chicken salad sandwiches made with soft white bread.

Amma sipped a cup of chamomile tea. "Sometimes we should treat ourselves."

"Look, tree!" Aleena pointed. Yusuf turned around. The Christmas tree in the town square was up, and people walked around, taking pictures. It was taller than all the downtown buildings, and covered head to toe with brightly colored ornaments.

"Christmas is coming," Amma told her. "It's a holiday some of our neighbors celebrate, and we're happy for them."

Yusuf was still staring at the tree. Next to it stood Mr. Grant, surrounded by his motorcycle friends. They were laughing and joking, but their faces were angry. How was that possible?

Amma tapped Yusuf's arm. "Don't look at them.

We don't want any trouble."

Yusuf gritted his teeth and looked away.

In the afternoon, Danial and Cameron came to wish Yusuf a happy birthday. "Your mom said there'd be cake," Cameron said, looking around the kitchen.

Danial slapped him lightly on the shoulder. "Be nice!"

"I'm being very nice. Please can I have some cake?"

Yusuf didn't know what was more painful: the fact that Danial had apparently found a new best friend, or that Jared was missing from this little impromptu party. Amma put out chips and soda, plus a chocolate cake with strawberry ganache they'd bought on their way back home from lunch. The three boys sat down at the kitchen counter and ate like they were starving. "This cake is amazing!" Cameron exclaimed.

Danial paused to take something out of his pocket. "Here's your gift," he said. "Happy twelfth."

It was a small Best Buy box. Yusuf ripped it open and dumped the contents on the counter. "A micro:bit! Thank you!"

Danial grinned at him with chocolate-covered lips. "Only the best for my best friend!"

Yusuf grinned back. He'd read about micro:bits online and had been dying to program one. "Wanna code with me?" he asked the others.

Danial shook his head. "Later. First, I brought some games to play."

In Yusuf's room, Danial set up his PlayStation while Cameron inspected the photos hanging above Yusuf's desk. "Your sister is hilarious," he remarked, pointing to a picture of Aleena dressed as a monkey.

Yusuf was looking through the micro:bit box for instructions. "I guess," he muttered.

"Sorry I don't have a present for you," Cameron continued. "I don't really get an allowance or anything, like Richie Rich here."

"Hey!" Danial protested. "I'm not that rich."

"You're the only kid in sixth grade who has a phone," Yusuf pointed out.

"Yeah, but I hardly use it."

Cameron moved some papers around on Yusuf's desk. "Anyway, just meant to say I wish I could give you something, but my parents don't have any cash for nonessential things."

Yusuf put down the box slowly. He remembered how Cameron had agreed to join TRC for the computer prize. Was Cameron poor? "Don't worry about it," he said. "Your friendship is enough."

Danial chortled as if that was a joke.

Cameron was still playing with the papers on Yusuf's desk. "What are these?" he asked, his voice suddenly hard.

Yusuf leaned forward, alarmed. Cameron was holding the notes from his locker in his hand. "Stop going through my stuff!" he yelled.

Cameron waved the notes above his head. "Are these the notes you were talking about at the Urooj Diner?" he demanded.

Danial put down the PlayStation and came over to them. "I want to see too."

Yusuf groaned and flopped down on his bed. "Ugh, go ahead. See all you want. I don't care!" he lied.

The other boys spent long, silent minutes reading the notes. There were six in all, written on the same lined notepaper, in the same loopy cursive handwriting. "Dude, this is messed up," Danial finally whispered. "I didn't know there were so many."

Cameron sat down on the bed next to Yusuf. "Did I ever tell you about the notes I found in my desk all through fourth grade?"

Yusuf opened one eye. "What are you talking about? Elementary school was awesome!"

"Maybe for you." Cameron scoffed. "For me it was awful. Ethan isn't the only bully in this town, you know."

"What did your notes say?" Yusuf whispered. He

should have been happy he wasn't the only one being harassed, but something in Cameron's face made Yusuf want to hug him. Hard.

Cameron shrugged. "Pretty much the same thing. I can't really remember. I threw them away."

"Smart man," Danial said. "Yusuf, you should throw these away too! Why are you keeping them?"

Yusuf wasn't sure why. "They're evidence, I guess."

Identical looks of alarm crossed his friends' faces. "Evidence?" squeaked Danial. "For what? Against who?"

"I don't know yet. But I'm tired of everything that's happening in this town. It's like I don't even recognize the place anymore." He remembered what Abba had said the night he'd signed the robotics permission slip. *"A wind that's blowing through Frey."*

Danial crossed his arms across his chest. "It's not just Frey. It's everywhere. All of the U.S. All of the world."

Yusuf hadn't known that. But it didn't make a difference, anyway. "Doesn't make it all right."

Cameron leaned closer. "Listen to me. There's only one way to survive this. To assimilate. That's what your dad and my dad are doing. That's what we all are doing."

Yusuf thought of Saba and her red hijab. Of Sameena Aunty and her sad face. Of Mrs. Levy and her Jewish ancestors. "I don't like that word," he whispered.

"Assimilate. It sounds like you have to give up every-thing that makes you, *you*."

"What other choice do you have?" Danial demanded. "Have you seen those Patriot Sons? Even our parents are scared of them."

Yusuf got up and took the notes from Cameron. Carefully he folded them up and put them inside a drawer at the bottom of his dresser. "That's what they're counting on," he told them grimly. "And that's what we can't allow to happen."

32

A package arrived from Uncle Rahman in the evening:
a rolled-up poster of Muhammad Ali with the words
FLOAT LIKE A BUTTERFLY, STING LIKE A
BEE across the bottom. Yusuf tacked it up on the wall
over his desk, just like he'd seen in Uncle Rahman's
room. Then, smiling, he went to work on the micro:bit
Danial had given him.

There were hundreds of different projects online for
this sort of tiny computer, and he wanted to try them
all. He played around a bit, coding and deleting, then
coding again. He finally found a program for a virtual
cat, complete with beeping reminders for feeding and
washing it. With a little glue and card stock, he could

even make the micro:bit look like a cat. Aleena would be so excited!

It took longer than he'd thought. The next day was Sunday, so he had to wait until he got back from the construction site to begin programming. He was still working past midnight.

On Monday, Yusuf pushed everything into his backpack when he went to school. He wanted to show Danial how much he'd programmed over the weekend. Just before he left home, Amma gave him a big hug. "Take care, okay?"

Amma never hugged him before school. She was always busy making breakfast and running after Aleena. "Love you," he said as he hugged her back. She smelled of vanilla and cinnamon.

Mondays were always chaotic at Frey Middle. Kids walked around bleary-eyed. Yusuf felt a yawn coming, and then another and another. He was late, so he decided to keep his backpack with him instead of depositing it in his locker. He couldn't find Danial anywhere, which meant Danial had overslept and would be arriving at school in his mother's Jeep.

Mr. Parker went over science notes from the week before. "Anybody remember how earthquakes are caused?"

Yusuf racked his brain. Something about plates.

His eyes were drooping and he blinked to stay awake. This was what happened when you stayed up all night making a toy for your little sister.

Mr. Parker was looking right at him. "Yusuf?"

"Um . . . tectonic plates?"

"Good." Mr. Parker went to the whiteboard to write something. Yusuf closed his eyes in relief. He'd never blanked on a science question before. He really needed to catch up on his sleep tonight.

By gym class, Yusuf was yawning nonstop. Danial stared at him. "You look exhausted, dude," he said.

Yusuf opened his backpack and showed Danial the micro:bit. "It's going to be a virtual cat when it's finished," he bragged.

"A virtual cat?" Danial's eyes popped. "How old are you, five?"

"For Aleena, of course."

"Of course. Do you ever do anything for yourself, like ever?"

Yusuf rolled his eyes at him. "You can't understand. You're not a big brother."

Coach Boston blew his whistle and shouted, "Change, everyone. Then laps!" Yusuf closed his backpack and groaned. "If I do laps now, I'm going to collapse."

Danial motioned to the door. "Go to the nurse or something. You don't look too great."

The nurse's office was at the other end of the school. He made a detour through the cafeteria, where a group of parent volunteers sat making banners for the Christmas concert. He walked slowly, his backpack on one shoulder. By the time he reached the nurse's office, he felt better. Maybe if he just leaned against the wall and closed his eyes for a second, he'd be well enough to go back to class.

The seconds were longer than he imagined. The next thing he knew, there was a ringing sound around him, followed by rising chatter. He opened his eyes wearily. The bell had rung, and gym class was over. Kids streamed out of their classes and surrounded him. He saw Ethan and Sammy in the distance, bearing down on him with dark, gleeful faces. A faint beeping sound emanated from around him like a warning signal.

Beep-beep-beep.

When Ethan and Sammy were just a few yards away, Yusuf realized something. The beeps were coming from inside his backpack. He fumbled for the strap, but it was too late. Ethan reached him and slapped a beefy hand on his shoulder. Ethan's face loomed close enough for Yusuf to smell his breath as he opened his mouth wide and yelled, "BOMB!"

Yusuf was bewildered. *Who has a bomb?* he wondered. He looked around at the other kids' faces. They were all looking at *him* with . . . fear and anger. Him? Yusuf Azeem had a bomb? What were they talking about?

Everything happened with lightning speed after that. Ethan continued to yell, his piercing voice drowning out all the other voices. Kids started to run away from Yusuf, but Ethan stood like a statue, still clutching his shoulder. Then Mel, the school security guard, rushed up, panting, and dragged Yusuf and Ethan with him. The hallway ahead was long and narrow, filled with kids who were staring, turning away, running. Running.

Yusuf wanted to run too, wanted to sleep forever, but Mel held on to his right arm and Ethan to his left shoulder. "BOMB! BOMB!" Ethan kept shouting, until Mel growled, "Shut up, kid!" at him.

Ethan shut up, but kept his gleeful eyes trained on Yusuf like a hawk. Yusuf wanted to punch him, but he knew something serious was going on. If only his brain would cooperate. If only he could think clearly. Why, oh, why had he stayed up all night?

It was only when the trio reached the parking lot outside that Yusuf caught his breath. His backpack was still beeping, and finally he realized what it was.

The half-built virtual cat inside was begging to be fed.

33

The first thing Mel did was throw Yusuf's backpack far away in the field next to the parking lot. The field was used for football practice by the Coyotes most days, but now it was empty, and muddy from rain the night before. Yusuf stared at the black lump of his backpack. He could still hear the beeping, so faint he wondered if it was just his imagination.

Beep-beep-beep.

Mel gave him a grim look, said, "Don't move," and stomped away with Ethan, back into the school building.

Yusuf couldn't help it. He ran to the field—to his backpack—until he was standing right next to it. Still, he didn't dare pick it up. The beeping was stronger now, more insistent. *Beep-beep-beep.* "Shut up!" he whispered in a furious tone.

The next second, the shrill sound of a fire drill blasted into the air around Yusuf. He whirled around and watched with miserable, bleary eyes as students streamed out of the school building, asking frantic questions.

"Is this for real?"

"Where's the fire?"

"It's a bomb this time!"

"No kidding? Oh my God!"

Yusuf turned away from them. A police car screeched to a stop near the kids, and Officer Strickland got out. He ran straight to Yusuf, eyebrows meeting grimly in the center of his forehead. "So . . . what's this about a bomb, eh, Yusuf?"

Yusuf tried to smile. "It's all a mistake. Of course it is. My backpack—" He reached down, but Officer Strickland put up a quick hand.

"Don't. Touch. That!"

"What? You don't really think . . . ?"

With slow movements, Officer Strickland picked up the backpack from the ground. It was muddy now, and bits of leaves stuck to the bottom. "What's that beeping?"

"My virtual cat." Yusuf tried to explain. "It's not really a cat, just a computer. A toy. It's beeping because it's time to feed the cat."

Officer Strickland gingerly opened the zipper and peered inside. "Looks like a computer chip to me. Not a toy."

"But it is . . . you can code this thing to be anything. A remote control for a vacuum, or a guitar player, or even a counting device."

Officer Strickland continued to stare inside. "Can you code it to be a time control for a bomb?"

"What? No!" Yusuf paused, horrified. "I mean, I don't know. . . ."

Officer Strickland held up one hand. "Better not complete that sentence, son." He sighed heavily and closed the zipper. "It's not a cat, I can tell you that. And it's still beeping."

"Yes, I'm sorry. It's not coded properly yet."

"I'd be happier if you'd hidden a real cat in there."

"But . . ."

He pointed to the parking lot. "Go back there and don't move. I have to discuss this with the police chief."

The police chief? Yusuf looked back to where Officer Strickland was pointing. A row of police cars were now parked helter-skelter, and at least ten police officers walked around with hands on their belts, looking grim.

A fire truck and ambulance waited with flashing lights on the road outside the school.

Yusuf tried to make sense of this situation. Why on earth did anybody need a fire truck or an ambulance? Then he remembered Ethan's angry, gleeful face, and the way his mouth opened wide to shout "Bomb!" over and over. He followed Officer Strickland slowly back to the parking lot, one foot in front of the other. Everyone was staring at him. Students. Teachers. Police officers.

Yusuf sank down on the ground at the edge of the field, where the parking lot began. This was all a misunderstanding, he told himself. They would look inside his backpack and see for themselves what a micro:bit was. Nothing special, just a tiny computer.

He squatted and hugged his knees. Eyes downward, no need to make eye contact.

"Don't move," Officer Strickland said again. He strode away, and two other officers came to stand near Yusuf. They both had blank faces, and they didn't look down at Yusuf even once. But he knew why they were there: to guard him. To make sure he didn't move or run away.

That's what nobody in Frey seemed to understand. This was his home. Where else would he go?

The noise around him continued. Voices. Sirens. Shouts. He didn't look up. What was the point? They were all probably staring at him. He closed his eyes and tried to rest.

"Are you okay?" It was Jared, his face haggard. He sat down next to Yusuf.

Yusuf wanted to say yes, but he wasn't sure if that would be a lie. "I guess."

"I'm sorry about everything."

"I don't have a bomb, you know that, right?" Yusuf whispered. "This is nuts! I don't know why I'm still sitting here."

"Officer Strickland tried to say something, but Uncle Trevor and his friends are here, yelling at everyone."

So that was what all the commotion was. Of course. The Patriot Sons. Everything made so much more sense now. In a way, Yusuf was glad. At least he wasn't losing his mind. "It doesn't really matter. There's no bomb. It's just my micro:bit."

Jared gave a ghost of a smile. "I got one for Christmas last year. I programmed it to play Christmas songs I could send to my mom overseas."

"I made a virtual cat for Aleena."

They sat together in silence, clasping their knees. Jared slipped a hand in his pocket and took out a card. "I'm sorry I didn't come to your birthday party," he said. "I made this for you."

Yusuf opened the card. It had a small painting of two

cats sitting together in a garden full of roses. Underneath them, he'd written *Happy birthday to my friend*.

Yusuf stared at the writing on the card. The curl of
the Y was so familiar, as if the person who'd written it
had tried cursive but given up halfway.

Who even wrote cursive anymore?

Something niggled in Yusuf's mind. The handwriting . . .

His breath caught in his throat.

The handwriting was just like the writing on the
notes in his locker.

Jared was looking at him nervously. "You don't like
it?"

Yusuf blinked hard, and then scrambled up with a
quick push of his legs. "You? It was you?" he almost
shouted.

Jared stood up too. "What do you mean?" he asked
faintly.

"The notes in my locker. *You* wrote them!" It wasn't
a question. It was a fact. A horrible, painful fact that
Yusuf could hardly wrap his head around.

Jared nodded, looking defeated. "It was before I
knew you. Ethan made me. He said we needed to send
a message to our country's enemies. He said I was
being a patriot!"

Yusuf felt sick. He sank down again, wondering what

fainting felt like. "A patriot?" he spat out.

"Yes, but now I know he's wrong. You're a good person. You're my friend. I stopped delivering those notes as soon as I realized that." Jared was almost begging, his hands clasped together like he was praying a desperate prayer. "I'm so sorry. I'm—"

"Shut up." For the first time ever, Yusuf said the words he'd always thought were rude. But now the whole school thought he had a bomb. The person he thought was his friend was actually his tormentor. So what if Yusuf said shut up? Who cared?

"Listen, Yusuf . . ."

There was a movement behind them. Yusuf turned away from Jared, his stomach heaving. Officer Strickland was coming back. Mr. Grant stood nearby with hands on hips, a thunderous expression on his face. "I'm sorry, son, we'll need to take you to the police station downtown," Officer Strickland said quietly.

Yusuf blinked hard. "Why?"

"Nothing to worry about," the officer replied. "Just to ask you a few questions."

Yusuf felt faint. "What about my parents?" he whispered.

"I've already let them know. They'll meet us downtown." Officer Strickland grabbed Yusuf's shoulder and pulled him up. Yusuf hoped fervently his shaky legs would keep him standing. Another officer pulled both of Yusuf's lifeless arms behind his back. He felt the cool touch of metal on his wrists.

Handcuffs.

Was he really being handcuffed like in the movies? Was this reality or a big, awful nightmare?

The last thing he saw before he was pushed into Officer Strickland's cop car was the shocked, crying face of his ex-friend, Jared Tobias.

Journal entry 11
December 11, 2001
Exactly two months from the awful events of 9/11, another awful thing happened. Only it didn't affect anyone other than my family. Jonathan came to school today furious. His uncle had been officially declared dead, after two months of being missing in New York City.

"It's all your people's fault," he yelled at me after school as we waited for the bus. He had tears on his cheeks and his hands were trembling, but he still gathered enough strength to push me into a wall. I put out a hand to grab his shirt as I fell, and we ended up tumbling onto the ground together like dominos.

"I'm sorry," I whispered into his ear, hoping to ease his pain. I thought of my uncle—Amma's elder

brother in Pakistan—who took me on piggyback rides even though I was too old for them. "I'm sorry, my friend," I repeated.

He struggled and stood up. "Don't call me that," he shouted, and ran away. I decided not to take the bus. Home is close enough to walk, if one of my sisters walks with me. I went over to the high school across the street and found Farrah baji just leaving.

"What's up?" she asked. But I just shook my head. "Come on, then," she said. "Let's walk home together. We can even get some fries on the way."

But that's not the real bad thing that happened today. The absolute worst thing was still to come. When we reached home, Silky lay on our front doorstep, cold, stiff, and dead. I sank to the ground and picked her up, but she felt like a wooden doll someone had dragged through mud and leaves. "Who did this?" I screamed. Farrah baji tried to hug me, but I screamed and screamed until I had no voice left.

34

Amma and Abba came to get Yusuf from the police station, their faces streaked with dried-up tears. He saw them from the window of the jail cell he'd been put in, walking like they were even older than Nani. They disappeared inside, and he waited. They probably had papers to sign and questions to answer.

It wasn't really a jail cell he was in. The downtown police station was a small building, full of cubicles for police officers and a holding area for criminals. Jared was a minor, so he got his own little room with a couch and a table. The window had bars across it, but otherwise it was just a small, plain room. Officer Strickland had taken off his handcuffs with an apologetic smile and promised to come back "when all this nonsense gets sorted out." That had been at least an hour ago.

Yusuf paced the room for a while, up and down, up and down. His hands were trembling, and he could feel his heart pumping in his chest like he'd just run a mile. *It's going to be okay,* he told himself, but he knew that was a lie.

He tried to focus on something else. Something good. He pictured his room. His desk, with the poster of Muhammad Ali that Uncle Rahman had sent him for his birthday. *Float like a butterfly, sting like a bee.* Had Muhammad Ali ever felt this heartbroken?

He finally sank down onto the couch and fell asleep, dreaming that he'd been handcuffed by a screaming Ethan. Then he woke up and realized it wasn't exactly a dream. The sky outside the window was dark now. He'd missed the asr and maghrib prayers. A trickle of fear grazed his spine. Had his parents gone home without him?

"Hello?" he called out, first in a whisper, then louder. "Is anyone there?"

An officer opened the door a crack and put a plate with two doughnuts on the floor. Yusuf got up, but the door slammed shut again before he could take more than a few steps. He squared his shoulders and told himself to stop being a baby. They were feeding him doughnuts. That was a good sign.

Wasn't it?

He went back to the couch, curled into a ball, and prayed.

He prayed all the prayers he'd learned at Sunday school. The prayer of Abraham as he faced his accusers. The prayer of Moses as he faced the Pharaoh. The prayers of the Prophet Muhammad, so many of them.

Eventually his heartbeat slowed, and his hands stopped trembling. When the door opened again around midnight and Amma rushed in, he didn't move. He could hear her weeping and calling his name. He could hear Abba behind her, begging him to get up. But he was so sleepy, he didn't reply.

The next day at the Azeem residence, a steady flow of visitors dropped by. First was Sameena Aunty, so early that Amma almost didn't open the door for her. "Some people have no consideration," she muttered as she went to open the door. But Sameena Aunty brought a big bowl of chicken pulao and a container full of beef samosas, so Amma let her in. Pulao was Yusuf's favorite.

"How is he?" Sameena Aunty whispered.

"I'm not sure," Amma whispered back. Neither knew he stood just outside the living-room door, blanket clutched in his hand, listening.

They sat together in the living room, talking of

nothing in particular. Amma cried a little bit, and Sameena Aunty told her to be brave. To be strong. Yusuf wanted to shout that he was the one who needed to be brave and strong. He was the one who'd been stuck in the jail like a criminal for hours and hours. Not Amma or Abba. But he went back to his room and tried to go to sleep.

One by one, all the Muslims of Frey visited, bringing food and well wishes. Yusuf was jarred awake every time the doorbell rang, loud and insistent. He was somehow grateful for the interruptions, though. Sleep brought nightmares, dark and echoing. Saba knocked on Yusuf's bedroom door at lunchtime, holding two paper plates of rice. "Time to eat," she told him firmly.

Yusuf wasn't hungry, but he got up anyway. It was embarrassing to have a female other than Amma or Aleena in his room. He smoothed his hair and clothes, and sat cross-legged with her on the carpet next to his desk. They ate in silence. "Are you doing okay?" he finally asked her.

She gave a surprised laugh. "You're asking *me*? Everyone is worried sick about *you*."

He shrugged. "What happened to me was a misunderstanding. Your thing was real."

She bent her head. "I'm fine. They wanted me to tell who pulled off my hijab, but I couldn't. I know you think that makes me a coward."

Yusuf picked at his rice with his fork. "I don't think so. I think you're brave for going to school every day wearing a hijab. I brought my micro:bit to school one day and look what happened."

They both smiled sadly at each other, then pretended to eat.

Danial and Cameron arrived in the afternoon with their parents. While the adults sat in the living room with serious faces, the boys crowded around Yusuf in his room, asking a dozen questions. "Did you tell them it was all Ethan's fault? Did they read you your rights? Did anyone interrogate you?"

Yusuf realized that nobody had, in fact, read him his rights or asked him to tell his side of the story. He felt his pain being replaced with anger, ever so slightly. He told Danial and Cameron about the room he was locked up in, and the police officer who brought doughnuts and left them on the floor, but nothing else. Nothing about his crippling fear, or the way he held in his pee for hours because he couldn't find the voice to call the police officer outside his door.

Cameron gave him an awkward pat on the back. "Next time anybody calls me a bad boy, I'm pointing to you."

"Yeah, we have an actual gangster in our group!"

crowed Danial. "Nobody will dare mess with us now!"

Yusuf wanted to smack their faces, but he gritted his teeth and said nothing.

"Shhh," Cameron whispered, pointing to the door. The adults in the next room were arguing.

"You're on the school board, why didn't you do anything?" That was Amma, her voice hard and brittle, like it would break any minute.

"I didn't know until this morning." That was Mr. Khan. He sounded sad. Yusuf looked at Danial, who was staring intently at his nails.

"Let's not blame anyone." That was definitely Abba, always trying to keep the peace.

"But they blamed my son for something he didn't do!" Amma's voice was so low, Yusuf wasn't sure anyone else heard it.

Cameron cleared his throat and said, "Play any new games lately?" Then Mrs. Khan called out to them, and the two boys filed out of Yusuf's room with weak smiles.

Yusuf was glad to see them go. He slept again, hugging his pillow, haunted by more dreams. The phone rang constantly while he slept, and he could hear it ringing over and over. He finally covered his head with a pillow to block out the noise. "Reporters," he heard Abba growl more than once. "They never called this much when I defeated the robber."

In the evening, Mr. Parker came by with pizza and his homework. He spent some time talking with Amma and Abba, then came into Yusuf's room. "How're you doing, buddy?"

Yusuf's back was stiff from lying in bed all day. "Everyone's treating me like I'm ill," he complained.

Mr. Parker smiled a little. "I suppose you are, just a bit. Emotionally. You need time to recover, I think."

"I'm fine," Yusuf insisted.

"I'm sure you are. Still, your parents have requested that you stay home until the winter break, and Principal Williamson agrees. It will help you heal, and give the school time to figure out what to do about this whole situation. Your assignments will be emailed tomorrow."

Yusuf sat up in bed, his forehead throbbing. "What situation is that, exactly?" he demanded. "That everyone thinks I brought a bomb to school?"

Mr. Parker looked startled. "Nobody thinks that, Yusuf. At least nobody who knows you."

Yusuf slumped back down. "They all treated me like a criminal," he whispered. "Everyone. Officer Strickland, who's my dad's friend, and the other kids who ran away from me when Ethan started shouting . . ."

He couldn't bear it anymore. He buried his head in his hands and cried. It was a hot, angry mess of tears, everything he'd kept bottled up inside since sixth grade had started.

He cried and cried, until he felt just a little bit better.

Mr. Parker sat on his bed and held on to Yusuf's hand. "I know it's hard, son. You're an example to me, you know. You stand up for what you believe in, even when everyone is against you. But some things are best left to the adults. We're working on it, we promise you. It's going to get better, you'll see. Most people see the Patriot Sons for what they are. We just need to stand united against them."

It sounded like the typical adult speech to Yusuf. All words and no action. He pulled his hand away and wiped his face. "Yeah, sure," he mumbled.

Mr. Parker sighed and stood up. "Take care of yourself, son. We want you happy and healthy for TRC after the holidays."

35

Yusuf couldn't stay sad or mad forever. Mr. Parker's parting words had reminded him that Miss Trashy's code still needed to be fine-tuned.

He woke up the next morning, ready to tackle life. "Will you have breakfast with us?" Amma asked when he entered the kitchen. She'd been walking on eggshells around him since the day before, but for the first time Yusuf saw how fragile she herself looked. Her lips were trembling and her eyes were downcast, as if one loud noise or harsh word would completely destroy her.

Yusuf enveloped her in a hug. "Amma, I'm okay now," he whispered.

She hugged him back so tight and hard, he had to

force himself not to wiggle. "Are you sure?" she asked. "Do you need anything?"

"Just breakfast."

She let him go with the beginning of a smile. "I was thinking parathas and omelets?"

"That sounds great." He looked around. "Where's Aleena?"

"Playing in her room. Want to get her ready while I cook?"

Getting Aleena ready for the day was just the soothing routine he needed. He stuck his head in her room and roared "Boo!" at her, then tackled her on her bed as she squealed in surprise and delight.

"Bhai okay now?" she asked, patting his cheeks.

"Yes, I'm fine," he nodded, kissing her palm.

She beamed. "Play dollies with me."

They sat on the bed and played for the longest time, until the aroma of parathas wafted into the room and Aleena sniffed like a puppy. "Food!" she announced. "Me hungry."

"You have to change first." Yusuf pointed to the bathroom. "And brush your teeth."

When they reached the kitchen table, Aleena and Yusuf were grinning. Amma saw them and breathed in relief. "So what are your plans for today? I have to work in my office—"

"You mean the garage?" Yusuf interrupted.

"Yes, the garage." Amma gave him a stern look. "And you're free to do whatever you like."

"Can I just play with Aleena all day?"

"Yayyyyy, we play all day!" Aleena shouted, clapping her hands in excitement.

Amma squeezed his hand. "I think that's a good idea, darling."

In the afternoon, Principal Williamson called. She spoke first to Amma, and then asked to speak with Yusuf. He took the phone with trembling hands. If she wanted to know whether he really had a bomb in his backpack, he was going to be very rude to her.

"I heard y'all had a real busy day in my absence," she joked, her voice hollow.

"I guess."

Her sigh was loud in his ear. "Listen, son, I'm sorry all this happened. I'd gone to Conroe for a district meeting and only checked my assistant's frantic messages after it ended. By the time I drove back to the school they'd already taken you. . . ."

Yusuf couldn't speak. What was there to say? "It's all right," he finally whispered, even though it wasn't.

The principal sighed again. "No, it's really not. And that's why I'm calling. Put the phone on speaker, so your mom can hear this too."

He put the phone on speaker and placed it on Amma's desk. Principal Williamson continued. "So, I talked to Officer Strickland—do you know him? Such a good man—and he said they didn't file any charges against Yusuf because . . . well, because it was just a false alarm."

Amma interrupted, her voice shaking. "A false alarm? They held my son at the police station for a total of twelve hours, for a false alarm?"

"I understand your concern—"

"No, I don't think you do!" Amma's voice was louder now. Stronger. "I'm not concerned. I'm furious. I'm shocked and stunned. I'm very, very upset!"

Yusuf held Amma's hand. He was glad to know he wasn't the only one going through so many emotions at the same time, like water running roughly down a steep hill.

"I understand, Mrs. Azeem. I really do," the principal replied after a pause. "Unfortunately, the police said they have to take measures like these if someone makes a credible threat. There was a consistent beeping from your son's backpack, and it's not a good idea to take this sort of thing lightly. We have the safety of the school to consider."

Yusuf sat down on Amma's office chair, holding on to

its arms for support. The school was worried about the students' safety, but not his own? Wasn't he a student too? "What about Ethan?" he finally croaked. "He goes around hurting students every single day, but nobody's concerned about student safety then?"

"We definitely are concerned. And I've spoken to his father many times. He's got several warnings in his discipline file."

"He never had to go to the police station, did he?" Amma cried.

Principal Williamson said, "No, he didn't," and it sounded like she was holding back tears too. "Look, I'm trying to do something about him, but his father is difficult to reason with, and the mayor seems to be doing his bidding."

"So there's nothing anyone can do?" Amma asked tiredly. The fight seemed to have gone out of her, and she sagged against the wall.

"That's not what I'm saying," replied the principal. "Listen, if you get any calls from reporters, don't turn them away. I think it might be a good idea to tell them your side of the story."

Amma shook her head. "You think so?"

"It's just a suggestion," Principal Williamson replied. "All I can say is, the local residents need to be really strong against this sort of behavior, and show true unity against the Patriot Sons."

Amma stood up a little straighter. "That's it? That's your message? Love will overcome hate, or some such nonsense?"

The principal's voice was loud and warm now. "That's a powerful message, ma'am. Don't you forget that."

Yusuf kept thinking about Principal Williamson's powerful message for the rest of the day. When Abba came home, they sat together in the living room and watched a documentary about space. "Do you agree, Abba," Yusuf asked during commercials, "that love overcomes hate?"

Abba nodded slowly. "The Prophet certainly taught that. You've heard the story about the woman who'd throw garbage on his head every day, but he went to inquire about her when she was sick? The Quran uses the words 'mercy' and 'forgiveness' over and over again."

"Yes, but the Quran also asks us to punish bad people so that they can't harm others."

Abba gave him a push with his arm. "Not us, the government. Punishment must come through laws, not you and me."

"That's not fair," Yusuf said. "What if the laws favor the bullies? Like during the Holocaust? Or after 9/11?"

"Then the people must unite against hatred, and choose love."

Yusuf tossed the television remote on the couch and stood up. "You sound just like my principal," he cried. "What power does love have?"

Abba gave him a gentle smile. "It's got the same power as hate. If one can do a lot of harm, then the other can do a lot of good. You just have to get your head out of the robot world and think like a human being for a change."

Amma came in and sat down on the sofa's arm. Her fragile look was gone, and in its place was determination. "That's why I think we should talk to the reporters who keep calling," she said.

Abba stared at the television screen for a while. Finally he nodded. "I'll call them back in the morning."

Yusuf groaned. He didn't want people to ask him more questions. He definitely didn't want to advertise the fact that he'd spent all day and half the night in the police station. But he could tell from his parents' faces that they'd made their decision. They'd talk to anyone who would listen. They'd tell his miserable story to the world, or at least to everyone in Frey.

The problem was, ugly, hateful voices were always louder than nice, loving ones. The reporters could only share his story. They couldn't guarantee anyone would listen.

There had to be another way to bring the Patriot Sons down. Yusuf went back to his room and signed on to Scratch's group messaging. Jared had sent twenty-five messages, all variations of "Sorry" and "Please talk to me."

Yusuf deleted all the messages and pinged Danial and Cameron. Then he remembered Madison and added her to the group chat.

Yusuf: Guys and gal, we need ideas.

Madison: For what? A new robot?

Yusuf: Nope. We need ideas to get our town back.

Cameron: What are you talking about, dude?

Danial: Yusuf, you need to focus on getting better. And TRC.

Yusuf: Sorry, Danial. We need to defeat the enemy.

Danial: What enemy????

Yusuf: You know. A certain boy and his dad. Plus his posse.

Danial: Wow, okay. You're officially nuts.

Yusuf: No, I'm not. My dad says love overcomes hate. Personally, I don't believe it, but I'm willing to try.

Danial: This guy is too optimistic for his own good. Cameron, tell him.

Cameron: No, he's right. We've tried everything else

and failed. Let's try love too. What's the harm?

Danial: Are you serious? We could end up in jail like him.

Cameron: That's okay with me. People think I'm a gangster anyway.

Danial: Unbelievable

Madison: I'm in too!

Yusuf: Awww . . . Love you guys!

Danial: Shut up, dude, don't be a hero.

Yusuf: Too late.

36

It was Cameron who stated the obvious. "We need Jared. We need his church to help us."

The three boys and Madison were squeezed into a booth at Dairy Queen, munching on jalapeño fries and drinking peppermint shakes. They were supposed to be strategizing for TRC, but the topic always seemed to turn to the Patriot Sons. "How to defeat them and win Frey back," Madison had said laughingly the other day.

"Don't say his name," Yusuf said with gritted teeth.

"I don't get it." Danial frowned. "I thought he was your friend."

Yusuf swallowed his nausea. "He was, until I found out he's the one who left those notes in my locker."

Danial's mouth dropped open. "Seriously?"

Yusuf nodded. He'd thought it would feel good to tell everyone about Jared's betrayal, but he just felt sad.

Cameron took a sip of his shake thoughtfully. "I bet Ethan forced him. He's really hard to ignore, that guy."

"I doubt that," Yusuf said, but his voice was uncertain. *Could it be?*

Cameron put down his shake. "Ethan had originally asked me to send those notes, offered me money, but I refused. I guess he found Jared easier to manipulate."

"That's why you kept asking about it," Danial guessed. "Wow, that's messed up."

"Yeah." Cameron nodded. "Plus, Jared is really scared of his uncle. I've seen how he gets all pale in his presence."

Yusuf scowled. Was he supposed to forget that his friend had turned out to be the one sending him mean, slightly threatening notes? Was he supposed to forgive and forget?

Abba would say yes.

He groaned and slammed his half-empty shake on the table. "Okay, fine. Ask Jared to help. But I'm not going to talk to him. Someone else do it."

Madison raised her hand. "I'll do it. He lives down the street from me."

"Can we get back to TRC now?" Yusuf begged.

A man around Abba's age walked past, smiling. "You kids ready for Christmas, eh?" He saw Yusuf and stopped. "Wait, you're the boy . . ."

Yusuf hung his head. "Yes, sir," he whispered. His face had been on the TV news on Monday and Tuesday, and on the front page of the *Frey Weekly* on Wednesday morning.

The man came closer, his face angry. "Listen, I hope you're doing okay. I have two boys your age. I was worried sick when I heard the news that you'd been hauled to jail. My entire family was."

Yusuf looked up. He realized he recognized the man. He was one of the city council members at the mosque zoning meeting. "Really?"

"Yes, of course. What do you think we are, son? Monsters?"

Yusuf managed a small smile. "No, sir."

Cameron cleared his throat and waved a fry in the air. "Well, maybe you should let the police know that what happened to my friend was wrong."

They all looked at Cameron, awed by his boldness.

The man looked thoughtful. "Maybe you're right," he said. "Maybe I can write a letter or something." The man's order was called, and he turned. "Take care of yourselves, kids."

They looked at one another in stunned silence. "You

know what this means, right?" Madison finally said, grinning.

"Yes," Yusuf agreed, thinking about the man and his angry face. He wasn't angry at Yusuf, but at Ethan and the Patriot Sons. At Frey Middle School. At the police. This was incredible. "Maybe we actually have a chance."

They went home with little smiles. Later, Madison sent a message on Scratch.

Jared's in. He'll call Pastor Nielson tonight.

On Sunday, the construction site was busy. Cameron's dad had brought more men this time, and they looked to be professionals. The frame of the building was complete, and the drywall was ready to be hung. Men walked around with ladders and tools, talking as they worked. After their lunch break, the New Horizons Church farther up the road opened its doors, and people streamed out. Pastor Nielson was with them, a happy look on his face.

"Howdy, neighbors!" Abba gave them his usual greeting as they passed.

"Hello, Mr. Azeem!" Pastor Nielson stopped right in front of Abba, and so did all the other churchgoers. Some carried hammers and saws, others wore tool belts. "May we come in?"

"Of course!" Abba cried and opened the gate wide. "Welcome, my friends!"

Jared slipped in and headed toward the kids who were sitting on the roots of the big tree. All of them smiled and waved, except Yusuf.

"Guess the pastor worked his charm, eh?" Cameron nodded toward the group of adults.

"Pastor gave such an amazing sermon!" Jared said, his face glowing. "He reminded us about Jesus' commandment to love our neighbors, and how we need to stand strong against hateful elements."

"Did he actually say 'the Patriot Sons'?" Danial asked, gaping.

"Not really." Jared shrugged. "But everyone knew what he was talking about. My uncle walked out of church during the service."

Yusuf hadn't known Mr. Grant attended church right next door to them. He shivered and looked around, trying to change the subject. "What are all these people here for?"

Jared's grin was as wide as a beam of wood. "To help, obviously."

They all turned to watch. The men from the church and the mosque—even a few women—went to work on the construction site as if they'd been doing so for months. The sound of nails being hammered into studs, of electric screwdrivers whirring quietly, filled the afternoon air. The Muslim aunties sprang into action, bringing water and snacks to the workers.

Pastor Nielson stood with a hammer in hand, smiling at the scene before him. "Perfect. This is what being a Christian is all about."

"I don't know how to thank you," Mr. Khan began.

"You are all too kind, really!" Abba agreed.

"We should have done this a long time ago," the pastor replied, putting up a hand to stop them from continuing. "I'm sorry it took a child to remind us of our duties as Christians."

"A child?" Mr. Khan frowned.

"Yes, a boy from my parish came to me a few days ago with the most passionate speech." The pastor smiled sideways at Jared. "I believe he is friends with your children."

Abba nodded. "Ah yes, Jared is a good boy. His grandmother told me he's been worried about my son ever since . . . the incident."

Yusuf stared at Abba. Incident? Was that all that had happened this past week? Why did his heart hurt so much then? Why did he have the most terrible nightmares and wake up screaming then? Why was he unable to look any of his friends in the eye any longer?

Pastor Nielson gripped Abba on the shoulder, his

face etched with grief. "Listen, Mr. Azeem, I'm really, truly sorry about what happened to your son. A few other pastors around town and I will be speaking about it the next few Sundays. Why don't you come visit us one day at our church? Maybe around Christmastime? They would love to hear from you."

Abba's back straightened, and his face lit up in a way it hadn't all week long. "Me?"

"Of course. You and your friends are welcome at my church anytime."

Abba told Yusuf that his new "church friends" were coming by every day to help with construction. In a few days, their number had swelled to three times the regular crew, and many of them actually knew what they were doing. The drywall was hung, and they'd started laying bricks on the exterior. It was hard work, but they told a lot of jokes and sang a lot of Christmas songs. "'Jingle Bell Rock' is my favorite," Abba said, smiling. "Although I know a lot of the older songs too, like 'Silent Night.'"

Yusuf blinked behind his glasses. "How come?"

"I went to St. Patrick's School in Karachi," Abba told him. The same abba who hardly ever talked about his childhood. "All the students sang Christmas carols at our annual concert, and we spent weeks memorizing those lovely melodies."

"What else do you remember about school?" Yusuf asked. "Did you have lockers like me? Gym class? Pizza for lunch?" They were sitting at the breakfast table, a rare thing for Abba. Since the "incident" a week before, Abba had started leaving for work later. He said he was training his assistant to open the store, but Yusuf knew the real reason: him.

Abba smiled as he ate his eggs. "Lockers are a very American thing, I believe. I only knew about them from movies like *Back to the Future*. Ah, what a movie! And yes, we had PE every week, where I was the volleyball champion. But lunch? Never from the school shop. My mother, your dadi, would pack the most delicious lunch for me every day for school. Shami kebab and pulao and cucumber salad . . . mmm!"

"Sounds nice," Yusuf told him, and it was true. Life in a Pakistani school did sound better than Frey Middle School at the moment.

"It was okay. I had my fair share of bullies, you know!" Abba's smile faded. "There was this one boy, Imtiaz, who'd flick ink on my uniform when the teacher wasn't looking. Once he pulled my chair from under me just as I was sitting down, and I fell on the floor with a big crash!"

Yusuf knew all about ink from a Pakistani television show set in the eighties. Ink could get very messy if you weren't careful. "Really? Did he get into trouble?"

Abba shook his head. "No. His father was some government minister. Imtiaz could do whatever he wanted and get away with it. I, on the other hand, would get punished for offenses like wearing an ink-streaked uniform to school."

"That sucks." Yusuf paused. "I mean, I feel bad for you."

Abba shrugged. "Life is full of all kinds of people, son. We just have to learn to avoid the bullies and stick with our friends." He scooped up the last of his egg with a bite of toast and opened the *Frey Weekly*. "Well, look at this!" he said, his smile back, brighter than ever. "Farrah, come here quickly!"

Amma came running from her garage office, coffee mug in hand. They read the headline on the front page of the paper together. *City Council Opens Investigation On Local Boy Locked in Jail without Charges*. There were two pictures with the story. One of Yusuf from his fifth-grade yearbook, and the other of the city council members looking seriously at the camera. Right in the middle of the group was the man Yusuf and his friends had met in DQ last week.

✳ ✳ ✳

Journal entry 12

December 25, 2001

Yesterday evening, our family dressed up and went to Sacred Heart Church at Pastor Hancock's invitation. Amma wore her favorite green shalwar kameez, and Abba put on a dark gray suit. "It's Christmas Eve," Amma protested. "Surely the priest wants to spend time with his friends and family." Abba told us it was a special gathering for the entire neighborhood.

"Everyone in the neighborhood doesn't even celebrate Christmas," Sarah said. Abba told her to be patient and see.

The church was filled with people, but they weren't all Christians. I saw many of our Muslim neighbors there, and a few of my classmates' parents. People who looked like me, and those who looked nothing like me. Father Hancock welcomed us with a big smile and took us to a table so full of food I worried it might fall down under the weight. We piled our plates high and sat down, and then the music started, a soulful sound that filled the air and made everyone quiet. I thought of Silky and realized her death didn't hurt as much as it had before. Maybe Amma was right. Maybe time would make me not miss her as much.

Father Hancock came up to the stage and made a little speech, then a rabbi spoke, and then it was

Abba's turn. He looked nervous, but he read from a note card and hardly made any mistakes. "The only way to fight bigotry and hatred is through accurate information," he told everyone. "Human beings fear what they don't know, so the best thing is to get to know each other."

When he finished, I stood up and clapped and clapped. After a few minutes, everyone else did too. Amma beamed at the crowd, and even Farrah baji was smiling. Abba almost dropped his note card in surprise.

37

Christmas arrived quickly and without warning. Yusuf and his family didn't celebrate, but it was difficult to miss the season in a town like Frey. Every house on Yusuf's street and beyond was decorated with lights and nativity scenes, as well as reindeer and inflatable snowmen. Winter break officially began on the Monday before Christmas, and Mr. Parker threw a party for Team Freybots in the gym after school on the last day. "Here's to TRC!" he said, holding up his apple juice box. "May we have a place of honor in the records of the contest!"

Yusuf munched on a bag of Cheetos and looked around. He'd sat as far away from Jared as possible. He knew they'd have to talk to each other at some point, but he wasn't ready yet. Being back on school grounds wasn't as scary as he'd thought it would be, though. It reminded him of how much he'd once wanted to be part of TRC. How much Mr. Parker still wanted it. "Let's take Miss Trashy for a practice run?" he said, wiping his hands on his jeans and standing up.

"Let us eat first, at least!" Cameron told him sternly.

"Yes, we're celebrating the holidays here, not your robot." Madison laughed.

"Correction, *our* robot," Yusuf told her.

After eating, they cleaned up and put Miss Trashy through the challenges. "Three minutes exactly," Mr. Parker announced. "It'll be harder with the competing team stopping you at every turn, but this is an excellent time."

The team members cheered and high-fived one another. "Less than a month to go," Danial said.

Mr. Parker nodded. "Let the countdown begin."

On Christmas Day, Abba packed his car with items from the dollar store. They weren't exactly toys, but practical items for everyday use. Yusuf saw paper plates and cups, hair accessories, diapers, notebooks, baby food, and much more. The entire back seat overflowed with boxes. "What's all this for?" he asked. Abba had taken him to the store that morning, saying he needed help with a special project.

"Our friends, of course," Abba answered as he locked the door, then started the car and backed out of the parking space.

Yusuf didn't know Abba had so many friends. They drove out to the construction site, which was empty for once. Yusuf was amazed to see how the building had transformed in just two weeks. The outside was covered with pretty grayish-brown bricks, and the sidewalk was laid with cement. "We'll be working on the inside next week," Abba told him. "Doors and windows and such."

"But there's no one here," Yusuf pointed out. "Why did we come?"

Abba drove farther, until they reached New Horizons Church. Pastor Nielson was clearly expecting him. He stood in the open entryway, arms outstretched, smile on his face. "Welcome, my friend. Will you be celebrating with us today?" His voice was loud and friendly.

Yusuf looked around. The service was obviously over, but people were still there, talking, laughing, their faces full of joy. Everyone was dressed in fancy clothes. The girls wore the most beautiful dresses, and the boys wore suits, with their hair combed back. It reminded him of Eid, the happiest time of the year.

Abba parked the car and got out. "I just have some gifts for your members," he mumbled, a bit embarrassed at the attention. He and Yusuf took the boxes out and placed them on the steps of the church. "Just a token of our appreciation."

Pastor Nielson was delighted. He took Abba by the arm and almost dragged him inside. "Come, you must eat with us."

A table in the hallway was set with all sorts of food and drink. Yusuf and Abba nibbled on some crackers while Pastor Nielson introduced them to some of the church members. Yusuf recognized the city council member who he'd met in Dairy Queen. He shook Abba's hand vigorously and said "Merry Christmas" about ten times before patting Yusuf on the head. "Glad to see you're doing better, my boy."

Abba gave Yusuf a little sideways hug. "He's doing fine. He's a brave lad. He's going to compete in the TRC next month, you know!"

The adults clapped Yusuf on the shoulder and began talking about the competition. "Lord knows we need something other than football in this town," somebody joked.

"Robotics, eh?" The city council member smiled approvingly at Yusuf. "That's exactly the kind of people we need in Frey. Smart and hardworking!"

Yusuf blushed. A woman who looked a bit like Amma held out a plate of chocolate éclairs for him to try. He took one and tasted it. Warm and sweet, with a hint of salt. He felt at home in this church, just like he did at his mosque. They could see the potential in someone, not just his skin color or religion. "Thank you," he whispered.

On Sunday, the construction was back in full swing. Most of the work was inside now, laying tile on the floors and installing fixtures. Yusuf and the other kids helped Sameena Aunty make sandwiches for the workers. "Faster, kids! Those people need nourishment!" Sameena Aunty scolded.

Yusuf slapped peanut butter on a slice of bread, muttering. Danial made a face behind her back, and he almost laughed. "She's not that bad," he told Danial.

"Since when did you become her friend?"

"Friend?" Yusuf paused. "I guess I've just been seeing everyone in a different light these days."

The lunch team had just finished when the workers came out for a lunch break, grabbing at whatever they could find to eat. Everyone was talking about the city council investigation. "They're not scared of making enemies, I suppose," an uncle said admiringly.

"Enemies? Those Patriot Sons can't do much more than make noise!" another uncle replied, shaking his head.

"They can also make our lives miserable." Danial pointed toward the street.

Yusuf turned and froze. A group of angry-looking people stood on the street just a few yards away, with Mr. Grant in the front like he was their angry leader. They had their placards and signs, and they chanted their usual slogans. "Go home!" "We don't want you here!"

"Forget them." Mr. Khan picked up a box of tiles and went inside. "They're just exercising their constitutional rights."

A few uncles—from the mosque and the church—muttered rude things at this. But Yusuf remembered how Mr. Grant had stood outside the school, arms crossed, with the same furious look, while Officer Strickland hauled Yusuf away to his police car. Mr. Grant had looked like he was mad at the whole world.

Pastor Nielson stood up and walked to the edge of the street. He was wearing a black T-shirt and jeans, and you could mistake him for any kid's dad right then. But when he spoke, his voice was fire and brimstone, loud enough to be heard over the noise of the protestors. "You're the ones who need to go home! These people are our neighbors, and they have a right to build their place of worship, just like we do."

The other men and women from the church joined.

Some shouted "Yeah!" while others clapped. Soon, all the people at the construction site were clapping and cheering. The kids screamed the loudest, their mouths open in joy and amazement.

Yusuf bit his lip. Then he too opened his mouth wide and screamed with all his might. *"Woohoo!"* With the shout, he felt all the anger and confusion leave his body and melt into the air around him. He felt lighter, happier.

They all stood there for the longest time. Finally the Patriot Sons put down their signs, got back onto their motorcycles and into their cars, and left. "Good riddance," old Razia Begum called out in her ancient, shaky voice, and everyone mumbled agreement.

38

School started again in January, with the TRC regionals in Conroe looming ahead like golden goalposts. Yusuf's legs trembled as he walked the school hallways once more, the blue lockers like something out of a bad dream he'd been trying to forget.

Principal Williamson had called another first-thing-in-the-morning gym assembly. She looked different than before: her jumpsuit was black, without a single decoration except for a red bow at the waist. Her usual bouncy smile was absent, replaced with something small and sad.

"Is this normal?" Danial whispered as he sat with Yusuf on the gym floor. "I thought assemblies were only on the first day of school."

Yusuf looked around. This was the place where he'd argued with Ethan, and where Coach Boston made them run laps until their breath rattled in their throats. But the gym was also home base for Team Freybots, a place full of memories of the robotics team laughing and working together, eating lots of snacks, and becoming friends.

"Ahem." Principal Williamson coughed. Her face was serious, and her eyes looked at each student in turn. "Welcome back from winter break! I hope everyone had a relaxing holiday with family and friends."

The students buzzed with chatter. Yusuf looked around, wondering if they were talking about what gifts they got for Christmas, or where they went on vacation. His eyes reached the gym doorway and stopped. Amma and Abba stood just inside, holding hands. He blinked and stared. What were his parents doing there?

Danial had noticed too. "Something's up, Yusuf. Maybe they're going to expel you."

"In front of the entire school?" Yusuf tried to grin, but his insides were shaking.

The principal held up a hand for silence. "I've called you all here for two things. One, we all know about the unfortunate event that happened in the school before Christmas. One of our students accused another of a very serious offense, and our school administration made some very hasty decisions that caused heartache and pain. I'm not going to say either student's name, but the whole town knows who they are. The boy who was accused is here; he is one of your classmates, and a very smart, caring young man."

Yusuf blinked. For some reason his eyes weren't able to focus properly.

Principal Williamson looked directly at him. "Today, to that boy and his parents, I want to say we're sorry. I'm officially apologizing on behalf of the school. On my own behalf. We let you down, son, and we should have done a better job protecting you."

Yusuf's shaking stopped, and he turned toward Amma and Abba. Even from the distance, he could see Amma's slumped shoulders, the tight grip she had on Abba's hand. But they were both smiling too, just tiny smiles that showed they were happy at the apology.

Words matter, Yusuf told himself. He turned back to Principal Williamson and nodded firmly.

She went on. "We're instituting a zero-tolerance bullying policy at our school from this point forward. We've already emailed the documents to your parents, but the summary is this: If there's a bullying incident, we won't wait until a student decides to complain. We will take evidence from teachers and onlookers, and we will take action on the first offense. If you have three bullying complaints against you, you'll be suspended until a committee can investigate." She paused, then almost shouted: "Nobody must be scared of reporting a bully, and nobody must be scared of helping someone else."

The students started talking again, excited and loud. Yusuf grinned at Danial; then he caught Saba's eye in the next row. She was looking . . . happy. Relieved. Yusuf wondered if he looked the same, like a big sack of rocks had been lifted from his back.

Principal Williamson tapped the microphone. "The second announcement is much happier, I promise. We are sending a team to the Texas Robotics Competition regional contest in Conroe very soon! We haven't had a team in almost ten years, so this is a really big opportunity for our school!"

The students clapped, and many turned to give Yusuf and Danial a thumbs-up. "They're clapping for us!" Danial said, shocked.

"Yes, they are."

That wasn't the end of it. Coach Boston blew his whistle, and the middle school cheer team ran up to the stage with Principal Williamson. Music began blaring from the loudspeakers, and the cheer team started to dance, kicking up their heels and clapping, forming lines and then breaking up, again and again. "Hey,

hey! Ho, ho!" they sang, and everyone sang with them. "Team Freybots, let's go!"

"That's their top routine," Danial said excitedly. "The one they do on Friday nights for the Coyotes!"

Yusuf was grinning now. "Guess we're the team to beat today."

That weekend was the last TRC club before the competition. Word about the competition had spread, and dozens of middle schoolers showed up at the gym on Saturday morning to watch the final rehearsal. Tony Rivera quickly set up the practice arena. Mr. Parker timed the challenges, while the audience crowded around, wide-eyed. "Normally we'd have another team with their robot here," Danial explained to everyone. "That will make the challenge much harder."

Afterward Madison sat in the corner, making final notes in her binder. She'd have to turn it in to the judges before the competition in Conroe began. "I should have taken more pictures," she groaned.

Yusuf sat next to her and surveyed the crowd. "You can take some now," he said. "This is a nice moment to remember."

"Tell me about it," she replied, rolling her eyes. "When was the last time these kids paid more attention to a bunch of nerds than to football players?"

Yusuf held up their robot. "Miss Trashy is better than any football."

"Hey, Yusuf!" Mr. Parker came up to them, huffing. A woman with a microphone and a man with a big camera over his shoulder walked behind him. "These people are from TNN. They're doing a segment on our team."

Yusuf remembered all the times he'd watched negative news on TNN shows. Maybe this time they'd showcase something good about Muslims. "Sure," he replied, standing up. "But I want to make sure everyone gets credit for their hard work."

Mr. Parker nodded. "I'll call the other members of the team."

The woman asked a lot of questions, mostly of Yusuf. They were all about their robotics team, and how they hoped to do in the regionals next week. But the last question was different. "You were arrested late last year, weren't you? What do you think that will mean for your future?"

Yusuf stopped breathing for a second. What did that have to do with robotics? But then he squared his shoulders and looked straight at the camera. "I wasn't arrested. It was all a misunderstanding, and the school apologized for it. It's in the past. It's got nothing to do with the robotics challenge or my future. I'm a part of this town, and my team's win will be a win for Frey."

Around him, the rest of his teammates nodded and clapped. Mr. Parker stood to the side, giving him a proud look. It was the same look Amma always gave him before any big exam: "I'm proud of you, no matter what happens."

The cameraman lowered his equipment, and the woman doing the interview shook the team members' hands. "Good luck next week," she told them. "I'm sure you'll do great!"

39

The competition was going to be held in a high school gym in Conroe. Since it was a big group, Mr. Parker had arranged for a school bus to take the team and their parents. Amma and Abba were there; Aleena stayed behind with Sameena Aunty. Mr. and Mrs. Khan sat in the row behind them, wearing business suits like they were at work. Mrs. Raymond was with Jared, beaming. Yusuf stayed away, giving a polite nod in her direction, but nothing else. If she wanted to know why Yusuf wasn't being friendlier, she'd have to ask her grandson.

They all waited for the bus in the school parking lot, huddled in their jackets in the early morning. "What time do we need to get there?" Danial asked for the tenth time.

"Just be quiet," Yusuf told him. "There's plenty of time."

The bus arrived with a rumble and a smell of gasoline in the air, and they climbed aboard. Yusuf, Danial, and Cameron stretched out together in the back seat. The driver checked the rearview mirrors and drank from his coffee mug until Cameron's dad told him to get going already. The bus roared to life and drove out of the school parking lot.

"TRC, here we come!" Mr. Parker shouted.

The adults cheered, and Madison began singing the cheer from the school assembly. "Hey, hey! Ho, ho! Team Freybots, let's go!"

Mr. Parker stood up in the middle of the bus and clapped his hands to the cheer's rhythm. "Hey, hey! Ho, ho! Team Freybots, let's go!" he repeated loudly.

"Sit down, sir!" the driver shouted, and Mr. Parker settled down on his seat again. But his grin was wide, and his eyes shining.

"What if we lose really badly?" Danial whispered to Yusuf. "He's going to be crushed."

Cameron leaned forward. "Then we better not lose, I guess."

Yusuf looked out the window. They were on I-45

now, and Frey was just a speck on the road behind them. "We're not going to lose," he whispered. "I can feel it."

They reached Conroe with plenty of time to spare. The high school was humungous, and its parking lot was already packed with cars and trucks. Registration was inside in the main entryway, next to a life-sized statue of Sam Houston, Texas's first president from the time when Texas was a country. Mr. Parker signed some paperwork and turned in Madison's binder. "Miss Trashy, eh?" the woman at registration said, looking at the team.

"She's going to clean up all that trash in record time," Tony Rivera said proudly.

"I'm sure she will," the woman replied. She handed Mr. Parker a small black folder and pointed to the gym entrance. "You're team eight. The opening ceremony is in half an hour."

The gym was bigger than anything Yusuf had seen, and more crowded than a Walmart on Black Friday. Mr. Parker led everyone to the bleachers, and they settled in near the back. Yusuf looked around, hoping to see some of the other robots. The crowd was too noisy and thick for him to see much. "Wonder who we'll be competing against?" Madison whispered, staring.

The program began late. The TRC event coordinator, a man in a gray suit, welcomed everyone to the competition with wide-open arms, like he was sending out a big hug. "We've gotten entries from ninety-three schools this year, almost double the year before," he boasted. "I'm happy to see the interest in science and robotics increasing each year."

They stood for the pledge of allegiance, first to the U.S. flag and then to the Texas flag. There were short speeches by two people: a high school principal from San Antonio and a college professor at UT Austin specializing in robotics. Abba listened with attention and delight. "He's saying his students get really good jobs," he whispered to Yusuf.

"I know, Abba."

The TRC coordinator came back to the microphone and announced the beginning of the qualifying round. "This is where we test your stamina, kids. Only ten teams go on to the final challenge. Only five teams advance to the finals! Five out of ninety-three, kids. The competition is tougher than an armadillo's hide!" He blew a big red whistle. "Good luck!"

Mr. Parker was rifling through his black folder. "We're in arena twelve," he announced.

Yusuf stood up. His feet felt heavy and his palms were sweating. "Well, this is it," he said to the others, trying to look confident.

Amma gave him a hug. "I'm proud of you for getting this far, darling."

"I know."

Abba clapped him on the back several times, grinning. "This is wonderful, son. See how many kids are here. All bound for early college, no doubt!"

Amma tugged at his hand. "Come, sit down and let the kids work."

They followed Mr. Parker out to the middle of the gym. Tony ran ahead and found arena twelve. Two judges, a man and a woman dressed in black-and-white-striped shirts, were already there, making notes on their clipboards. "Team eight?" the woman asked. "Please set up as quickly as you can."

Yusuf took deep breaths to calm his nerves. Danial looked ready to pass out, and Yusuf gave his shoulder a little shake. "Get your laptop," he told him gently but firmly. Danial sprang into action. He and Yusuf would sit on the side with their laptops, ready to adjust the code if needed. The others would stand around the arena, watching Miss Trashy like hawks.

While Danial set up his laptop, Yusuf studied the competition. Team Jaguars was a group of South Asian kids from Houston, dressed in identical blue jeans and green T-shirts with a bunch of company names. Yusuf was glad his team was wearing their white Freybots shirts with a photo of Miss Trashy in the center. He thought it made them stand out. He saw Mr. Parker talking to the Jaguars' coach, and the judges inspecting the arena and the two robots. He heard someone ask, "Ready?" and he nodded without even knowing who had said it.

Was he sweating? He wasn't sure if it was nervousness or excitement. Or both. He could hear his own heart beating until he realized that a cheer team in the front of the gym was stomping their feet to the tune of "We Will Rock You."

Great. Now that tune would be stuck in his brain for the rest of the day.

The judges placed items randomly on the board: red circular chips for plastic trash, black ones for food trash, and brown cardboard squares for traffic obstacles. The teams would be allowed one trial race with their robots before the actual competition.

Miss Trashy got stuck in five places on the board, but Yusuf quickly adjusted the code to make her smoother. The Jaguars' robot got stuck eleven times, and they had to spend ten minutes working on it after the trial. Yusuf saw one of the team members looking at him, a long-haired boy who looked like an older version of his cousin Saleem. Yusuf offered him a reassuring smile. "You did good."

"Not as good as you guys," the boy remarked. "Seems like you spent a lot of time practicing."

Yusuf shrugged and turned back to his laptop. With everything going on with the Patriot Sons, he knew he hadn't been able to give his team the attention they deserved the last few weeks. If they lost, he'd never forgive himself.

"Let's go!" Cameron nudged him. The judges signaled the start of the competition, and the robots were off. Miss Trashy gathered all the trash while neatly avoiding the traffic obstacles, and piled it in the corner as she'd been programmed to do. Her arm never wavered, and her wheels never stopped. The Jaguars' robot was fast, but not fast enough to keep up, and it stumbled twice over traffic obstacles. The judges were keeping track. When they hit the buzzer to signal the end of the race, Miss Trashy had collected all but two chips. The Jaguars had almost half of theirs still on the board.

"We will, we will rock you!" They didn't need the judges to tell them the results: they'd won this round easily. The Freybots clapped one another on the back as the Jaguars walked away with slumped shoulders.

Yusuf couldn't help but grin. *One down, two to go.*

They stayed at arena twelve, waiting for the next two races to be announced. In between races Yusuf worked on his laptop and checked Miss Trashy dozens of times to make sure everything was perfect. The next team was a group from Pasadena, loud and gangly kids who shouted every time their robot, Drake Junior, collected a chip. Yusuf wished he'd brought earplugs. The shouting was constant, but Miss Trashy collected two more chips than Drake Junior. "Win for the Freybots!" the judges announced, and the Pasadena kids slunk away.

They waited a long time for the third race. Many of the judges were being replaced, and some kids were asking for breaks. Cameron and Tony took Miss Trashy outside for some small fixes. The rest of the Freybots team sat on the gym floor, listening to the hum of excitement around them. "We will, we will rock you!"

"We're doing great, aren't we?" Madison said, hugging herself.

Danial shrugged. "Even if we win all three races, it doesn't mean we qualify. Depends on how all the other teams do."

"Way to be negative, dude!"

"Come on, you guys!" Yusuf interrupted. His head was aching with all the noise in the gym, but it was a buzzing sort of ache, just enough to make his heart beat faster. "These are the TRC rules, and we've known them forever. We just have to focus on collecting as many chips as possible, and then see where we place on the leaderboard."

Madison gave him a nod. "Yes, Captain."

A whistle blew somewhere, and the break was over. Their third competition was set up in arena five, with another team from Houston. "Hey," a boy from the other team said. "May the best team win!"

Yusuf inspected their robot, SuperGirl II. She was half the size of Miss Trashy, and when the race began, she zoomed away as if propelled by lightning. Miss Trashy rumbled along behind her, slowly picking up chips. Yusuf felt nauseous. They had to win this last race, they had to.

"Don't worry, we have lots of points," Jared whispered in his ear.

Yusuf turned away as if he hadn't heard.

When the race ended, SuperGirl II had won. Yusuf shook hands with the other team captain, trying to act cool. But his heart was thumping, and the ache in his head was fiercer. "Congrats," he whispered, looking down. He knew this wasn't the end, but he was still worried.

Mr. Parker pointed to the leaderboard on the gym wall. The Freybots watched with anxious eyes. The noise in the gym had been sucked out, and silence echoed around them. Yusuf tried to swallow. He didn't want to look over at his parents, or at his teammates. Would their two wins be enough to move them into the main competition?

After ten of the slowest minutes in history, the scores were tallied and the leaderboard lit up. The Freybots were in! Danial and Cameron hugged each other over and over. Tony shook hands with Jared, while Madison danced a little jig like an excited toddler. Yusuf let out a deep breath, feeling as if a huge burden had been lifted from his shoulders. Still, he didn't want to get anyone's hopes up. "We still have the actual competition to get through after lunch," he told his team.

Danial scoffed. "Since when did you become a pessimist?"

"Just being careful."

Mr. Parker turned to Yusuf and the others. His eyes were shining, and his face was full of joy. "No matter what happens after lunch, I'm incredibly proud of y'all."

Journal entry 13
January 1, 2002
It's finally 2002. I'm going to turn in this journal to Mrs. Clifton after the winter break, so this will probably be my last entry.

Abba said we should all make New Year's resolutions, just for fun. "You don't have to tell anyone," he said. "Just know what you want to change in your heart."

So I did. After lunch, I went to Jonathan's house to wish him a happy New Year. It's been so long since I walked on his street, but everything is familiar. The tree stump we'd use as a launching pad for our toy rockets. The rosebush I fell into last summer while we raced our bikes . . .

The palms of my hands were sweaty as I knocked. Jonathan's mom opened the door and gave me a glare, then turned to get Jonathan. "That Muslim kid is here!" she shouted, and I wanted to run away. Still, I waited for him.

We sat on his front porch together, not talking. "I just came by to say Happy New Year," I finally told him.

"I'm sorry about hitting you," he replied.

I said, "It's okay," because it was.

Then he said, "I can't be friends with you anymore. I hope you understand why. I just can't."

I got up to leave. I told him, "Yes, I understand." I wasn't lying. I truly did. His uncle's death had left a wound in his heart, just like Silky's death had done to me. There was no way we could forget something

349

like that. A wound that would never heal.

"I'm sorry about everything," I told him, and then I left.

There wasn't anything else I could do.

40

After lunch, the ten finalist teams went head-to-head in battles in separate arenas. The music was blaring now, and the gym was echoing with a multitude of sounds. Yusuf sat on the floor at the edge of the gym, studying the code on his laptop. He wondered if he could somehow make Miss Trashy faster, more accurate. He didn't notice when Amma came over to him. "I think you've done enough," she whispered quietly in his ear. "Just relax and leave the rest to God."

Yusuf chewed on his lip. He was finally at the TRC regional contest. All the other teams were much better than they were. Two of the Houston schools had dedicated robotics programs. How could the Freybots compete against that?

Amma pointed to the others near the board. "You're their captain. They need you."

Yusuf sighed. She was right, as always. He got up from his spot on the floor and walked over to his teammates. "Ready, guys?" he almost shouted, trying to stop his voice from trembling.

They nodded. Madison gave a little smile and yelled back, "Ready!"

"Good," Yusuf said. "Listen. We've done our best. We never would have imagined being a finalist among ninety-three teams, but we're here. Team Freybots will be in the TRC records forever as a finalist. We've already done our school and our town proud."

Cameron nodded. "That's true."

Yusuf grinned at them all, then let out a huge breath. "This is the time to have fun, okay? This is a challenge for us, but we want to also enjoy being here, right now. Okay?"

"Okay!" the others shouted, grinning back. "Okay!"

The opposing team took their place. It was a group of kids from Fredericksburg, a town near Frey. They were three boys and three girls, all dressed in Catholic school uniforms. TEAM YONDER LIGHT, their placard said. Yusuf nodded at them politely, then took his place near the laptop. "Ready," he told the judges.

"Miss Trashy versus Robomaniac!" a judge announced. He blew his whistle, and the robots were off. Yusuf tried to focus on the board, but the noise of the students around them cheering, and the music thumping, came at him in waves. He narrowed his eyes until all he could see was Miss Trashy, rumbling on the board like a faithful servant, collecting plastic chips and making piles on the side. Robomaniac was right on her tail the entire time, not only picking up trash but also blocking Miss Trashy more than once. "That robot is good," Cameron whispered.

Three minutes seemed like three hours, and when the judge blew his whistle again, it was echoed by all the judges around the gym. The final race was over.

It was done. Not a single plastic chip was left on the board.

Yusuf's backbone sagged like it had been transformed into a liquid. He looked around for Amma and Abba and found them nearby, looking as exhausted as he was. Then his eyes widened. Next to Amma stood a tall, bearded figure. Uncle Rahman.

Yusuf beamed. "You came!"

Uncle Rahman hugged him. "That was an incredible game, kiddo!"

The judges tallied up the scores. "Team Freybots, one hundred and ten points," the female judge noted.

"Team Yonder Light, ninety-five points."

Team Freybots went wild. They hooted and clapped and cheered loudly. Mr. Parker looked equal parts excited and ready to faint. Yusuf hugged Danial once, then twice, grinning like a person who'd won the lottery. Last year's TRC high score had been one hundred and thirty points. Could they actually win this thing?

There was another break while the scores were reported and calculations made. Team Freybots went back to the bleachers with their parents, waiting. Yusuf tried to ignore the tension, thick like a fog, around him. *Quick, think of something else to distract yourself,* he thought. "I finished reading your journal," he told Uncle Rahman.

Uncle Rahman stilled. "Really? What did you think?"

Yusuf paused, unsure. Everything in the journal had been so huge, so emotionally wrecking. "You seemed . . . very lonely in the journal. How come you never told anyone how you were feeling?"

"Like who? We were all grieving in our own ways—9/11 was too . . . disastrous to share."

"It's been twenty years now," Yusuf pointed out. "Maybe if we talk about it now, we can get past it. Learn from it."

"I think for those of us who went through it, the past still hurts a lot."

Yusuf remembered something from the journal.

"Like a wound that never healed."

"Exactly."

Yusuf picked up his laptop and wrapped up the charging wires. "Did you ever become friends with Jonathan again?"

Uncle Rahman's eyes flickered. "Not really. He stayed away from me after that. I made other friends."

"What other friends?"

"Muslim friends. Kids who were going through the same sorts of things in a world changed by 9/11." Uncle Rahman cleared his throat. "Seems like my journal helped you, eh?"

Yusuf nodded quickly. "Yes! It helped me understand my enemies a little bit better."

A ghost of a smile crossed his uncle's face. "Enemies? What are you, a pirate?"

Yusuf felt himself grow warm. He wasn't sure what he was. He shrugged awkwardly. "Kids can have enemies too."

The TRC coordinator was walking up to the stage, microphone in hand. "Come," Uncle Rahman said, turning away. "You can tell me all about your enemies later."

The announcements were short and dizzyingly exciting. "Third place goes to Team Freybots!" the TRC coordinator roared.

Yusuf couldn't breathe. He took gasps until Uncle Rahman slapped him on the back, and then he screamed at the top of his voice. *"Woohoo!"* Everyone turned and laughed a little. The team went up to the stage to get their trophy, while Mr. Parker and all the parents took pictures. He stood with Danial on the left and Cameron on the right, smiling until his lips felt sore. Jared stood at the far end of the line, tall and silent.

Back on the bus, the team sang the victory cheer over and over until they were hoarse. The parents took pictures and talked loudly about how amazing their kids—and grandkids—were. Mr. Parker called Principal Williamson on the phone to tell her the good news, and her squeal came through the speaker loud and very clear. "We'll get ready to ce-le-brate!"

"Seems like you kids will get quite the welcome when you reach home," Mr. Parker said as he hung up.

"They deserve it," Mr. Khan replied, taking some more pictures.

Yusuf turned slightly and saw Jared looking at him. Maybe it was time to forgive and forget. He didn't want to lose a friend like Uncle Rahman had.

He couldn't find the words, though. He practiced what he'd say for miles, but nothing seemed right. What Jared had done was wrong, but it was before they'd known each other. Before they'd seen each other as human beings, rather than enemies.

When he could see Frey in the distance, he took a deep breath and went to the front row, where Jared was sitting alone, away from his grandmother and everyone else. "Hey, congratulations."

Jared nodded, looking down at his shoes. "Thanks, you too."

"Thanks."

They sat in silence until the bus turned into the school parking lot. "I know you're sorry about what happened," Yusuf began, rubbing the frame of his glasses.

"I am."

"Want to be friends again?" Yusuf held out his hand.

Jared's eyes widened. "I've been your friend all this time," he replied.

Yusuf thought about this. Was it true? A sudden image of Jared's happy face as they dunked Father Robbins at the pumpkin patch loomed in his mind. "Sorry it took me a while to figure that out."

Jared finally smiled. He shook Yusuf's hand once, firmly. "Don't worry about it. I'm not going anywhere."

"Good. We still have to win the TRC nationals."

A NOTE FROM THE AUTHOR

The inspiration for this story came from a real event that happened in my home state of Texas in 2015. Ahmed Mohamed, a fourteen-year-old boy in Irving, was arrested at his high school because of a disassembled digital clock he brought to school to show his teachers. Nicknamed Clock Boy, Ahmed became an overnight sensation for all the wrong reasons. He was a smart young man who was betrayed by those who should have protected him, including his school. His arrest, release, and the resulting media outcry showed the world how people view Muslims: Dangerous. Suspicious. Not to be trusted.

Ahmed's story was heartbreaking, but it also reminded me of the days after 9/11. I was in my twenties when that attack occurred, and I still remember how Muslims were treated in its aftermath: as the enemy. The Clock Boy incident brought home to me that even now, twenty years later, things haven't changed much. We are still viewed with suspicion.

After 9/11 I had a choice. I could sit and complain, or I could do something to change things. I began working with other people in my community to hold events and discussions, to share my faith as a Muslim and learn about those who are different from me. My hope with this interfaith work was to build bridges, to show Muslims in a positive light—as neighbors, friends, family. As Americans.

With the twentieth anniversary of 9/11 approaching, we must ask ourselves: What has been gained and lost in the last two decades? Have we progressed as a nation? Do we treat others better than we did in the days and months after the attacks? Or are we still the same, maybe even worse? The answers are complicated. I believe that there are many people in our country who are working hard to build bridges, like me. But there are also many people who are trying to destroy those bridges. This book highlights both sides, and helps kids understand why an event that happened before their lifetimes still resonates in our culture and politics today.

Ahmed Mohamed was so traumatized by what happened that he left the U.S. and settled in the Middle East. His family tried to sue the high school and the police department, but nothing came of it. When I wrote this book, I wanted to explore whether the incident could have had an alternate ending. A better conclusion. In my story, Yusuf has a stronger support system, including a school that decides to do the right thing.

I hope this book will teach us all—parents, teachers, school administrators, community members—how to stand up to the bullies in our communities, be they kids or adults.

—Saadia Faruqi

ACKNOWLEDGMENTS

I want to thank all the people who led to this book, but I don't know who most of them are. Living in this country post 9/11 as a Muslim American has not been easy, but I gained a lot from the experience. I've met tens of thousands of people in my work as an interfaith activist, and they all left some sort of impression on me. A few became lifelong friends, such as my interfaith partner in crime, Nancy Agafitei, with whom I had countless conversations about interfaith work and how imperative it was if we wanted to defeat the hatred that arose after 9/11. Thank you, Nancy, for taking a chance on me so many years ago when I stepped into your library office and asked to hold a book exhibition.

A tremendous thank-you as always to my family, especially my husband, Nasir, who always supports my dreams and urges me to keep going when things get tough and I want to give up. To my amazing agent, Kari Sutherland; my wonderful editor, Rosemary Brosnan; Courtney Stevenson; and the rest of the team at Harper: You are all brilliant and such strong supporters of my stories. I couldn't do this without you.

I'm grateful to all those I interviewed about their 9/11 memories. Y'all are brave for being willing to relive a horrible day for the sake of my book. Finally a big thank-you to Alysa Wishingrad, for the invaluable advice and feedback. This is a better book because of you!

Turn the page to start reading Saadia Faruqi's
A Thousand Questions, a middle grade novel about
two girls navigating a summer of change and family
upheaval with kind hearts, big dreams,
and all the right questions.

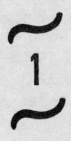

1

MIMI
SUMMER VACATION IS OVERRATED

Imagine an oven, like 400 degrees. Then imagine crawling inside and closing the door behind you. That's what Pakistan feels like in the summer. Who'd be dumb enough to crawl inside a superhot oven, you ask?

Good question. Nobody with brains, that's who.

We're standing outside the Jinnah Airport in Karachi, trying to get a taxi from a small kiosk with dirty windows. There are a million people around me, all talking faster than I can understand, and anyway they're talking in Urdu so I have only a vague idea of what they're saying. Mom fans herself with a *Parents* magazine, the blonde model on the cover all creased as she tries to keep her mom-cool. I try fanning too, but my copy of the new Dork Diaries is too thick and short to give me any air. "Ugh!" I grunt, and Mom turns to frown at me.

"No complaining, Mimi," she reminds me, patting my nose with her finger. That's been our rule since I was a little girl. No complaining, no matter how hard things get. Not when Dad left us when I was five. Not when I crashed my bike in the street outside our Houston apartment at age seven and broke my leg in three places. Not when Mom lost her teaching job at the Houston Art Institute last year and went on a million interviews, always returning with a smile on her tired face, saying, "It's fine. Something will turn up soon."

But this forced vacation in Pakistan, the land of my ancestors . . . This is not the something I'd been expecting to turn up.

I swat angrily at a big fly that's been trying to land on my face for the last ten minutes. "Not easy," I hiss at Mom. The fly glares at me with its hundred eyes, daring me to catch it.

Mom turns back and offers an apologetic smile to the man in the window. "So how much?" she asks in Urdu. I can't speak it too well, but I've heard it enough to know what she's saying. How much to go to Grandma and Grandpa's house?

That's another thing. I've never even met these Pakistani grandparents of mine. Mom's parents. They call us on Skype once in a while, but mostly in the middle of the night, when I'm already asleep, because of the time difference. I have to stay up late on my birthday to talk to them, but it's always an awkward moment when they stare at me through cyberspace. A stern woman with glasses and arched eyebrows. A man with a shock of white hair and twinkling eyes.

Mom is still haggling with the man in the kiosk. He says something, and she shakes her head. "Too much, that's insane!" she says, firm and clear.

"It's nothing in dollars, ma'am," he tells her firmly, almost mocking. I gasp. How does he know we're American? Is it my Old Navy backpack, or my colorful Skechers sneakers? Is it Mom's dangly earrings or her white embroidered tunic worn over jeans? I'm pretty sure it's the clothes. I survey the women milling around us. Almost everyone is dressed in shalwar kameez of a dizzying variety of colors. Blues and greens like the ocean. Reds and yellows like the leaves in fall.

I do have the traditional Pakistani dress, a black linen kameez with silver embroidery on the sleeves and a plain white cotton shalwar that's too short for my legs now. I wore it twice last year for the two Eid celebrations, and then stuffed it in the back of my closet. I prefer jeans and T-shirts with funny messages. Right now, for instance, I'm wearing a white T-shirt with a purple poop emoji. It's holding its nose and asking *WHAT STINKS?*

I can smell so many things at the moment, none of them good. Garbage spoiling in the early sun. Sweat. Muddy shoes. My T-shirt suddenly doesn't seem that funny. I take my blue cardigan from around my waist and put it on over the poop emoji. "What do you think the temperature is, Mom?" I ask. "Probably a hundred degrees. Or do they use Celsius here?"

Mom shushes me with a finger. She and the man in the kiosk have decided on a price. I never knew one could haggle over taxi fares. Another man walks out, picks up our luggage, and takes it to a white sedan with a broken bumper, covered in dust, and we climb in. "Thank you," I say in English, and he stares at me.

"Is it okay to say thank you?" I whisper to Mom as we settle in and the driver starts the taxi slowly, honking the horn every few seconds to alert people on the road. Wait, is this a road or the sidewalk? It's hard to tell because there are people everywhere.

Mom gives me the side-eye. "Please, can we take a break from your thousands of questions, just this once?"

"Mo-om!"

She leans her head back and closes her eyes. "Yes, Mimi, you can say thank you. Or shukriya."

"Really? I feel like that guy didn't understand me

when I said thank you to him. Or maybe he's just not used to getting thanked. What do you think?"

She doesn't reply. "Mom?" I say, louder, then feel the driver's eyes on me in the rearview mirror.

"Just look out the window, sweetie," Mom murmurs. "You don't want to miss any details for your travel journal, do you?"

I grimace, thinking of the journal Mom gave me a few weeks before we left Houston. I'm secretly planning to write to Dad about my trip, even though I haven't heard from him in years, but she doesn't need to know that. Somehow I doubt she'll be thrilled. She always mutters about him and says "good riddance to bad rubbish" or something like that if anyone asks. But maybe if I write to him, he'll start writing back.

I turn toward the window, shutting my mouth firmly. At least the car isn't too hot. The crowds outside have disappeared, and we're cruising down a big road with neat little trees on each side. The traffic is heavy, though. There are small cars, motorcycles with loads of passengers, and big buses with men sitting on the tops and hanging from the sides. Billboards line the sides of the roads, advertising everything from the latest fashions to cell phone service. A few signs in English proclaim *DON'T FORGET TO VOTE ON AUGUST 1*, with dozens of Pakistani flags surrounding the words.

5

My eyes are literally popping out of my head; I can feel them. It's all so strange, but also cool and bright, an explosion of color so sharp it reaches inside me and draws out a little sigh.

I realize I'm pressing my face against the window and force myself to sit back and relax. This is Karachi, the largest city in Pakistan, the birthplace of my mom and the grandparents I've never met. This is my home for the next month and a half, whether I like it or not.

We pass through congested intersections filled with cars and motorcycles, trucks and donkey carts. I see squat buildings that are obviously offices, and tall glass structures that may or may not be offices. One is definitely a mall, and it rises to the sky. Soon, the streets broaden; the cars thin out. We must be in a different part of the city.

I squint at the street sign. Sunset Boulevard. Funny, Dad once sent me a postcard from Sunset Boulevard in California, a year after he left. It was the only time he ever sent me anything. Is this an omen? He's a journalist and travels a lot, so he could be anywhere in the world right now. Thanks to Google, I know he's traveled to lots of cool (and some hot) places. The last time I checked, about six months ago, he was the Asian correspondent of a fancy-pants newswire service somewhere in China. Still, I like to think of him in sunny California, surfing the waves and reporting on shark attacks.

I lean my face back against the window, taking in the big houses and the towering boundary walls with barbed wire on the top. This journey is never-ending.

I look sideways at Mom. She's breathing deeply from her mouth, a sure sign she's asleep. Her hands are folded neatly in her lap, fingers stained deep blue from the last painting she worked on before we left Houston. She can never get the stains out properly.

I rummage in my backpack and find my little square journal. It's got a gray leathery cover, and thick lined paper. My purple gel pen is tucked inside, serving as a bookmark.

Dear Dad,

You won't believe that I'm on a different continent from all my friends, right this minute. I'm awake while they're all sleeping, dreaming of who knows what. It's early morning here in Karachi, all the way in South Asia.

We're taking what Mom calls a long-overdue vacation. She's finally got a job at a private school as the art teacher, and we have the whole summer to celebrate instead of worrying about money as usual. My best friend, Zoe, is spending the summer in Italy. Isn't she L-U-C-K-Y? I would give my left arm to go to Europe.

Instead, I'm in Pakistan, which Mom says means "land of the pure." Ugh. It's pure, all right—pure haze, pure dust. Pure heat.

    Have you ever been to Pakistan? Somehow I doubt it. A white man with light brown eyes and blond hair would really stand out here. Mom says this place will grow on me if I just give it a chance, but at the moment I'd give anything to be with you. Would you give anything to be with your family again?

    Love,

    Your daughter, Mimi

The taxi screeches to a stop in front of a sprawling white house with a balcony on the second floor and huge windows covered with metal bars. There are more *VOTE!* posters plastered on the boundary wall, along with colorful graffiti. "Is this it, ma'am?" the taxi driver calls out in Urdu.

Mom straightens up, yawning. I'm always amazed at her ability to take cat naps and wake up refreshed. I, on the other hand, wake up grouchy as a cat without whiskers. "Still the same," she says quietly, staring at the houses outside with a dreamy expression.

I scramble out of the car without being told and stretch on the street. "This is practically a mansion," I whisper in awe.

Mom joins me and grins. She's standing up straighter than I've seen in a long time. "Welcome to my childhood home, Mimi, my darling!" she says, and strides up to the gate to ring the bell.